BEHIND CLOSED DOORS

A DANIELS BROTHERS ROMANCE

SHERRI HAYES

Behind Closed Doors

Daniels Brothers Series

Sherri Hayes

First published by The Writer's Coffee Shop, 2011

Cover Design by Get Covers

ABOUT THIS BOOK

Falling For His New Neighbor Was Never Part of the Plan

Chris Daniels is single, and he prefers to keep it that way. Women are trouble. One look at his new neighbor has all his warning bells going off. He needs to stay away from her for his peace of mind.

Elizabeth Marshall is hoping for a new start where she can heal from the scars of her past and rebuild her life. That is, until she comes face-to-face with Chris. He's all male with broad shoulders and dark brown eyes that seem to look into her soul. She needs to keep as much distance between them as possible.

Too bad fate, and their meddling landlord have other plans. Before she knows it, Elizabeth is working at Chris's construction company, helping him in the office. Their forced proximity means she can't avoid him, and before too long she realizes she doesn't want to.

Just as Elizabeth thinks she might get her happily-ever-after, someone from her past decides they aren't ready to let her go. Can Chris keep Elizabeth safe, or will her past end their relationship before it can begin?

CHAPTER 1

Elizabeth Marshall drove her red Honda Civic into the little town of Springfield, Ohio. The simple name was one of the things that attracted her. It wasn't complicated, and that was exactly what she needed in her life right now: no complications.

She wanted a fresh start, far away from all the memories of the city she'd left behind. Away from the person everyone thought she was. A person she'd really never been, before or after. At the age of twenty-seven, she would be reborn. Reborn into someone she could be proud of again. Someone who didn't pretend to be something she wasn't. Someone her parents could be proud of.

Springfield was big enough to have all the basic necessities without any of the flashy extras you'd find in larger cities. It was just over an hour away from the place she'd called home for the last ten years. Far enough away that she didn't think anyone here would recognize her, but near enough that she could visit her parents' graves whenever she wanted. In some ways she was glad they couldn't see her now. Yes, she missed them, but they'd also missed the mess her life had become. She felt moisture pool in her eyes as she thought of them, and knew that if she didn't redirect her thoughts soon she'd be a bawling mess by the time she arrived at her destination.

Her destination. As she wove through the side streets, she focused on her surroundings. Springfield felt like a completely different world. No longer would she have to attend cocktail parties or ladies' teas. Her hair and makeup didn't have to be perfect before going outside to retrieve the morning paper. Here she could just be herself.

In her search for the perfect place to start this new chapter in her life, she'd stumbled upon an old home that had been turned into apartments. When she'd received the e-mail back from Mrs. Weaver, her new landlady, she knew this was the place for her. The three-story building had been around for over one hundred years, but it looked to be in good repair. She loved old buildings. It was one of the few things she'd enjoyed about where she'd called home for the past five years. In her new home, Mrs. Weaver occupied the bottom level, and Elizabeth would be on the second floor. The third floor had an occupant as well, although she hadn't thought to ask for details.

She felt good about having her own space. *I need my independence,* she reminded herself.

Even with that mantra, it was hard to block out what had led her to this small town surrounded by corn and soybean fields, but there was a new life waiting for her in Springfield, she just knew it.

With a few more turns, she found the road she was looking for and followed it, as the houses once again became farther and farther apart. There was a line of trees to her right and a soybean field on her left when a mailbox came into view. Sitting back off the road, the large Victorian house was tucked between two soybean fields and surrounded by a small grove of trees.

As she drove up the long gravel driveway, she noticed someone looking out the first-story window.

"You can do this," she said to herself, figuring if she said it enough she could make it true.

Pulling her loose button-down shirt tighter around her, she got out of the car and went to the trunk. There wasn't much to retrieve, just two bags. That was all her life consisted of now. All she had chosen to bring with her. The rest of her old life was either in storage or had been donated to Goodwill. She didn't need reminders. She had enough of those all on her own.

A woman with salt-and-pepper hair met her at the door and opened it wide. She looked to be in her mid to late sixties, old enough to be Elizabeth's mother if she were still alive.

"Hello, my dear. You must be Elizabeth," she said, reaching out to take one of her bags.

"It's okay, I've got it. They're not that heavy." *You could also use the exercise*, her inner voice chastised.

The woman waved her concerns away and took the bag. "Nonsense. I may be old, but I'm not completely useless. Not yet anyway." Extending her hand, she introduced herself. "I'm Janice Weaver, but you can call me Jan. Everybody does."

Taking the offered hand, Elizabeth said, "It's nice to meet you."

She took a quick survey of her surroundings, noting that the pictures online hadn't done the place justice, and followed Jan into a foyer decorated in cream and soft blue. The ceiling soared high above her, creating an open and inviting space. She loved it already, and she wasn't even in her apartment yet.

"Over there is my apartment should you ever need anything," Jan said, pointing to a door just to the right. Elizabeth nodded. "And you're up here." She continued up the stairs as Elizabeth followed, eager to see her new place.

At the top of the stairs were two more doors: one to the right and one to the left. Jan stopped at the door on the right and retrieved a single key from her pocket.

As Jan put the key into the door, curiosity got the better Elizabeth. Looking over her shoulder she asked, "What is the other door for?"

Jan turned slightly to see what she was talking about. "That's the staircase leading to the third-floor apartment."

Then, as if the brief conversation hadn't occurred, Jan opened the door, motioning for Elizabeth to go inside.

Elizabeth looked around, very pleased. While there was a certain modern flair to the place, it was like stepping back in time. The architecture was beautiful, with a vast wooden arch separating her living room from her new kitchen.

"Do you like it?" Jan asked from behind her.

She'd been so caught up she hadn't even heard Jan approach. That hadn't happened in a long time. She was usually overly aware of her surroundings. It just reaffirmed her decision. "I love it."

Jan smiled and Elizabeth relaxed a little, but old habits were hard to break. While it might be true the danger was gone, one didn't just forget being afraid.

An hour later, Elizabeth stepped back to admire the small air mattress she'd just blown up in the middle of her new bedroom. It was only big enough for one person, but it would do until she could get a bed delivered. She needed to pick up some sheets and blankets. Sleeping directly on the vinyl didn't hold great appeal. Not even for one night.

Next she went to the kitchen. It was a nice size and had everything she needed, including a dishwasher, and there were plenty of cabinets lining the walls, waiting to be filled with food and dishes, both of which she currently lacked.

There's no time like the present.

Jan had given her directions to the nearest market, so she grabbed her purse and started to leave, but just as she was about to descend the stairs, she heard an angry male voice say, "I don't care what you have to do, Terry, just get it done." Every word was punctuated by heavy footfalls coming up the stairs, closer to her apartment.

Elizabeth's breathing quickened as her chest tightened, and she automatically huddled in on herself. The man's voice changed in her mind. It wasn't some stranger anymore; it was Jared, her husband.

She leaned her forehead against the wall next to the door, trying to push the memories away. *He's not here. He's* not *here*, she kept repeating to herself.

Just as she was starting to calm, the door only a few feet away was wrenched opened and then slammed shut. It didn't take much to put together that the man must be her new neighbor or one of them at least. She hadn't thought to question Jan about the third-floor residents and felt stupid for not asking more questions.

It was too late now. She was here, and she wasn't going to let something like a disagreeable man chase her out of her new home. She would deal with her neighbor even if he didn't seem like a nice man. Maybe she could avoid him altogether. It wasn't as if they really had to cross paths, right? She'd learn his schedule and then avoid him. That would work.

With renewed determination, she opened her door and ran down the stairs and out to her car, her speed of flight having nothing to do with the man upstairs. At least, that's what she kept telling herself.

This day had to be one of the worst of Christopher Daniels' life. His assistant had just up and quit without notice, and then his foreman, Terry, had failed to order enough materials to finish the interior drywall for the house they were in the process of building. On top of all that, he'd managed to run over a nail somewhere and had to change a flat halfway home.

It was two o'clock, and he had more work than he wanted to contemplate waiting on his desk for him, but for just a few minutes he was going to try and not think about it. *Yeah, right*, he thought as he pulled out the lunchmeat, cheese, and mayo from his refrigerator. He took the bread out of the cabinet, hurriedly made a sandwich, and took a huge bite.

Leaning back against the counter, he forced his mind to think of something else, anything else but work, and settled on the new neighbor Jan had told him about. She'd said the woman seemed nice enough and had moved down from Columbus, but that was all Jan knew. He really wished she had gotten more information so he could have had his brother Paul run a background check or something. But that wasn't Jan Weaver. She was a great woman, just too trusting.

Chris had known Jan and her husband, Charles, since he was a kid. They'd lived across the street from his parents until they'd bought this house fifteen years ago. Fate had brought them together again when Chris' short-lived marriage had come to an end right around the same time Charles' health had taken a turn for the worse. In exchange for decreased rent, Chris helped out with minor repairs when needed. Living there was beneficial for both of them.

He hadn't had a downstairs neighbor for three months, and it was going to take some getting used to. *No more running out in just my boxers*, he thought, laughing to himself.

It had happened years ago, but Jan never let him forget it. He'd been living there only a few months when, on his way in, he'd dropped some papers. Later that night he was getting ready to climb into bed with his usual mound of paperwork, when he'd realized something was missing. Instead of putting his clothes back on, he decided to duck out into the hallway and check.

Unfortunately, the papers were just out of reach and as he stretched to pick them up, he heard his door click shut, locking him out of his apartment. He'd had to run down the stairs in nothing but his boxers to retrieve the spare key from Jan. It was embarrassing enough, but at least there hadn't been anyone else living there at the time to add to his humiliation.

That was three years ago. In that time he'd separated himself from all distractions. All he had left was his work, Terry being the only one he'd become friendly with, and his family, of which he considered Jan a part.

He looked at the clock. Only twenty minutes had passed since he'd walked in the door, but it was all he could afford.

After popping the last of his sandwich into his mouth, he took a glass from the cabinet, quickly filled it with water, and downed it in one gulp. He placed it in the sink, retrieved his cell phone from off his belt, and dialed as he walked out the door.

By the time Elizabeth made it back, it was almost seven. It had taken her a lot longer to find everything she needed because she'd had to go to three places before finally finding the bedding she was looking for. What she'd found was perfect. It was mostly white, but with red and gray clovers all over it, a far cry from the browns and creams Jared had insisted upon.

Thankfully, the rest of her trip had gone smoother. She'd found a nice little restaurant and had dinner there. Then she went to the grocery store and filled her cart, anxious to get home, put everything away, and make her house feel like a home.

With her arms full, she managed to get the front door open and the first load up the stairs. It was the first time Elizabeth was thankful for all those years Jared had made her go to the gym. No. She was having such a good day she would not let her thoughts wander down that path. Resolute, she marched back down the stairs and was just reaching for the doorknob when Jan came out. "Did you need some help, dear?"

"Uh, no. I—"

She was almost knocked over when a large man came barreling through the door. He didn't seem to notice Elizabeth at all, as he focused on Jan. "You can't leave the front door unlocked like this. It just isn't safe."

His voice was gruff, and she instantly recognized it as the one she'd heard this afternoon. It was not as angry as it has been before, but still intimidating. She backed toward the stairs without thinking. It was then that he noticed her, appraising her from head to foot, and his scrutiny made her uncomfortable. Even though she was completely clothed, she felt the need to cover herself.

He was huge, taller than Jared or her father. His hair was a dark brown, only a shade darker than his eyes, and he looked dangerous, more dangerous than her husband. Her frightened expression must have been apparent. She closed her eyes tight, willing everything to go away: her memories, her fear, this man before her.

"Chris, you have perfect timing." Jan walked over to the man and placed her hand on his arm. "Elizabeth," she said, motioning in her direction, "just went shopping and needs some help getting everything up to her apartment. You'll be a good neighbor and help her now, won't you?"

The man looked down at Jan with an expression she didn't understand. Then he sighed, turned to her, and in that same gruff voice said, "Come on. Let's get your stuff inside. I've got work to do."

Before she could say anything, he was back out the door and halfway to her car. She looked over at Jan. "Go on," she said. "He won't bite."

Cautiously, she followed him outside where he was already unloading what was left and had most of it in his arms before she reached his side. "I . . . I'm sorry. You don't . . . have to help me," she said, almost hoping he'd drop everything and leave her alone.

"I said I'd help and I'll help," he replied curtly. "I think I got everything. You might want to check."

He stood, waiting, so she glanced in quickly. "Yes. That's looks like everything," she said, and he gave her a firm nod before marching back into the house.

By the time she caught up with him, he was waiting impatiently outside her apartment door, and she fumbled with the key several times before finally managing to get it into the lock and open the door.

As soon as she stepped over the threshold, he brushed past her as if he owned the place and went straight to her kitchen. She stood stunned for a few seconds. How did he know her place so well? Elizabeth fought with her nerves once again before following him. *Of course he knows the layout of your apartment*, she told herself. *He lives upstairs. It's probably the same. That's all.*

He turned, catching her off guard, and she stumbled backward, but he managed to catch her in time. As soon as she was upright, however, he released her as if she were poison, and shoved his hands roughly into his pockets.

"If you don't need anything else, then," he said, already walking to the door.

She watched his retreating back, not understanding what had happened. When he'd touched her it had felt, well, odd. Not unpleasant, just strange. But he'd acted like she'd hurt him. His eyes had held a pain that she didn't understand. It didn't make any sense.

She had no idea how long she stood there just looking at the closed door before making herself move. She put all the groceries away and made her air mattress look as inviting as possible before deciding to go ahead and get ready for bed. It was early, but she had nothing else to do. She didn't have a television and she had no friends there.

Sinking down into her makeshift bed under her new sheets, she rolled over to watch the last of the sun fall below the horizon outside her bedroom window. She could see the tops of a few trees, but not much else. The view was so different from out her old bedroom window where she could see nothing much more than the house next door. One day was behind her. Tomorrow she would find some furniture and, after that, look for a job. Even though she didn't need one thanks to Jared's careful planning and his life insurance settlement, it was something she needed for herself.

This would work—her new apartment, her new life. All she had to do was avoid her new neighbor and pray no one figured out who she was. She could do that.

She hoped.

CHAPTER 2

CHRIS SAT in his office two days later, more frustrated than he thought possible. He couldn't seem to find anything.

Tara, his assistant—*former* assistant—was always able to find whatever he needed quickly, but for some reason nothing was where he thought it should be. He had to get payroll done today, and it took him three hours before he finally found it.

He'd offered to get a babysitter for Terry's wife if she could come in for a few days, but their kids were sick, and she didn't feel comfortable leaving them. Chris understood, but it didn't help his situation. There was filing to be done, mail to sort through, messages to return, and the list was growing.

Terry did manage to get the drywall delivered this morning, so that was a move in the right direction. His foreman had even offered to stay late tonight and help him, but he'd turned him down. If the kids were sick, Jessica would need him at home.

No, it was up to him to figure out this—whatever this was—by himself.

By eight o'clock, he'd reached his limit. He was hungry and tired, and the rest would just have to wait until tomorrow. Besides, he had to finish a bid waiting for him at home.

After locking up, he drove home.

He should have known he'd never make it up to his apartment unnoticed. Jan was waiting for him as soon as he came through the front door, her arms folded with a look of disapproval on her face. "I'll bet you haven't had dinner yet, have you?"

"No. I haven't," he admitted.

Jan shook her head. "I won't take no for an answer, young man. You look dead on your feet." She ushered him into her apartment and pointed at her table. "Sit. I'll bring you some food." Chris was too tired to argue. He might be thirty-two years old, but Jan, much like his mother, had a way of making him feel like a naughty child, so he did as he was told.

It wasn't until he got a whiff of what she pulled out of the microwave that he realized he'd missed lunch, too. As soon as the plate was put in front of him, he ate with gusto. Jan was a great cook, even better than his mom, if he was being honest, and she just watched him eat while shaking her head and clicking her tongue.

When he finished, he pushed the plate away. "Thank you, Jan. That was delicious."

She came over and sat across from him, still not looking all that pleased. "You're welcome. I promised your mom I'd look after you, but what am I supposed to tell her when you aren't even eating?"

In truth, Chris felt a little guilty. After his divorce, his mother had been beside herself with worry, begging him to move down to Cincinnati to be closer to them, but his business had just started gaining momentum. Moving in with Jan and Charles had not only worked for him, but eased his mom's mind as well.

He gave Jan a grateful smile. "I'm sure you'll think of something."

Chris had meant to lighten the mood, and thankfully it did. A slow smile spread across Jan's face, and she shook her head in amusement before getting up to put his empty plate into the sink. "You're not too big for me to turn you over my knee, Christopher Daniels."

He laughed deeply and soon Jan was laughing just as hard.

As she wiped tears from her cheeks, she said, "Okay. Maybe you are, but you *do* need to take care of yourself."

"I know."

For the next twenty minutes, he talked about his day and his business, and Jan shared the latest gossip from her bridge club. After the week he'd had, he was enjoying the downtime, but unfortunately he couldn't put off work forever. When he noticed it was nine o'clock, he knew he had to excuse himself.

"Thanks for the dinner, Jan, but I really have to be going."

"Do you think you could find the time this weekend to look at the kitchen sink on the second floor? Elizabeth said the water is slow going down."

At the mention of the new tenant's name, Chris felt a lead weight in his stomach. He'd been doing his best to forget about her with the chestnut brown hair and curves that made his fingers itch no matter how much she'd tried to cover them. Why did it have to be her apartment and why so soon? She'd just moved in.

"Sure. I'll make some time tomorrow."

They said good night, and he headed up the stairs.

As he passed Elizabeth's door, he cursed whatever had brought her into his life. He knew what he'd felt when he'd seen her, touched her, how his body had responded, and he didn't like it. He didn't need the complication of a woman again. Carol had taught him that much.

He liked being single. There was no one telling him all the things he did wrong or acting as if she loved him when in reality she was screwing his best friend. He didn't want or need a woman. She was just someone living in the same building, and she would stay that way. No matter what his body was telling him.

Elizabeth was feeling pretty pleased with herself. In the last two days, she'd filled her place with furniture. Rush delivery had cost her a little more, but it was worth it. The space was really feeling like hers now.

There were splashes of color everywhere. Her curtains were a deep red, which matched the rug she'd found for the living room. Bowls and flowers in shades of yellow and blue accented the room.

The colors made her feel alive, and she never wanted to be without them again.

The only thing not yet delivered was her bed, and that was coming today. She wasn't a vain person, but sleeping on an air mattress wasn't something she wanted to repeat in the near future. Every time she moved, it made a squeaking noise that would wake her up.

It was Saturday, so she took her time making a big breakfast for herself. Cooking relaxed her. There was just something satisfying about it, and it reminded her of her mom.

As she washed out a dirty bowl, she remembered telling Jan about the slow drain. It wasn't anything major yet, but it could turn into something more serious, and she wanted to catch it quickly.

There was a knock on the door. *My bed!* A smile lit her face. The delivery guys hadn't called, but maybe Jan had let them in.

She rushed to the door, taking a deep breath before opening it, but it wasn't the men with her new bed staring back at her. It was her upstairs neighbor. He was just as big as she remembered from their first encounter, but instead of the refined dress shirt and slacks, he was now dressed in faded blue jeans and a black T-shirt that pulled tight against his chest. He'd never bothered to introduce himself, but she'd heard Jan refer to him as Chris.

Without thinking, she took a step back, and he must have taken her action as an invitation because he pushed his way into her home. She stayed where she was, unsure of what to do as he walked into her kitchen, stopped, and turned to face her.

"Jan said your sink needs to be fixed."

That was when she noticed his tool belt, and she tried to push away her fear. "Y-yes. She said she'd get someone to fix it," she whispered feebly.

"And here I am." He sounded impatient.

She was at a loss. When Jan had told her she'd get someone, Elizabeth had assumed a plumber would be called. Why would her upstairs neighbor be here to fix her sink? "I-I just thought—"

"Look, I don't have all day. Do you want your sink fixed or not?"

All she could do was nod. The moment Chris turned his back, she practically ran into the living room. She didn't feel comfortable being in the same room with him and his tools, but didn't think it was a good idea to leave him alone either. This way she could still see him, but he was far enough away that she didn't feel crowded. Plus, there were things she could easily use as weapons if she needed them.

She picked up a book and pretended to read. Over the top of it, she watched as he took different tools from his belt. She relaxed a little. He seemed to know what he was doing, and if he was helping her, he couldn't be all that bad, right?

It's not like you could stop him if he wanted to hurt you anyway.

Chris was trying very hard to keep his mind on what he was doing. What in the world had that woman been thinking opening the door looking like that? Her hair looked like she'd just taken a tumble between the sheets, and even though she'd thrown a loose-fitting shirt over her yoga pants, it didn't lessen the effect. She still drove him crazy.

All he wanted to do was fix this drain of hers and get as far away from there as possible. He didn't need this type of distraction, especially from his neighbor. His body was just going to have to learn to live with denial because there was no way he was getting involved with Elizabeth Marshall. Normally he would work from home on Saturday, but today he was willing to make an exception. As soon as this was done, he would grab his things and leave.

Immediately.

Just as he was finishing up, there was a knock at the door and Elizabeth padded barefoot toward the door. He noticed that she keep sneaking furtive looks at him.

What? Does she think I'm going to jump her or something? He quickly placed a wrench back in his belt before walking toward the door where she was standing with two men carrying what looked to be a headboard.

Great! All I need are more visuals.

He knew he had to get out of there. "Your drain's fixed," he snapped, and her eyes widened in response. He didn't like it when she looked at him like that. It made her appear more vulnerable, innocent. "Just let Jan know if you have any more problems," he said in a softer tone.

Her posture didn't relax, and he felt his anger surge.

What is with this woman? Whatever it was, he wasn't sticking around to find out. He wasn't getting sucked in. As he pushed his way through the men and out the door, he got a look at the queen-size mattress propped against the stairs and cursed as he nearly ripped his door off its hinges before slamming it shut behind him.

Elizabeth was stunned when Chris stormed out of her apartment. She didn't understand him. She wondered if he was always this angry or if it was just her. One of the deliverymen caught her attention, and she showed him where her bedroom was. It felt odd having strange men in her home. Even though she was alone with the delivery men, her nerves were more on edge with Chris gone than with him there, which made no sense at all since she was more afraid of Chris.

She went back into the living room to wait. Back near her weapons.

The men weren't long, thankfully. They knew what they were doing and had her bed together in no time. She saw them out the door and then watched from the living room window as they walked to their delivery truck and drove away.

Her shoulders relaxed. They were gone. She could breathe. Then she heard a door open and movement on the stairs. She tensed again until she realized the sound was moving away from her. Chris must be leaving.

She stayed by the window and watched him walk out to his black pickup truck. From up here he didn't seem so intimidating. It didn't look like he could crush her with his little finger. Okay, maybe that was an exaggeration, but he was so much bigger than Jared.

Her fear, she decided, was a combination of the fact that he looked like he could bench-press her and his angry demeanor when he was around her. That he also lived upstairs didn't help matters.

The thought sent a shiver down her spine. Even though Jan seemed to like him and she couldn't see the older woman letting a violent man live there, she was still unsure. It was probably irrational, but emotions weren't always logical.

Her reaction to him was getting to her. She didn't *want* to be scared all the time.

In a split-second decision, she grabbed her keys and ran downstairs to Jan's apartment. Maybe if she found out more about Chris, she'd feel better. Besides, she needed to thank her landlady for getting her sink fixed so quickly.

When Jan came to the door, she seemed surprised to see Elizabeth. "Well, hello, dear. Is everything all right?"

"Oh, yes." Elizabeth quickly assured her. "I just . . ." She paused. "I just wanted to thank you for getting my sink fixed so quickly."

"Chris stopped by, then?"

"Yes." Although part of her reasoning for coming down there had been to learn more about Chris, she was still uncomfortable talking about him for some reason. She felt like she was snooping on her neighbor, but that was the point, wasn't it? How was she going to find out about him if she didn't ask?

They stood there for a few awkward seconds. Elizabeth started to rethink her plan and was just about to excuse herself when Jan said, "Would you like to come in?"

"Yes, please," she said with a sigh of relief.

Jan's apartment looked a lot more lived-in than hers did. It was still the same basic setup, but the furniture was older and little touches gave the place a warm, welcoming feel. She only hoped that one day her place would feel the same way.

She sat at Jan's table with a glass of iced tea in front of her. "How are you liking your apartment? Are you getting settled in?"

"Yes, thank you. All my furniture was delivered, so it's starting to feel like home."

"That always helps," Jan said, and took a sip of tea. "Hard to feel truly comfortable in an empty place."

It was quiet as they both just sat there. *It's now or never*, she thought. "Has . . . Chris"—*it seems odd saying his name out loud for some reason*—"lived here long?"

Jan looked up and there was an odd expression on her face. "About three years."

She nodded when Jan didn't go on. It didn't seem like she was going to find out much this way.

"You're from Columbus, aren't you?"

"Yes." She gulped as the cold liquid slid down her throat a little too fast.

Jan didn't seem to notice her reaction. "It's a nice city. I have some friends there I visit from time to time."

Elizabeth froze. Did Jan know?

But Jan eased her worries when she went on to talk about her last visit to the capital city. "We even went to see a hockey game!" she exclaimed and laughed. "If that isn't an excuse for grown men to fight, I don't know what is."

Jared hadn't liked hockey. He'd preferred golf. Personally, she found it to be the most boring sport imaginable, but as with everything else in her past life, she hadn't been given much of a say.

"So what did you do back home?" Jan asked.

Elizabeth didn't answer right away. Although it wasn't unheard of for a woman to not work outside the home, since she had no children it wasn't common either. Most women her age held a job of some sort. She wondered how Jan would react to her lack of employment over the last five years. "Community work mostly. My husband and I were heavily involved in fundraising for the local university."

"Are you married, then, dear?"

"No."

Thankfully, when she didn't elaborate, Jan didn't press, but instead steered the conversation to some volunteer work she did at the local senior center.

As they continued talking, Elizabeth realized she was enjoying herself. The time flew by and before she knew it, it was after five. "Oh, I'm sorry," she said. "I'm keeping you from dinner."

"Don't apologize. If I'd wanted to kick you out, I would have." She winked. "Besides, I like having company. Chris is much too busy these days to come visit much."

"Oh, sorry." She didn't know why she was apologizing so much, but it just felt right.

Jan laughed and shook her head. "Do you have plans for tomorrow?"

"Uh . . . no."

"Good," Jan said as she began taking what Elizabeth soon realized were leftovers out of the refrigerator. "You can come have dinner with us. We eat at two." She popped the first plate into the microwave. "It's nothing fancy. Just come hungry. I put out quite a spread on Sundays. It's always more than Chris and I can polish off on our own."

She didn't know how to respond but didn't feel like she could say no, considering how hospitable Jan had been. Plus, wasn't learning about Chris the whole point of coming down here in the first place?

Well, she was getting her wish, one way or another. Tomorrow she would find out more about her upstairs neighbor.

CHAPTER 3

Chris' life wasn't getting any easier. No matter if he stayed late at the office or if he brought his work home, he couldn't seem to do anything but fall more and more behind.

There was no two ways about it; he was going to have to call a temp agency first thing Monday morning. Placing an ad and doing interviews himself would just take too long. He needed someone now.

He was sitting at his kitchen table surrounded by stacks of paperwork. To his left were three potential jobs he needed to research and decide if he was going to put in a bid. On his right sat bills that he'd discovered during one of his frantic searches for something else, which now urgently needed to be paid. Directly in front of him were three different piles with everything from accounts receivable to a message from his mother.

For the next four hours he tried to get through as much as he could and even managed to get checks written and envelopes made out for all the unpaid bills. All he had to do was take them to the post office and mail them come Monday. He'd also been able to look at two of the three jobs up for bid and dismissed one right away.

It was only his stomach's rumbling that caused him to look up at the clock. It was Sunday and that meant dinner with Jan. She'd been feeding him every Sunday since he'd moved in, except for when he drove down to see his parents. It was a tradition they both enjoyed.

And according to the clock, he was late.

After putting the finishing touches on her pineapple upside down cake and making sure she was dressed appropriately, Elizabeth carefully walked downstairs. She was nervous, but it didn't make a lot of sense, really. Jan was going to be there, and it wasn't as if Chris was going to attack her or anything. With one last deep breath, she knocked on Jan's door.

Faster than she would have thought possible, Jan opened the door and ushered her inside. "You didn't have to bring anything, dear. I invited you."

"I know, but it didn't feel right coming empty-handed."

Jan chuckled. "Why don't you find a place to put it in the kitchen? I think there's a little space left on the counter, although you might have to move things around a bit."

She nodded and walked with her cake into the kitchen. Almost every surface was covered, but with a little maneuvering, she was able to find a spot big enough beside the refrigerator.

There was a small picture sitting on a shelf over the sink that caught her eye. The woman in the picture was Jan—a much younger version, but still recognizable. The man in the picture towered over her, but it wasn't their difference in size that caught her attention. It was the look on his face. Something she had longed for in her own marriage. Joy. The couple in the picture appeared to be totally absorbed in each other. It was almost magical.

A tear rolled down her cheek.

When she heard Chris arrive, her nerves took over again. Then she reminded herself that she knew he'd be there, and she could have declined. Her original plan to avoid him had already failed anyway. It had been less than a week, and they had crossed paths more than she had in a month with her previous neighbors.

She was going to have to work through this fear that gripped her every time she saw him. It might help if he didn't act angry every time he saw her. Maybe all they needed to do was get to know one another. Not too much, though. She just wanted him to stop being angry with her and for her to stop jumping out of her skin every time she heard him walk past her door or bumped into him on the stairs. With a steadying breath, she walked back out.

What's she doing here? That was his first angry thought when she walked into the room. Okay, that wasn't true. His first thought involved doing things to her that might even make Jan blush, and that was mighty hard to do. Of course, that just made him even angrier. Why couldn't he simply block out this woman's effect on him or something? He didn't even know her.

"Did you find a place for your cake?" Jan asked her.

Instead of answering, Elizabeth continued to stare at him like a deer caught in headlights, eyes wide.

"Elizabeth, dear? Are you all right?"

She finally snapped out of it. "Oh. Yes. I did, thank you."

Chris watched her chest rise and fall under her shirt. Even though it was loose fitting, like all her clothes seemed to be, it didn't help, and in fact only made him more eager to find out what was underneath.

What the . . .

He stopped those thoughts right in their tracks. Elizabeth Marshall was off limits. It was already decided. But for some reason, his body was having difficulty grasping that concept.

Thankfully, Jan asked him to help bring the food to the table.

Over dinner Jan kept the conversation going, and he kept a covert eye on Elizabeth but tried not to address her directly unless he couldn't avoid it. Jan seemed to want them to get to know each other, but it was the last thing he wanted. She'd suck him in just as Carol had, and that wasn't happening again.

Jan asked what her plans were now that she'd moved to a new

town, and Elizabeth mentioned she was going to start looking for a job tomorrow. That's when Jan very nicely informed her of his need for a new assistant. She played it up, sharing how much he'd been working lately, how desperate he was. He began to get suspicious.

Sure enough, she dropped the bomb he might never forgive her for. "Elizabeth would be the perfect solution to your problem, Chris. She needs a job and you need an assistant. These long days are going to catch up with you soon."

He just looked at Jan, dumbfounded and coming dangerously close to yelling at the woman he'd always thought of as a second mother.

"Don't you think she'd be perfect?" she said again, looking at him with innocent eyes.

Perfect. That was a word he didn't want to explore when it came to the woman sitting across from him, since his body was currently telling him the exact same thing.

He contemplated all the reasons he shouldn't offer her a job, even if it was just until he could find someone else, but Jan was right. He was going to run himself down quickly if he continued to work these long hours.

Finally he took the plunge, hoping he didn't regret it. "I could use the help if you're up for it—just until I find someone else," he said hastily. There was no way he could handle seeing her every day and *not* drag her into his office and—

Closing his eyes, he willed those thoughts out of his head.

Elizabeth didn't answer right away. She was stunned. How did a simple invitation to Sunday dinner become a job offer? And from a man who scared her on a level she couldn't even begin to understand.

She realized they were both staring at her, waiting for her answer. The job itself sounded simple enough. It didn't have anything to do with her degree in public relations, but she'd answered phones in a vet's office the summer after high school. It couldn't be that different. Besides, she had to start somewhere, right? Jared had forbidden her from working. For one, it would have given her too much independence, and for another, there was his reputation he wanted to protect. She wasn't even sure her degree would mean much now since she'd never used it. "I . . . don't know. I mean, I don't really have much experience."

Jan waved her hand dismissively. "Nonsense. You're an intelligent person and quite pleasant. You can file, can't you?"

"Well, yes," she said.

"Answer the phone? Take messages?"

"Yes."

"Can you count money? Balance a checkbook?"

"Of course I can," she said indignantly, sitting up straighter.

"It's settled, then." Jan smiled, looking pleased with herself.

As the impact of what just happened hit her, she turned introspective and didn't say much for the rest of the afternoon, excusing herself as soon as she could manage without being impolite. She needed to think.

What in the world have I gotten myself into? Chris thought as he watched Elizabeth leave. Some part of his brain acknowledged the logic of Jan's plan, but it was getting lost in all the reasons why this was a bad idea.

"Do you mind telling me what it is you find wrong with Elizabeth?" Jan asked as soon as they were alone.

He stood and took his dessert plate to the sink. "I have no idea what you're talking about."

"Go sell that line of bull to the guys that work for you, 'cause I'm not buying."

He loved Jan, he really did, but this was not a discussion he was going have with her. Besides, there wasn't anything *to* talk about. He'd just hired Elizabeth Marshall despite his better judgment. Now all he had to do was find a way to keep his hands off her and his mind focused on his work. No problem. He hoped.

CHAPTER 4

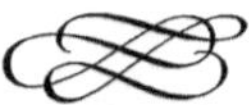

THE ENTIRE MORNING, Elizabeth was a nervous wreck. Every time she replayed yesterday in her mind, she panicked again. Jan had somehow made working for Chris sound like a good idea. What had she been thinking? It wasn't as if she had to get a job right this very minute or face starvation or anything.

But Jan had mentioned how much Chris had been working lately, and how desperate he was in need of help. Maybe his anger wasn't anger at all. Maybe it was frustration due to how overwhelmed he was at work. Stress could do funny things to people.

Trying to calm down, she concentrated on getting ready. This was only temporary after all. She could do this. Besides, it would be worth it if it made for a better neighbor.

After searching her entire closet, she picked out a pair of cream-colored pants with a blue shirt that looked very professional.

As she looked at herself in the mirror, she could hear Jared's voice telling her that while her breasts looked good, she needed to spend more time at the gym toning her butt and thighs. The tears formed in her eyes before she could stop them.

Why can't he just leave me alone?

Pulling herself together, she went back to getting ready. She was just putting her new earrings in when there was a knock on her door. The sound brought with it a whole new wave of anxiety.

Chris was driving her to work today. It only made sense, but she had no idea how she was going to be in a car alone with him. He'd been nice enough yesterday, not as scary as before, but still, between his size and always being angry, he made her nervous.

I can do this, she said to her reflection, and with one last calming breath, she went to answer the door.

Chris waited impatiently for Elizabeth. He wasn't late, but he had a nervous energy he only got when he was running late for a meeting or under a hard deadline. He pulled on the collar of his dress shirt, willing her to hurry up already so he could get this over with.

He'd done a lot of thinking last night and had decided that the best way to handle this was to show Elizabeth where everything was and then leave her to it. There was more than enough work on his desk to keep him busy for the rest of the day, and once she got her bearings, he wouldn't need to have much contact with her. Although he knew he was being naive, he was trying to find a silver lining to this situation he'd gotten himself into.

Just as he was about to knock again, she opened the door.

From the moment he saw her, he knew he was in trouble with a capital *T*. What she wore had him shifting uncomfortably in his seat the entire drive.

What got him most of all was that the outfit was completely appropriate for work. Carol had been all about pushing the boundaries of what was acceptable, especially with the clothing she wore. Elizabeth was driving him crazy without having gone to much effort. *So why am I ready to press her down into the seat and devour her?*

It was better once they got to work. At least he could get a little breathing room.

She was better than he'd expected. By noon she had all the filing caught up, and when he'd asked her for a phone number, she'd been able to produce it in less than five minutes. To say he was impressed was an understatement.

Five o'clock rolled around, and for the first time in a week, he didn't feel as if the weight of the world were pressing down on him. There was still work to take home, but it was a third of his usual load, and it was all thanks to Elizabeth.

So far she'd been nothing like Carol. She was smart, beautiful, and willing to work. It still didn't mean he was thrilled with her being his employee, his neighbor, or the woman who was haunting his thoughts, but he was willing to admit that maybe he'd been wrong about her. Maybe.

Her first day had not been what Elizabeth had expected. Chris had shown her around and then left her to her own devices except when he'd needed something.

The first thing she'd noticed was just how disorganized everything was. It was a wonder he could find anything in that mess. Only one corner of her desk was visible for all the stacks of paper. At least fifty sticky notes littered the desk and were scattered among the papers. Thankfully, she noticed the majority were from the same people. It would make resolving those issues much easier if she didn't have to make fifty calls.

Filing became her number one task. She couldn't get a clear picture of everything until the papers were off her desk.

The morning passed by in a blur as she learned where everything went and put it in its proper place. Chris came out to check on her at noon, and informed her that he'd ordered in lunch and it would arrive soon. Other than that and having her track down a phone number for him in the afternoon, he'd left her alone.

When they arrived home that night, he'd politely said good night to her before disappearing into his own apartment. She was left completely confused when it came to him. Nothing about Chris appeared to be simple. It was difficult to fit the man she'd worked for today with the one who'd all but bitten her head off last week. She was beginning to think her theory about his mood being work related, and not about her, was correct.

Elizabeth slipped off her heels and walked into the kitchen to make dinner. As she chopped and sautéed the vegetables for her stir-fry, she thought of her parents. She needed to visit their gravesite. It had been too long. With everything else going on in her life, she'd not made the trip to the old cemetery since she had decided to move. That had been two months ago.

After putting the finishing touches on her dinner, Elizabeth took her plate to the small kitchen table. So much was different now, but it was for the better. She wanted to share that with her parents. She needed to. Without thinking about it further, she made plans to make the thirty-minute drive to the cemetery just outside London that weekend.

Chris woke up on Friday drenched in sweat, just has he had for the last three mornings. Elizabeth was haunting him, truly haunting him. He couldn't get away from her.

Every morning when she'd answer the door, he'd hold his breath to see what outfit she had on. Yesterday it had been a pencil skirt and blouse. Again, everything was completely work appropriate. Her skirt came down to her knees with only a small slit in the back. It wasn't her fault the slit showed off just enough skin to drive him nuts. Her blouse was beyond conservative, but it couldn't hide what was underneath. Every time she moved, it seemed, his body reacted.

He wanted to peel those layers of clothes from her body to see what lay hidden, and that wasn't good at all. He was her boss. As if that wasn't enough, she was a woman. Okay, that was a given otherwise he wouldn't be having issues below his belt. That didn't change the facts. She was torturing him. Women were nothing but trouble and to be avoided. Life was much simpler without them.

His brain broadcasted that message loud and clear. Now, if he could only get the rest of him to get with the program.

Turning on the shower, he tried to push the thoughts of Elizabeth out of his mind. He had a meeting today with the Beckmans, a couple who wanted to construct a home on their own lot. It seemed straightforward, but you never knew in this business. It was good to expect the unexpected.

The drive to work had been another quiet one. Elizabeth rarely spoke, but then again, neither did he. It was almost as if the confined space of his truck was too much, too close.

At ten, the Beckmans walked through the doors of the small office. Elizabeth greeted them, and he was, once again, amazed. He could tell the couple was nervous by the way each was shifting from one foot to the other as they waited, but Elizabeth managed to put them at ease. By the time he'd picked up his notes and walked back out to greet them, they were both smiling.

Elizabeth sat in on the meeting, taking notes and offering advice when the couple openly included her in their discussion. He found himself fascinated by her smile, something she rarely did around him. A yearning to see more of it gripped his chest before he forced his attention back to the paper in front of him. In the end, the couple signed the contract. He had a new client. And if he was honest with himself, Elizabeth played just as big a role in that as all the marketing brochures on his company had.

Elizabeth tucked her purse under her arm before exiting the vehicle. The cemetery was empty as far as she could tell, but she never felt comfortable leaving her belongings unattended in a public place.

The walk to her parents' grave was short. Their tombstone was only about twenty feet from the small drive. She stopped once she reached them and knelt down, running her fingers over the engraved letters. *Marshall. Gary and Beth.*

She could feel the tears well up in her eyes as she felt the cool granite. It happened every time she saw their names.

"Hi, Mom and Dad. I miss you."

The wind carried her words away, but that was okay. She knew her parents had heard her anyway.

"I moved. You'd like the house. Only the second floor is mine, but it's really nice. And I got a job. I'm not sure how I feel about that yet. I like the job, but Chris . . . my boss . . . well, he's a little confusing." She paused not sure she wanted to go there even with her dead parents. Instead, she took a deep breath and whispered, "I really wish you two were here."

She lay down on the soft grass and continued to talk to her parents. They'd been close once. Before she'd married Jared. She had many regrets in her life, but that was perhaps the biggest. So for the next hour, she gazed up at the sky and told them all about her new life. She only wished they were able to respond.

CHAPTER 5

Over the next two weeks, Elizabeth found herself looking forward to work. Chris still didn't talk to her much and overwhelmed her with his presence, but he didn't use his size to gain a situational advantage. He also hadn't snapped at her since she'd started working for him. She'd observed him interacting with Terry, his foreman, and some of the other guys on the crew, and they all seemed to like and respect him. She was beginning to relax. A little.

He also hadn't brought up replacing her. Although he'd insisted that her job was temporary, he hadn't asked her to schedule one interview, and except for his employees, nobody else had come through the office.

Then one day a woman showed up. Her long blond hair looked as if it had taken hours to style, and her dress revealed a little too much.

As the woman marched past, Elizabeth asked, trying to be polite, "May I help you?"

The woman stopped, turned, and glared. "Who are you?" Her voice had a nasty sneer.

Elizabeth's eyes widened with shock. "I'm Mr. Daniels' assistant. Did you need to see him for something?"

"What happened to Tara?"

Something about this woman bothered Elizabeth. She didn't like her one bit. In fact, the woman reminded her of the ladies she'd met at the parties Jared used to drag her to—gold diggers who chased after men who could spend the most money on them.

"Tara no longer works here," she said, delivering the standardized answer.

The woman snorted as she turned toward Chris' door and barreled her way through without knocking.

Elizabeth immediately followed her, ready to apologize to Chris for the woman's intrusion, but when she entered the office, she found a very different woman than the one she'd just encountered. Gone was the holier-than-thou attitude. In its place was the picture of an attentive and flirty female. The woman leaned seductively against Chris' desk, showing more of her leg than was decent.

He looked up at the new arrival with an irritated expression on his face. "It's okay, Elizabeth."

"Do you want me to—"

"No. Please, stay. Carol won't be here long."

The woman glared at Elizabeth over her shoulder before turning flirty eyes back to Chris.

Who was this woman? Carol made her interest in him clear with the open flirting. That thought brought with it an unpleasant feeling in the pit of Elizabeth's stomach.

"What do you want, Carol? I have work to do."

Carol feigned offense. "Can't I just *want* to see you, Chris?" she said seductively.

Ugh! This woman was making her sick. Elizabeth had seen this game played many times and by women who had skill.

He frowned as he pushed away from his desk and away from her. "No," he said. "You can't. You gave up that right three years ago."

She pouted, but his determined expression didn't change. Then she sighed, pushed away from the table, and leaned on the arm of his chair, showing more of her physical attributes. "I've missed you," she whispered. "I thought maybe—"

"You thought what?" he said in a hard voice.

"I thought maybe you'd like to take a *long* lunch." She ran her finger in a seductive line from his shoulder down his arm.

He caught it and pushed her away from him. "Leave."

She tried pouting again, but he wasn't swayed. "Okay. I get it. You're busy right now," Carol said, strolling to the door and shooting daggers at Elizabeth the entire time. "Another time, then." She walked out with her nose literally up in the air.

"Not likely," Chris said under his breath.

They both remained silent until Carol opened the front door and left. "I'm sorry about that," they said at the same time, causing them both to chuckle. It was the most comfortable she'd ever felt with him.

He sighed. "That was my ex-wife, Carol. I should have warned you about her, but she hasn't shown up in a while. I thought she'd given up."

"Your ex-wife?" Her voice broke.

He smiled wearily. "Yes, unfortunately. She's a force of nature when she wants something."

"I can tell." Her dislike for the woman was growing by the second. Then, thinking she should probably change the subject, she said, "I guess I'll get back to it. There's still a lot to do."

Chris seemed relieved. "Okay then, thank you."

Aside from the difficulty Chris had keeping his hands to himself, things were going remarkably well. Elizabeth was good at her job. She kept things in order and stayed out of his way. She also got along great with the guys. Too well, in his opinion. He'd started to notice it last week.

There was rarely a reason for any of his crew besides Terry to come into the office, but they did anyway. First it was Mark wanting to know if she had some extra pencils, then Chad saying he was going to pick up some lunch for the guys and wanted to know if she'd like some. Yes, it was nice, but he'd never done that for Tara. None of them had. And it didn't escape his notice that it was all the single men on his crew.

He didn't like it. He knew there was no logical reason, but it didn't change the facts. Every time he heard one of his guys at her desk, he wanted to punch them. Not exactly the best reaction for a boss to have, but there it was.

He contemplated what was happening to him. Elizabeth was beautiful, but beyond that, he realized she was nothing like Carol. When he'd offered to have them drive separately to work since he'd be putting in long nights, he hadn't expected her to offer to stay and help. They'd even had a few pleasant conversations during their late nights. It had surprised him.

Carol had been all about what was most convenient for her. It was one of the many reasons his business hadn't picked up until she was out of his life. Every time he would need to stay late, she'd find some way to make him leave. It was a never-ending fight, and one he always lost. She was a master at getting what she wanted, one way or another.

Elizabeth was different; so much so that he found himself letting his guard down with her, and that wasn't good at all. Even if she was different, and even if she was the sexiest thing on legs he'd ever seen—

There was a soft knock on his door and Elizabeth came in. "I'm sorry to bother you, but there's a Mr. Jacobs on the phone. Says it's urgent."

Bryan Jacobs was the lead architect on a project they were about to start. The plans had been finalized months ago. He'd also been one of Chris' best friends in high school. They'd kept in touch over the years and sent jobs each other's way when they could.

"Hello, Bryan. What can I do for you?"

"I just found out something and wanted to call you right away since I knew you were starting construction on the Tanner project."

"We marked the foundation today and if the weather holds, we'll start digging tomorrow."

"Oh, good. I caught you in time, then."

"Caught me in time for what?" Chris asked with dread. He had a feeling he wasn't going to like this.

"Mr. and Mrs. Tanner came tearing through my office about an hour ago with a designer they hired, insisting that all the plans had to be redrawn because the current ones didn't provide the correct *flow*," Bryan said in a way that told Chris that Bryan was rolling his eyes.

This had to be more extensive than just an addendum to the plans. "How much do they want changed exactly?"

"Everything."

"Everything? You can't be serious."

"Unfortunately, I am. And given the time frame, I was hoping you could come to my office tomorrow so we can all sit down together and get this hammered out in one session. It'll be a long day, but I figure it's best to get everyone together at once rather than trying to piece it together through e-mails and faxes. Besides, you owe me a drink, remember?" Bryan said. The attempt at humor didn't work.

Chris rested his face on his hand. *This is* not *happening, just as I'm starting to get caught up.*

But it was happening and a part of owning a construction business. "My assistant and I will be there about nine thirty tomorrow. Will that work?"

"Perfect," Bryan said, exhaling loudly. "I'll see you then."

As soon as he hung up, Chris looked up hotel information and made a reservation for two rooms. He had no idea how late things would go tomorrow, but he was certain that he wasn't going to feel like driving home after the meeting. Besides, if Bryan wanted to get a drink afterward, who knew if he'd even be in any condition to drive.

Chris had summoned her to his office. Once she'd taken a seat, he said, "Do you have any plans for tomorrow night?"

Elizabeth was beyond perplexed. "Uh, no," she said tentatively. Her fear of him had subsided over the last month, but that didn't mean she felt entirely comfortable around him either. Every nerve in her body seemed alive when he was around, and that scared her even more. Her reactions weren't normal. They couldn't be.

"Good. I need you to go to a meeting with me tomorrow, and it will most likely run late, so I've booked us rooms at a local hotel."

She swallowed nervously. "Okay."

"I'll pay you overtime, of course, and I'll be driving us to and from. I just need you there to take notes and keep in touch with Terry during the day to make sure all is well here. I doubt I'll be leaving the meeting for much more than bathroom breaks."

"Is everything all right?" she asked, concerned that he seemed distressed.

"No. A client has decided to completely change their layout. We're going to have to sit down and begin again on everything."

"Does that happen often?"

"No, thankfully. Minor changes are common, but not like this. Even with this meeting tomorrow, it's likely to set the construction schedule back at least two weeks. That reminds me, I'll need to let Terry know."

Elizabeth bit the inside of her cheek. She didn't know how she felt about their little trip. Then Chris stood and she followed.

As he strolled toward the door, she asked, "Where are we going?"

"Bryan Jacobs' office in Columbus."

Columbus!

Thankfully, Chris didn't see all the color drain from her face or her death grip on the back of the chair in order to remain standing on her now less-than-sturdy legs.

Tomorrow she would return to the place she'd hoped to never see again. She was now thinking that Springfield might not have been far enough.

CHAPTER 6

WELL, that was interesting.

Over the last month Elizabeth had been working for Chris, they had found a good balance, and he was seriously considering offering her the job permanently. Besides, it wasn't as if he was making great strides to replace her.

He still wanted to ravish her on his desk. Often. But she'd lost that wide-eyed look she used to give him that did funny things to his instincts. This morning that look was back.

The moment he'd picked her up at her door, he'd known something wasn't right. She was paler than normal, and she kept tugging at the hem of her blouse. On several occasions he'd asked her what was wrong, trying to get her to talk about it, but she would just mumble that she was fine and look out the window. It was infuriating.

Before they got out of his truck, he asked one more time. "Are you sure you're okay?"

She swallowed nervously, seeming to have trouble focusing on him, as if waiting for someone or something to jump out at her. "I'm . . . fine," she said meekly, yet again.

He hadn't believed her the first ten times she'd said it, and he sure didn't believe it now. Unfortunately, he didn't have the time to coax it out of her. They had a meeting to get to.

They walked side by side into the tall gray building that housed Bryan Jacobs' office. Chris had been here many times, but it never ceased to amaze him. Originally built in the late eighteen hundreds, the building had lost all vestiges of its original beauty thanks to the previous owners. It had become Bryan's mission to restore it, and the result was nothing short of magnificent.

Bryan's office was on the tenth floor where his assistant, Karen, greeted them. "It's good to see you again, Mr. Daniels."

"Likewise, Karen. Is Bryan ready for us?"

"Yes." She led them down a long hallway. "Everyone is in the conference room." She stopped and nodded toward a closed door. "Can I get you anything? Coffee? Water?"

"Water would be good, thank you." Chris looked over at Elizabeth, who was even paler than before. Her lips looked almost purple. He wrapped his fingers around her arm, just above her elbow, pulling her just a little closer to him. "For both of us," he said before guiding them both into the room.

He made sure she wasn't going to fall out of her chair before turning to address everyone else, including the Tanners' new designer.

"Good. You're here," the person who had fueled this meeting said in a somewhat snarky tone. "Now we can get to work fixing this joke of a blueprint and get my clients into their dream home."

Chris chose to ignore the designer's comments, and concentrated on the papers in front of him.

"Yes," Bryan said. "Well . . . let's get started, then."

By the time they broke for lunch, he was even more worried about Elizabeth. Okay, worried had left the building about two hours ago.

Since he'd known her, he'd never seen her like this. Every sound made her jump, and every time someone spoke to her, she tensed as if preparing to defend herself. He wanted to get her alone and make her tell him what was going on, but that just wasn't possible. Bryan had offered to take them out to lunch, and it wouldn't have been right to refuse.

The restaurant was close, and the day was nice, so they decided to enjoy the sun and walk. Chris held on to her arm the entire way there, stealing covert glances. She didn't look like she was going to fall, but he wasn't taking any chances.

After the hostess seated them and their orders were placed, the two men fell into an easy conversation. Since they had gone to high school together, they always had fun reminiscing when they got together. It was hard to believe almost fifteen years had passed.

They were just finishing when there was a loud gasp. He looked up and saw a blonde with long hair, staring with wide eyes at Elizabeth. When he glanced at Elizabeth, he saw shock and possibly fear on her face.

"Liz? Is that you?"

He stared at Elizabeth and her muscles tensed as if ready for fight or flight.

"Hello, Stephanie. How have you been?" Her voice was controlled and emotionless, more so than he'd ever heard it before.

This woman obviously knew Elizabeth, but how? It didn't look like she was all that happy to see this Stephanie either.

Stephanie smiled. "Oh, you know. Same old, same old. Rich is taking me away in a couple of weeks to New York for some shopping." Elizabeth didn't comment, but it seemed to go unnoticed by Stephanie. "So are you back? I'd heard you'd *left town,*" she said, the last two words coming out in an exaggerated whisper. "I was rather disappointed. I thought we were friends, and you just disappeared without saying a word."

For the first time that day, he recognized sadness on Elizabeth's face. "I'm sorry," she said. "I'm . . . I'm not back. I'm just . . . visiting. I just thought . . . well, I thought you wouldn't *want* to talk to me."

Stephanie waved a dismissive hand in the air. "Don't be silly."

Elizabeth seemed to relax. "I'll call you?"

This got a large grin out of Stephanie. "You'd better. I'd hate to have to track you down." Then she glanced at her watch. "I'd better get going." She leaned down and gave Elizabeth two air kisses. Elizabeth stiffened but plastered a smile on her face.

"Call me," Stephanie called as she strutted away.

The entire walk back Elizabeth was lost in her own thoughts. She knew Chris was trying to get her attention, but she just couldn't deal with it right now.

Stephanie was her best friend. Or had been, anyway. Before.

But after that night, she had closed herself off. She'd encountered a few of her old acquaintances, sure, and none of them had been pleasant. She'd even received a few less-than-pleasant phone messages calling her every name under the sun and that they hoped she burned in hell. After that, she'd cut off contact with everyone except the police. Stephanie was in Europe at the time, traveling with her husband. By the time she'd returned, Elizabeth had isolated herself completely.

So when she saw Stephanie at the restaurant, she'd been sure that a cold shoulder or a slap in the face would be her reception. Did Stephanie still consider her a friend? It appeared that way.

She was distracted for the rest of the day, so she wasn't paying as much attention as she should have been. Chris placed a hand on her shoulder, and she nearly fell out of her seat.

"Sorry," he said. "It's almost five. Can you call Terry again?"

"Sure," she mumbled before excusing herself.

The phone call to Terry didn't last any longer than the other three she'd made earlier. Everything was fine. No need to worry.

She closed Chris' cell phone and was about to go back into the conference room when she noticed Karen walking toward her with a tray full of coffee, so she opened the door for her. Karen smiled politely and thanked her, but it there was something else there, too. Elizabeth just couldn't figure out what.

The meeting didn't wrap up until after seven, and she was surprised to see Karen still behind her desk when the group dispersed toward the elevators. Chris lagged behind with Bryan, so she waited over to the side for him.

That was when Karen made her move. As she approached, Elizabeth could tell by the look in her eyes that she knew. Elizabeth backed up instinctively.

"I *knew* you looked familiar," Karen said.

"I don't know what you're talking about," Elizabeth said, trying to remain calm.

"Deny it all you want, but I know who you are, Mrs. Carter." Hearing her married name again sent a shiver down her spine. *Mrs. Carter* had died with Jared.

Before she could respond, Chris and Bryan appeared, neither one of them looking happy. "Are you ready to go?" Chris asked. That gruff tone was back. She flinched, and he seemed to notice her reaction and softened his tone. "Bryan and I are finished. Are you done?"

"Yes," she said, barely above a whisper.

He took her by the elbow and led her to the elevators. By the time Chris told her to get into the truck, she had no desire to argue with him. They rode to the hotel in silence, and she watched him covertly. The way he kept tightening and releasing his fingers around the steering wheel scared her.

Once they arrived at the hotel, he still appeared agitated, but at least he wasn't using that angry voice that made her want to cower.

She didn't know what to think. The safety she'd begun to feel around him had quickly changed back to fear.

Her mind was blank. She couldn't think. So instead, she just let him lead her to wherever he was going. She remembered he'd booked them separate rooms, so she was hoping he'd just drop her off and leave. She'd figure everything out tomorrow. Maybe he'd be back to the Chris she was starting to like by then.

When they came to the room, however, he told her to get inside and then followed her in. Her panic hit a new high as he carelessly threw their belongings by the door and walked toward her.

"Now," he said through clenched teeth, "you are going to tell me what the hell is going on, and you are going to tell me now."

"I—" Her voice shook as she backed herself up against the wall.

"Now, Elizabeth."

Her eyes filled with tears as she sank to the floor and curled herself into a ball. "I can't," she cried.

For a long moment, he was silent, and all she could hear was their breathing. Her mind raced with what he would do next. She didn't think he would hurt her, though. Over the last month, she'd seen how Chris dealt with stress, and it wasn't by using his fists.

When he finally spoke again, his voice was softer, calmer. "Why not?"

"Because . . . because you'll hate me," she admitted. For some reason, his good opinion of her mattered. He was her boss, sure, but he and Jan were the only two people she'd gotten to know on any level since moving. She didn't know what she'd do if he could no longer bear to even look at her. Then there was movement, and she felt him on the floor beside her.

"I will not hate you, I promise. Please tell me."

She hesitated. "Why do you want to know?"

He sighed. "You've been acting strange all day, and then just as we were getting ready to leave, something obviously happened with Bryan's assistant. I'm sorry if I scared you, but I don't like being told everything is fine when it isn't. I don't like being lied to. Tell me what's wrong and maybe I can help."

She looked up, trying to gauge whether or not to just tell him. It was then she realized that she didn't care any longer. What difference would it make? If he really wanted to know, all he had to do was ask Karen or do a little research.

Her gaze drifted back down to the floor. "I killed my husband," she whispered.

"What?" The loud boom of his voice reverberated off the walls of the room.

Elizabeth recoiled, putting distance between them.

"I'm sorry," he said, remorseful. "What happened?"

Elizabeth stared at him for a long time, not speaking. She didn't know which Chris to believe. One was angry and scary. The other was kind and not scary at all.

"Why do you look at me like that?" he said.

"Like . . . like what?"

"Like I'm going to hit you or something?"

"You're not?"

"Of course not," he said, shocked. "Why would you . . ." He seemed to realize something. "Someone hit you."

It was a statement, but she nodded anyway.

"And you thought . . . Elizabeth, I'm so sorry. I would never hit a woman. I promise you that."

Chris seemed so sincere that she relaxed a little, getting closer.

Voices in the hall and a door closing nearby were the only sounds to permeate the silence for a long time.

"Do you still want to know?"

"Yes."

She looked up at him, tears once again welling in her eyes. His hand twitched at his side before finally coming to rest on top of hers, offering her comfort. She took a deep breath.

Chris sat patiently as she explained how her husband had been a prominent lawyer in Columbus, a junior partner by the age of twenty-seven. "Jared changed after my parents died. He'd always been controlling, but after it was . . . more."

Her crying had stopped, but she was still trembling. Chris lifted her chin, making her look at him for his next question. "He was the one that hurt you?"

She nodded, and he felt the need to hit something, preferably her husband's face. Too bad he was already dead.

"How long?" he demanded, trying not to raise his voice. "How long did he hurt you before you fought back?"

"Three years."

Chris balled his hands into fists and closed his eyes, willing himself to stay still. He didn't want to frighten her. Once he got himself back under control, he asked, "What made you decide to fight back?"

She was quiet for a long time, and he was starting to think she wasn't going to answer. Then she said, "I know it sounds silly, but I found out he was seeing someone else."

"He was cheating on you?"

She nodded. "I don't know why, but that was just the last straw. I'd given up everything for him and he betrayed me, so I left." She grew quiet and then said, "He came after me."

Chris was proud of her for getting the courage to leave even if it had taken three years, but he wished for her sake the ending had been different. She was obviously disturbed by the fact that she'd killed her husband, even if it had probably been in self-defense.

They fell into silence; the only sounds in the room came from their breathing and the soft hum of electronics. It charged the air around them.

She turned her face, angling it into the crook of his neck. It was innocent, but the feel of her breath, her skin, sent shivers rippling through him. Even in her distress, he felt his body calling out for what it wanted. *Her*.

Chris was getting good at denial, but there was only so much even he could take. "Why don't you go get cleaned up and ready for bed? My room is just next door if you need me."

She sat up and wiped her eyes. "I'm sorry," she said.

"No. Don't apologize."

She nodded, and stood. Halfway to the bathroom, she paused. "Would you mind staying? I mean, in my room. I just . . . I don't want to be alone."

Her back was still toward him, so he couldn't see her face, but he knew to admit something like that to him or anyone had to be difficult for her. This beautiful woman had been through so much. And whether he was willing to admit it to himself or not, he would do anything for her. "Sure. I'll stay if that's what you want."

Seconds later, the bathroom door closed and he was alone.

CHAPTER 7

THE NEXT MORNING, Chris awoke to the bathroom door slamming firmly shut.

He sat up and ran a hand over his face. After Elizabeth had drifted off last night, he'd just sat and watched her sleep while thousands of thoughts flooded his mind from her revelations.

With the morning light, he was still trying to make sense of everything. She obviously had a lot of baggage from her past to deal with, and for some reason he felt a compulsion to comfort and protect her. He didn't *want* to be the one to protect her. That sounded too much like something a boyfriend would do, and that wasn't what he wanted. She might not be like Carol, but he just couldn't go there with her. She was his employee. It bothered him that *that* was barely even a consideration. What was this woman doing to him?

Chris couldn't forget the look on her face when she'd told him that he would hate her. It made him wonder what type of people she'd dealt with before moving to Springfield. Anyone who knew her would surely know that she was not a violent person, but he was guessing that wasn't the case.

When he heard the shower shut off, he knew it was time to get up and moving. Sitting there reliving last night was not doing him, or her, any good.

He grabbed the small duffel bag he'd brought with him and pulled out his clothes. Thankfully, he didn't have any meetings scheduled once they got back, so he could be a little more casual. Though a meeting might have been a welcome diversion.

When she exited the bathroom, Chris was already fully dressed and ready to leave. She quickly gathered her things, put them in her bag, and let him know she was ready. The drive back to Springfield was quiet, too quiet, a charged silence filling the air.

Elizabeth's mind was racing. She knew better than most how a minute, an hour, or a day could completely change everything. During the twenty-four hours she'd been in Columbus, she'd run into an old friend, was confronted about her past, and had to tell her boss and neighbor that she'd killed the man she'd been married to for five years.

As they put more and more distance between themselves and Columbus, she couldn't help but wonder what he thought of her now. What would he do with what she'd told him?

As they passed the one-mile marker for their exit to Springfield, she still hadn't come to any decisions where Chris was concerned. She only prayed that maybe he'd just pretend as if it had never happened.

Chris couldn't seem to get Elizabeth or her past off his mind. Every morning he'd wake up with the memory of how she felt beneath his hand. He'd barely touched her, and yet it was burned into his brain.

As quickly as he was able, he'd push those thoughts away. What he couldn't do was let what she'd shared with him go. In fact, every night since their return he searched the Internet for any mention of the incident.

Why, he had no idea. He didn't want to care about her life, past or present.

He avoided her as much as possible. Occasionally, he'd still go out to a worksite and get his hands dirty. They were a few days behind on the Percell job. His guys had started putting up the drywall the day before, so it was the perfect excuse. Plus, he needed something physical to do, but with all the work of running the company, it didn't happen very often. So any excuse to get out of the office was good. That was how Terry found him at the worksite on Friday, covered in drywall dust and joint compound. "Chris," he said.

He wiped a bead of sweat from his brow and nodded hello to Terry before returning to what he was doing. Terry grabbed a dust mask from the supplies and settled in beside Chris.

Neither man said anything for the next hour as they worked their way around the room, making good progress. They used to work together like this all the time in the early years. Now that the business was going strong, Chris was often too busy handling the paperwork and meeting with clients to come out and get his hands dirty. Terry had been hoping his boss and friend would open up on his own and tell him what bug had crawled up his butt since his return, but that didn't appear to be happening. He'd had five guys come to him over the last three days, each apologizing for whatever it was that they had done to make Chris upset. They were going to lose good men eventually if he didn't get to the bottom of it.

Terry stepped away and walked to where he'd left his cooler just inside the door. Pulling out a water bottle, he moved his mask out of the way and downed half of it before coming back up for air.

"So how've you been? I haven't seen much of you since you got back."

"Good," Chris answered in a clipped voice, barely looking over his shoulder. "Fine."

"I stopped into the office earlier today. Elizabeth said you'd been out most of the week. Didn't know where you were, though. I had to drive around to a few jobsites before I found you since your cell doesn't seem to be working."

The knuckles on Chris' right hand tensed as he tightened his grip on his trowel. "Left it in the truck," he muttered.

"Hmm. Well, good thing there wasn't an emergency or something."

"What are you, my mother?" Chris snapped.

Terry's back stiffened. "No. I am, however, the person who needs to be able to get a hold of you if something comes up. You're the boss, remember? Act like it."

They had known each other for almost ten years, and not once had he spoken to Chris like this. But since nothing else had worked, he didn't feel he had a choice. He'd never seen Chris like this. Not even after Carol.

The trowel flew from Chris' hand and hit the nearby wall with a thud, leaving a gash that would need to be repaired. As Chris marched over to Terry, his anger seethed with each step. "Maybe I should fire you. Then I would be *acting* like the boss."

Terry took a deep breath, but didn't back down. "If that would solve whatever it is that has become permanently stuck up your ass then go ahead."

The two stared each other down, neither giving an inch.

Then, suddenly, Chris turned and walked away, leaving Terry standing there gaping after him.

Chris was avoiding her; that much was obvious. The first month Elizabeth worked for him, he'd spent most of his time in the office doing paperwork or meeting with clients. He'd been nearby, and it wasn't until now that she realized just how much she'd liked having him close. Since they'd returned from Columbus, he'd been in the office twice: once to sign off on a stack of paperwork she'd lain on his desk the previous day, and the second—well, she had no idea. He'd just walked in, not saying a word to her, and went straight to his office.

His reaction had been better than she'd expected. He could have fired her, but instead he just ignored her. She'd lived with a man for five years who, with a good night's sleep, went from Mr. Hyde to the respectable Dr. Jekyll. Chris' reaction was a much better alternative.

Why am I comparing the two?

Sadness took over as she packed up. Chris hadn't been in at all today. Terry had come looking for him around one, and she'd felt rather silly not being able to give him any information. Chris was shutting her out, but she understood that. Who would want anything to do with a murderer, let alone have one as an employee? She turned off the lights, making sure to lock up behind her, and walked to her car.

The driveway was empty in front of the house, so she slowly made her way up the stairs to her apartment. She walked into her bedroom and changed out of her work clothes. Looking in the mirror, she tugged at her shirt, trying to pull it away from her curves.

You're gaining weight. You know what that means.

She closed her eyes and willed the voice in her head to go away. Unfortunately, it was no use. So instead of the pasta she'd planned on fixing for dinner, she grilled up some chicken and made a salad.

Two hours later she was sitting on her couch, reading, when her phone rang, startling her. No one but Chris and Jan had her number.

Cautiously, she went to answer it. "Hello?"

"Did you think I'd let you get away that easily?"

"Who is this?" she whispered into the phone.

There was laughter and then, "It's me, Stephanie. Seriously, Liz."

She breathed a sigh of relief. "Sorry. I didn't recognize your voice. How'd you get my number?"

"Come on. Have you forgotten who you're talking to?"

She knew her old friend was probably standing in a designer suit with her hand on her hip, looking indignant. She couldn't help but laugh at the image. "Sorry. I guess I had a memory lapse or something."

"That's okay," Stephanie said. "I forgive you. I was calling to find out what you were doing for lunch Sunday. I figured maybe we could hit some shops in Dayton or something afterward. Catch up."

She wasn't sure. For the last month she'd had Sunday dinner with Jan, but just the thought of sitting in the same room with Chris and his silence filled her with dread. "Sure," she said, not dwelling on it anymore. "I'd love to."

CHAPTER 8

THE FIRST THING Chris had done after calming down from his confrontation with Terry was to call his mom and see if she was up for a visit this weekend. She was, of course. Marilyn Daniels always had an open door when it came to her children.

Friday night had been difficult. He'd avoided going home for as long as he could. After swinging through a drive-thru for dinner, he'd gone to the hardware store, taking his time picking up things he really didn't need. When he couldn't avoid it any longer, he'd climbed back into his truck and drove home.

Once there, however, he hadn't been able to sleep. The walls felt like they were creeping in on him.

Finally at six he hadn't been able to take it anymore and got up. After throwing some clothes and bathroom supplies into his duffel bag and letting a concerned Jan know where he was going, he hopped into his truck and put some distance between him and Elizabeth Marshall.

He slammed the door of his pickup truck and walked up the short path that led to his parents' front door, where his mom stood just inside waiting for him as she had years ago when he and his three brothers were growing up. She hadn't changed much aside from the addition of the gray that now streaked through her dark brown hair. Her arms opened, pulling him in for a warm hug.

"It's so good to see you, Chris," she said, ushering him to a kitchen chair. "Do you want some coffee? Or maybe some juice? I think I've got some of that white grape juice you like so much."

Chris chuckled. "I'm fine, Ma."

She gave him a look that clearly said she doubted he was telling the truth.

"Really, I picked up some coffee on the way here. I'm good."

She nodded, closed the refrigerator door, and sat next to him. "All right then, tell me what's wrong."

"What do you mean?"

"Christopher Allen Daniels, do not play stupid with me. We've lived in this house for almost ten years now, and I can barely get you to come one Sunday a month. Last night you call out of the blue, wanting to come for the weekend. Something is up."

He took a deep breath and ran his hand over his face. Maybe coming here hadn't been a bright idea. Maybe he should have just gone fishing or something. He grimaced. Fishing. Yeah, right. Just what he needed; endless hours with nothing but his thoughts that seemed to center on the one woman he was trying to *not* think about.

With a heavy sigh, he met his mother's concerned eyes, feeling a sense of guilt for putting that look there, but he had no intention of dragging her into this mess. Besides, if she knew about Elizabeth, she'd only encourage him to go after her, which was the last thing he wanted.

Eventually, his mother sighed and stood, wrapping him in another hug. "I'm here if you want to talk and so is your father, but I understand if you feel you need to figure this out on your own. Whatever it is." And then she left to go wake up his dad.

Chris spent the rest of Saturday working with his dad, Mike, out in the backyard. It was busywork like mowing the lawn and weeding the garden and flowerbeds; just the type of thing he needed to keep his mind busy. He missed the solitude of mind manual labor provided. Trent usually came over to help their parents with the yard work since he lived a little closer, owned his own landscaping business, and had all the right equipment. Their parents just weren't able to keep up with it anymore on their own.

Dinner was a quiet affair. After working outside all day, the food was more than welcome.

He helped his mom clean up before going upstairs to the guest room where he'd stashed his things. The room was littered with pictures of his family. The newest picture was taken about five years ago and included the whole family. He picked it up and studied it. Everyone looked so happy. Gage had just signed with Tennessee. Trent was standing proud, just having finished his first full year as a business owner. Paul stood with his arms wrapped around his wife, Melissa, whose belly was swollen with Chloe, still three months away from entering the world. And even he stood with a smile. He was newly married and happy. Even though Carol hadn't made it to the family barbecue, times were still good. Everyone was happy. So much had changed in five short years.

Before he could let his mind travel any further down memory lane, he dug through his duffel for a clean pair of boxer shorts and T-shirt. What he needed was a shower and a good night's sleep. He walked into the bathroom and turned on the water, watching the hard spray hit the tiles. Showers were simple and guaranteed. He wasn't holding his breath on the sleep.

Somehow he did manage to get a solid eight hours of sleep. The only reasoning he had was all the physical labor he'd done the day before. Even with that, the first thought that crossed his mind as he worked toward consciousness had been Elizabeth lying on the hotel bed, sleeping, her face relaxed, her hair feathered out on the white pillow. No matter how much he tried, he didn't seem to be able to escape her. Not even at his parents'.

Even though his mother hadn't pried any more the day before, she'd obviously decided to take a more direct approach this morning. Seconds after she set his breakfast in front of him, she said, "Jan told me you have a new assistant."

He didn't answer right away, but eventually responded with a quiet, "Yeah."

"How's she working out? Is she as efficient as Tara?"

"More," he answered honestly. Tara had been good at her job, but Elizabeth went above and beyond. Whenever a client had called in, she'd gone out of her way to get all the information he needed, sometimes even thinking of things that would have never crossed his mind until much later in the process. Whenever she'd made a fresh pot of coffee, she'd asked if he'd wanted some even though she didn't have to. Everything in the office was now organized and labeled so he could locate it quickly. She was clearly overqualified for the job, and he knew he should encourage her to find something more suitable, but if he was honest, he didn't want to. And what did that say about him?

His mother nodded. She didn't seem surprised.

"So you like her," she said matter-of-factly.

He nearly spat out his coffee. "What?"

"Well," his mother said, wiping off the counter behind her, "good people are hard to find. You just make sure to take care of her, treat her right."

He didn't respond. All that work he'd done yesterday to push Elizabeth to the back of his mind went out the window.

The coffee in front of him turned cold and he didn't care. His mother's words rang loud and clear. Terry had been right; he'd been a jerk all week. He couldn't keep doing that and expect people to keep working for him. But more importantly, he'd been avoiding Elizabeth. He'd forced her to tell him her past and then he'd left her, just like everyone else in her life had. No matter his feelings, he couldn't continue treating Elizabeth as he had this past week.

Suddenly he didn't feel so good.

He walked over to the sink and dumped the rest of his coffee down the drain before rinsing it out. He wanted to get home and apologize. Elizabeth deserved that from him at least. Without saying a word to his mother, he slipped out of the room to retrieve his duffel bag. Once he had everything, he intended to say goodbye to his parents and be on his way. When he turned the corner, he crashed into his younger brother Trent, nearly bowling him over.

"Hey, there you are," Trent said, getting his footing again and pulling Chris into a hug. "I thought I'd have to send out a search party or something."

Chris snorted. "Sure you were," he said, returning the hug. "Maybe you ought to work on your footwork first. I'm sure Gage can help you with that if you want."

Right away Trent went to grab Chris' shoulder, but Chris was quicker and managed to sidestep him easily and wrap his arms around Trent's waist.

"Now, now, boys. Behave yourselves," their mother said, shaking her head.

The brothers straightened up and smiled, responding as they always did. "Yes, ma'am."

Marilyn Daniels didn't stand more than five feet four, but that didn't mean she was to be underestimated. Her four boys had learned at a very early age that when their mother spoke, they listened.

She walked over, giving them each a loving pat on the cheek, and left the room. Chris turned back to his brother. "I didn't know you were coming."

"Yeah, well, Mom called me last night to see if I wanted to come for dinner today." Then he gave Chris a sly look. "Maybe she didn't want to be alone with you, big brother."

"Funny," Chris said, punching Trent on the arm for good measure.

Just then, their father yelled from the back of the house, "Boys, come help me move the grill. I'm not gonna fry in this sun today." They both smiled and went to help him.

"So . . ."

"So, what?"

"Don't act like you don't know what I'm talking about, Liz. I mean, Springfield? You used to live in Columbus. I know it's not New York or anything, but come on—at least there are decent stores," Stephanie said, her nose wrinkling in disgust as they walked through the local mall. "Why would you pick Springfield of all places?"

She shrugged. "I don't know. It just felt right, I suppose. Plus, I'm not a big shopper. You know that."

"Something I've never understood," Stephanie said as she guided Elizabeth into yet another clothing store.

An hour later, they were sitting inside Ruby Tuesday's waiting for their lunch to arrive. "Tell me about this man you were with," Stephanie demanded.

"There's nothing to tell," she said, taking a bite of her biscuit. "He's my boss."

"Why are you working? I thought Jared had life insurance, and with his job, his bank account couldn't have been that shabby either."

"He did. And no, I don't have to work, but I want to. Sitting at home just isn't for me. I'd go stir crazy." Trying to steer the conversation to something lighter, she said, "And like you pointed out earlier, there isn't all that much to do in Springfield." They were both laughing as the waiter brought their lunches.

By the time Elizabeth walked through the door of her apartment, she was exhausted. After lunch, they had picked up right where they'd left off, putting in another two hours of shopping before Stephanie had to drive back home.

She had mixed feelings about the day. It was good to have a friend again, but Stephanie was from her past and only knew the Liz that Jared created to fit into his world. She didn't know the woman who spent two hours finding the perfect bed sheets with clovers on them. Or the woman who liked to veg out on the couch in front of the television with a huge bowl of double chocolate ice cream.

With a sigh, she took her bags to the bedroom.

It was dark by the time Chris pulled up to the house. Every time he'd tried to leave, his mother or Trent would pull him into a conversation, or his dad would say he needed his help with something.

He loved his family, and no matter how much his mom tried, they never were able to spend a lot of time together. Trent had just turned thirty and owned his own landscaping business that kept him busy. They'd worked together many times over the last few years. Most people didn't want to move into a brand new house surrounded by mud.

Paul, the eldest brother at the ripe old age of thirty-four, was a police detective in Indianapolis. Between his job and his daughter, Chloe, he didn't make the trip to Cincinnati often.

Twenty-six-year-old Gage was the baby of the family and was lucky to make it to Christmas dinner. He was a professional football player and lived down in Tennessee, so he rarely made it home, even during the off-season.

Needless to say, when his mother got some of her kids home, she tended to hang onto them for as long as she could. Chris was almost willing to bet that his mother had called Trent just to get Chris to stay longer.

It was now nine o'clock, much too late to pay a visit to Elizabeth. He'd just have to wait until tomorrow. His eyes lingered on her door as he passed, and for a brief moment he reconsidered before forcing his feet to keep moving.

His apartment was dark and empty. Nothing looked different, but for some reason it felt that way.

He emptied his duffel and then went into the bathroom to take a shower as he thought about the woman downstairs. He still didn't know what he was going to do about her. His attraction to her had not diminished, but no matter how difficult it would be for him, he was determined to be her friend. She deserved that much from him.

Feeling a little better now that he was not only clean but had resolved to set things right with Elizabeth, he slipped into bed. Closing his eyes, he felt his mind begin to float toward the same dream that had been haunting him for the last week, but this time he didn't fight it. This time he let the feeling of her in his arms override everything else.

CHAPTER 9

"Good morning, Elizabeth." Chris smiled in greeting as he paused to pour himself a cup of coffee before walking past her into his office on Monday morning.

She sat there with her mouth open and stared at his retreating back.

What the . . .

Chris had not spoken more than a handful of words to her since they'd returned from Columbus. He'd been distant, moody, and insisted that they start driving the short fifteen-minute drive to work separately—this after they'd driven to work together for over a month. Now he greeted her as if the last week hadn't happened.

Before she could put too much thought into it, she jumped up and followed him. Entering Chris' office had always been a little nerve-racking for her. No matter how many times she'd done it, the act left her with that nervous fluttering in the pit of her stomach. Over the last week, however, she'd realized that she'd been disappointed every day when he didn't come in. It was frustrating, and she didn't understand it. She found she'd missed seeing him every day.

She set his messages on his desk, just to the right as she always did. Before she was able to retract her hand, however, he stopped her. The gesture was innocent, just a light touch to halt her movement, but she could feel the heat of it seeping through her skin.

"Thank you, Elizabeth."

She swallowed nervously. His hand felt warm and comforting while making the anxious feeling in the pit of her stomach explode. "You're welcome," she managed to say.

"Do you have a minute?" His hand didn't leave her wrist.

"Y-yes. Sure."

Chris stood, releasing her, but her stomach didn't settle. He still seemed so close, and yet not.

She wasn't even making sense to herself. Maybe she was going crazy.

"I wanted to apologize. The way I've been acting is inexcusable. I hope that you can forgive me."

"There's nothing to forgive," she said, unable to meet his eyes. No matter how you looked at it, the last five years of her life hadn't been pretty. She wasn't surprised by his reaction, just disappointed. He'd been kind and had listened to her talk about her past. She'd opened up to him about things she'd never told anyone but the police. The budding friendship they'd started to build had been ripped away and left her with that feeling of abandonment again . . .

Chris stepped closer. The look on his face suddenly made it hard for her to breathe. "You're wrong," he whispered back.

The space between them disappeared, and he was so close she could feel his breath on her face. Her head was spinning.

His gaze lowered, and she thought for a moment that he was looking at her lips. *Is he going to kiss me?*

They just stared at each other for a few moments before the phone rang, breaking the connection holding them.

"Excuse me," she said, nearly tripping over her own feet and her mortification on her way out of his office.

Chris was in a daze as he watched her scurry away as fast as her feet could take her.

What just happened?

He honestly had no idea. One minute he'd been trying to apologize, and the next he'd felt this overwhelming desire to kiss her.

Falling unceremoniously back into his chair, he buried his face in his hands. This was not good. He didn't want a relationship, not with Elizabeth, not with any woman right now, maybe ever. Why, then, was his body betraying him like this?

She'd left the door open in her haste, and her voice floated pleasantly into his office as she greeted the caller. He didn't know what to do. Staying away from her wasn't an option. She worked for him and lived in the same building. It was a no-win situation no matter how he played it.

As he contemplated his options, he realized that things had gotten eerily quiet in the other room. He looked down at the phone and saw the light was on; she was still talking to someone. Curiosity got the better of him, and he walked out to see if there was a problem.

When he saw her, he knew something was very wrong. She'd lost all color in her face and her knuckles had turned white as she clutched the phone.

In two long strides he was by her side, that need to protect her rushing through his veins once again, and she locked eyes with him, full of fear.

He knelt down in front of her before reaching for the phone. Putting it up to his ear, he said, "Who is this?"

No one answered.

"Hello?"

Still nothing.

She sat motionless, staring off into space.

No longer caring who was on the phone, he placed it back on the cradle and took hold of her arm, forcing her to face him. "Are you all right?" he asked, trying to remain calm.

"Yes," she said. "I just . . . I wasn't expecting . . ."

"Who was on the phone?"

Like a switch had been flipped, she pulled away from him, grabbed her purse, and bolted out the door.

She didn't exactly know where she was going; she just knew she had to leave. Chris and his mood swings were confusing her to no end. She didn't need that right now, especially after the phone call she'd just received.

What she hadn't expected was for Chris to follow her. She'd just reached her car when she felt his hand on hers. Fear ripped through her, and she pulled away, spinning around to face him.

"Elizabeth, what's wrong? Tell me," Chris asked.

"Why do you care?" she yelled. "Until this morning you'd barely said two words to me!"

"I told you I was sorry about that."

"And I said you didn't need to be." She could feel the tears building and just wanted to be able to shed them without witnesses.

He took a deep breath. "Whether you believe me or not, I *am* sorry."

She didn't answer, and he seemed to get frustrated with her nonresponse. "If you don't tell me who called, I'll just call the phone company. Whoever it was obviously upset you. I *will* find out one way or another." His voice was determined, and as she looked into his face, she knew he meant it.

What does it matter if he knows? she thought, defeated. He already knew about the biggest skeleton in her closet. What was one more thing?

"It was my mother-in-law." Her chin jutted out in defiance.

"Your mother-in-law?"

"Yes."

His face was full of confusion, but finally realization dawned along with understanding. For some reason that just made things worse. She didn't want his pity, his anger, or whatever emotion he decided best fit this new information. She couldn't deal with it right now.

She took advantage of his distraction, opened her car door, and slipped inside. He knocked on her window, but she ignored him as she drove away.

A minute later, she had to pull over because she couldn't see the road through her tears. Jared's mother had never liked her much. Abigail Carter always thought her little boy could do better. Her perfect son. And Elizabeth had taken him from her.

Although the things Abigail had said weren't anything new, they still hurt. She wasn't a horrible person. She'd loved Jared in the beginning. He'd made her feel special, like she was the only woman in the world for him, but Abigail could never believe her baby boy was beating his wife and that what Elizabeth had done was purely in self-defense.

Anger began to replace the fear and the hurt. She wasn't sorry she'd fought back. She only regretted that it had ended with the loss of a life. Jared had been terrible to her, but she could never bring herself to wish him dead. All she'd wanted was to leave, but he wouldn't allow her. She'd had no choice. She knew that. Unfortunately, that didn't make it any easier.

She had no idea how much time passed before she glanced at her surroundings. Nothing looked familiar. She had no idea where she was.

She dug through her purse for a tissue and then angled the rearview mirror so she could wipe the tears and streaked makeup from her face. After she pulled back onto the road, it didn't take her long to find a sign for Route 40. All she wanted to do was get home and have a large bowl of chocolate double fudge ice cream.

As soon as she left, Chris locked up the office, jumped in his truck, and peeled out of the parking lot.

He pushed the speed limit as much as he dared to get to the house. He figured he'd try there first. If she wasn't there, he had no idea where to look, but he'd cross that bridge when he came to it.

Luckily for him her car was in the driveway, and as he hopped out of his truck, he realized she was still sitting inside. Slowly, he walked over and knocked on the glass.

She jumped and just stared at him, looking shocked. Her eyes were red.

Seeing her hurting caused an odd pain in his chest, and he felt compelled to comfort her. Before he could think it through, he opened her door and guided her out of the car and into his embrace. Her arms hung limply at her sides at first, but then she wrapped them around his waist and rested her head on his shoulder.

She felt good against him—right. She always smelled feminine. He wasn't sure if it was her perfume or just her, but it pulled him in no matter how hard he tried to resist.

Suddenly, as if realizing where she was for the first time, she stiffened and he released her. She stared up at him, but neither spoke. Minutes passed, and that pull he felt for her returned again, even stronger than before.

Ever since Elizabeth Marshall had walked into his life, he'd wanted her, and no amount of avoiding or denying was working. At that moment, he didn't want to avoid. He didn't want to deny. He wanted her. Now. Even if he woke up tomorrow kicking himself, he'd take it. All he wanted was to stop fighting whatever this was, just this once.

When he finally kissed her there was an energy surrounding them that he'd never felt with another woman, and something inside him wanted to get as close to her as humanly possible.

The moment their lips met, she couldn't think clearly. His lips were soft, gentle, and tentative in such contrast to his size. He cradled her cheek as if she were the most precious thing before sliding his hand back into her hair to pull her closer to him.

The feel of him so close wasn't as scary as she'd thought it would be. Jared had never touched her like this. He'd never made her feel alive like she did now. She felt vulnerable and strong at the same time. Chris guided their movements, but allowed her to lead.

She gripped his shirt as she lost herself in the sensations. A warm, tingly feeling ran from her lips down to her feet.

He pulled back and she opened her eyes. He stared at her with a strange look on his face. His hand was still in her hair, sending warm pulses down to her feet. She wanted him to kiss her again.

They stared at each other until the spell was broken by the sound of a car door slamming.

"I knew you were screwing her!" Carol stomped toward them with a look of fury in her eyes.

Chris took a step back but didn't release Elizabeth completely and kept a hand protectively on her waist. "What are you doing here?" he demanded.

"Not even going to try and deny it, are you?" Carol was acting like a jealous wife.

"If memory serves, you're the one who had trouble keeping your pants on, not me. We aren't married anymore, so what I do or who I do it with is none of your business." His voice held an eerie calm, but Elizabeth felt his fingers flex against her back. "So I ask you again, what are you doing here?"

Carol stood motionless as if waiting on Chris to apologize or beg her forgiveness. But judging by his expression, he looked like he'd rather eat glass.

Then, before Elizabeth's eyes, Carol's features changed, becoming both pouty and flirty at the same time. She'd witnessed this earlier when Carol had stormed into Chris' office.

Suddenly, Elizabeth was furious, and she had no idea why. Chris leaned down and whispered in her ear, asking her if she could give them a minute. She didn't want to leave that nasty woman with him, but she did. She turned on her heel and marched inside, leaving them on the front lawn.

Once inside, the stairs seemed taller than usual as she trudged up them. It was as if a rubber band were inside her and with each step, it was stretching, pulling. She didn't know what was causing the feeling, but she didn't like it.

When she stepped inside her apartment, she walked straight to the kitchen for some water. Her mouth felt dry, and she wanted to lie down. It was only eleven in the morning, and she already felt as if she'd run a marathon.

As she walked into her bedroom, she kicked off her shoes. It wasn't until she was halfway across the room that she noticed something wasn't right. The sun was shining brightly outside, and yet her room seemed dark in comparison. Had she closed the curtains this morning?

She looked over to the window across the room. It took only seconds for her brain to take in what it was seeing. She screamed as she dropped her glass and heard it shatter on the floor.

CHAPTER 10

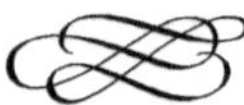

CHRIS WATCHED as Carol drove away. For whatever reason, she obviously wanted him back, but that was so *not* going to happen. *Fool me once, shame on you. Fool me twice . . . yeah.* She was not going make a fool of him again. Once was more than enough.

He turned toward the house, looking up to the second story windows. He'd kissed Elizabeth, and there was no question he wanted to do it again, but all his doubts were still there. He wasn't sure he could handle what happened with Carol again.

But she wasn't Carol. That was the whole point, really. Elizabeth was genuine. She didn't hide behind falsities. He never had to wonder if she was being honest with him.

Could he give whatever this was between them a chance?

He opened the main door to the large Victorian as he thought about the possibilities, but before he made it to the stairs, he heard Elizabeth scream. He raced up the stairs and burst through her door.

Hearing a noise coming from her bedroom, he raced in to find her kneeling on the floor and surrounded by broken glass.

She was staring, transfixed. Something was covering her window. He walked over to get a closer look. He was no expert, but it looked like blood and small pieces of flesh running down the smooth panes of glass and onto her floor.

Someone had been in her apartment, in the house. His mind raced, thinking of the implications. Alarms would need to be installed. He couldn't let anything happen to her or Jan.

He knew not to touch anything and, turning his back on the mess, he went to Elizabeth. She was clearly shaken, but he needed to get her out of there. He wasn't about to make her stay there looking at that window. Without thinking, he knelt down and scooped her up. She didn't fight him; just lay stiff and unresponsive in his arms.

He carried her up to his apartment. Once inside, he dialed 911. The dispatcher informed him that, since no one was in any immediate danger, a police officer would be there in an hour or two.

He hung up the phone and glanced over at Elizabeth. She hadn't moved. Her legs were still slightly bent, her back against the arm of his couch, her head tilted to the side leaning against the cushions. Just exactly how he'd left her.

She was in shock, and he couldn't even imagine what was going through her mind.

He walked into his kitchen and got her a glass of water. When he returned, she didn't even acknowledge him. "I brought you something to drink."

Nothing.

"Elizabeth?" he said, touching her shoulder.

She turned around sharply, eyes blazing, muscles tense, ready for a fight.

"Easy. You're okay. I thought you might want something to drink."

She looked down at the water in his hand, but it was almost like she didn't recognize what it was. A few seconds later, he saw her shoulders relax as she reached out. "Thank you," she said, taking the glass from him. She took a sip and then brought it down to rest in her lap.

"I called the police. They'll be here later to look at things and take a report," he said. She just nodded, so he stood and went over to the chair across from her to sit down. All they could do was wait.

After spending the day volunteering at the senior center, the first thing Jan noticed when she pulled up in front of her house was a police car.

She'd checked her phone after leaving the senior center and noticed Chris had called. Since he hadn't left a message, she hadn't been concerned. Now she was wishing she'd called him back.

Given that Jan and her husband had not been blessed with any children of their own, she'd always looked after Chris as if he was her own son. The thought of anything happening to him, or Elizabeth for that matter, sent a jolt of fear through her.

Both Chris' truck and Elizabeth's car were in the driveway nearly blocked by the police cruiser. Her mind was flooded with awful scenarios, but she knew she needed to calm down and stop jumping to conclusions.

She grabbed her purse, rushed inside and up the stairs, and her heart skipped a beat when she saw the open door to Elizabeth's apartment.

Quietly, she took the last few steps up to the landing and looked inside. Chris was standing just inside the entryway, his arm around Elizabeth as if supporting her weight. They both stood with their backs to the door.

Her attention shifted as a police officer in full uniform walked out of the bedroom. In one hand, he held a plastic baggie with a specimen cup filled with some kind of red blob, and had a camera in the other. "I've got everything I need. I'll get this to our forensics lab and have it analyzed. I'd be surprised if it's human, though. Looks more like someone was just trying to scare you," he said, looking directly at Elizabeth.

Elizabeth only nodded. The poor thing truly looked frightened, and Jan wondered what in the world had happened.

The officer reached into his pocket and handed a business card over to Chris before giving a curt nod to Elizabeth. "Someone will be in touch when we know something. Call us if you think of anything else." Then he turned and came to the doorway where Jan stood. "Ma'am," he said, nodding to her before going around her and out the door.

Jan watched as the man descended the stairs before turning back to Elizabeth and Chris. "Are you two all right?"

Chris said, "Yeah. We're okay."

"What happened?"

Instead of answering he said, "I called my security guy, the one I use on jobsites. He'll be here in the morning to take a look at what we need."

It took Jan a second, but then she understood. "Someone broke in? How?"

"Don't know. There was no sign of forced entry."

Jan went over and pulled Elizabeth into a hug. "I'm so sorry, my dear. Is there anything I can do?"

Elizabeth allowed Jan to hug her, but didn't return it. When Jan released her, she leaned back against Chris, and he immediately put his arm around her shoulders. No matter what he said, Chris wasn't as impartial to Elizabeth as he'd wanted Jan to believe.

"I need to clean it up," Elizabeth said in a dead voice.

There was one thing Jan was sure of: whatever the mess was, she didn't need to be dealing with it. "You don't worry about that, dear. Chris and I will take care of it. Why don't you just sit down and relax?"

"No, I couldn't—"

"Jan's right," Chris said. "You don't need to be dealing with cleaning up that mess. Come on, you can wait upstairs."

As soon as they were out of sight, Jan walked into the bedroom. One look and she knew why Elizabeth had been so shaken up. Jan had grown up on a farm, and her dad had a room in the back of one of their barns where he'd slaughter their pigs. What was on her far wall looked like the stuff that was left on the concrete floor after her father was done slaughtering a pig.

Whatever it was, it was not a house-warming present. This looked personal to her. Someone was trying to send a message, but who would want to hurt a sweet woman like Elizabeth?

Elizabeth was numb. She hadn't felt like this in a long time. Not since the night she'd killed Jared. Chris had helped her upstairs to his apartment and guided her to his couch. After giving her another glass of water and making sure she'd be okay alone for a while, he'd gone back downstairs with Jan.

There was a part of her that knew she should be the one cleaning it up and not them. They were too good to her, and she didn't deserve it. She stared at the glass of water until Chris returned and knelt down in front of her, frowning as he took the full glass from her hands.

"Are you hungry?" he asked.

She shook her head. She didn't think she could eat anything if she tried.

"Tired?"

Yes. She was tired. Although she knew it was only midafternoon, she felt as if she'd been up for days. She nodded and the next thing she knew, Chris had lain her down on the couch and covered her with a blanket. She began to cry. It had been so long since anyone had taken care of her.

Chris said, "I'm right here. You're safe." Callused fingers brushed lightly against her face as she let sleep take her.

By the time she woke from her nap, the sun was going down. She sat up, unsure where she was.

Looking around, she located Chris sitting at a table surrounded by paperwork. Memories of what had greeted her in her bedroom came rushing back. She closed her eyes and took a deep breath. Safe. No one was trying to hurt her right now.

Her eyes opened again. Chris hadn't noticed that she was awake, and she enjoyed a moment of just watching him.

She watched his hands sort through the pages and remembered the feel of those fingers on her face, in her hair. She recalled the gentle pressure of his hand on her back as he'd kissed her. A shiver ran down her spine. Only hours ago she was having trouble feeling anything. But now, seeing him across the room doing something as simple as sorting through paperwork created that fluttery feeling in the pit of her stomach. What was happening to her?

Her gaze traveled up to Chris' lips. His mouth was open slightly. It was something she'd noticed he did when he was concentrating on something. She couldn't help but remember the feel of his breath against her lips just before he'd kissed her. And no matter how wrong the moment was, she wanted his mouth on hers again.

She was so lost in her thoughts that she didn't realize Chris had caught her staring until he shifted his position. She glanced up and her eyes met his heated stare.

Gone was the fear she used to feel in his presence. Now there was this need to be closer to him.

Even though she'd run from him, he'd helped her, comforted her. He'd let her lean on him when everything seemed like too much. And he'd brought her into his home when the thought of being in hers had terrified her.

The invisible pull toward him was getting stronger. Suddenly, Chris pushed back from the table and their connection was lost. She immediately felt empty.

He doesn't feel it.

"Jan brought some dinner if you're hungry. Chicken and noodles." He walked toward what she assumed was his bedroom, given the layout of her own apartment. "I'm going to go grab a shower," he mumbled and then disappeared behind a closed door. She stared at the door until she heard the shower.

Reluctantly, she pushed herself up from the couch, folded the blanket she'd been using, and shuffled into Chris' kitchen. It was the exact reverse of her own, and the crockpot filled with Jan's chicken and noodles was on the counter by the stove.

She located a bowl and refilled her glass of water. Finding the silverware was easy enough, and once she'd scooped a healthy-sized helping into her bowl, she went to the table and sat down.

The food was good, but that wasn't a surprise. Jan was a great cook. She was still hungry once she'd polished it off, so she went to get more. *That's the last thing you need.* She ignored her inner voice and scooped another large portion into her bowl.

Finally after fifteen minutes, the sound of water cut off, and it seemed like forever before Chris came out, not looking at her as he found a bowl and filled it. He seemed to debate whether or not to come sit with her at the table before remaining at the counter. Not sure what to do, she switched her focus back to her own food and finished eating. The second bowl didn't taste quite as good as the first.

After they were both finished, she was at a loss. She knew she should really go back down to her apartment. It was getting late, and she was sure Chris would want to go to bed in the not too distant future. But the thought of being alone in her apartment sent chills up her spine.

She was still trying to give herself a pep talk when Chris left the room and then came back with a pillow under his arm. He walked to the couch she'd been lying on earlier and threw the pillow down at one end. "I made up the bed with clean sheets for you. I also laid out a toothbrush in the bathroom for you to use." Chris stretched out on the couch and turned away from her.

As much as she didn't want to, she had to say it. "I can go back downstairs. You don't have to give up your bed for me."

He turned and his stare was hard, determined, and somewhat angry. "No. Until the alarms are installed, you stay here."

CHAPTER 11

THE KINK IN CHRIS' back left little doubt that he'd spent the night on his couch. Rolling over, he stretched out his limbs as far as he could, given the limited space, and glanced at the clock. It was only five thirty, an hour before he had to get up. *Looks like today will be starting early.*

He threw the blanket off, sat up, and aggressively rubbed the sleep from his eyes. Jim had promised to be there first thing this morning to discuss security options, but that still meant eight o'clock at the earliest.

What he wanted was a shower, but that wasn't going to happen. She was asleep in his bed, and he'd have to walk through his bedroom in order to get to the shower, so that would have to wait. There was no way he could handle seeing her in his bed. Knowing she was there was bad enough.

Since he had time, he went into the kitchen to make breakfast. He pulled out all the stops, fixing bacon, eggs, pancakes, and even frying up some hash browns. Just as he was ready to plate the eggs, he saw movement out of the corner of his eye. She was standing there in one of his T-shirts and a blanket wrapped around her.

It was only with great effort that he managed not to drop the eggs.

Trying to distract himself, he said, "I made breakfast. Hope you're hungry." When he looked up, she smiled and his heart slammed against his chest, making it difficult to breathe. If he thought she'd been nearly irresistible before . . .

Knowing he had to get out of there and soon, he set the plates down on the counter. "Everything's ready. Help yourself. I'm going— I'm going to grab a shower first." Then he quickly brushed past and locked himself in his bedroom.

The problem was his bedroom was no longer safe. He could smell her everywhere, and that was before he noticed the tangled sheets.

It had been more than three years since he'd been with a woman. After seeing Carol in bed with his best friend, the last thing he wanted was any type of female companionship. He'd been tempted, sure, but even the thought of reliving what he'd been through with his ex-wife had turned his stomach and easily quashed any desire he had. He could honestly say he'd never been tempted like this. Elizabeth Marshall was something he'd never experienced before, and he wasn't sure that was a good thing.

He wanted her. There was no doubt about that. The physical attraction had been obvious from the first moment he'd laid eyes on her. But he'd dealt with that before. This . . . was something else, and he had no idea what he was doing. All he knew was it was driving him insane.

Now someone was toying with her. Even though the cop hadn't done much yesterday other than get their statements, take a few pictures, and collect a sample, he couldn't fault his assessment that someone had been trying to scare her.

That thought cooled his jets like nothing else. But, of course, it also brought that driving need to protect that seemed to come out whenever he was around her.

Given what he knew about her, which wasn't a lot, and the phone call she'd received yesterday, it was clear that people from her past didn't like her very much; people who might think it within their right to mess with her. But whoever had done this had entered her home. That didn't sit well with him. What if she'd been there?

He needed to find out more about what her life had been like before she'd moved to Springfield. She didn't like to talk about it, he knew, but it couldn't be avoided now. If someone was willing to go to this extreme once, who's to say they wouldn't do it again?

He let that uneasy thought settle into his bones as he rummaged through his drawers to find a change of clothes.

She watched Chris disappear behind his bedroom door, shutting it a little harder than necessary. He seemed preoccupied this morning, although considering what had happened yesterday, she couldn't blame him. She was, too.

She took her plate over to the table still cluttered with the paperwork Chris had been going through last night and made some room. It surprised her was how hungry she was both this morning and last night. Normally when she was stressed, she ate less. With that thought came the nagging voice telling her she'd need to spend more time in the gym, working off the pounds she'd shoveled into her mouth. She tried to ignore it, but that was easier said than done.

She thought of Chris and how different he was from Jared. Their kiss yesterday had felt really good. So gentle. She had no idea if he'd enjoyed it as much as she had. Jared's kisses were always hard and forceful from the very beginning. When Chris kissed her, she'd felt special. When Jared had, she'd felt marked.

Even when Chris had been angry, it was different. Jared used to grab her by the hair and pull her roughly against him. He'd tower over her just to scare her. It was as if he fed off her fear. When Chris had realized he was frightening her, he'd backed off.

Hearing the water turn on again in the other room, she wondered what Chris looked like naked. Just one look told her he was well built. She had never showered with a man, not even her husband. She'd never had the desire to. But for whatever reason, the thought of doing that with Chris left her feeling flushed.

Then reality hit her. If she could see him, he'd be able to see her, too.

Okay, maybe that's not such a great idea.

She took her dishes to the sink and then grabbed her purse. She needed some air and some clothing. Without allowing herself time to talk herself out of it, she ran down the stairs and dashed into her own apartment.

She stopped just inside the door. It was the same space and yet it felt different. Everything was in its place. Even when she walked into her bedroom, it was just the way she'd left it the morning before.

She went to her closet and selected a nice pair of slacks and a pretty top. It would be dressy enough for work, but still comfortable if she stayed home. As she closed the closet door, something nudged at her subconscious. She opened the door again, and looked inside, but nothing appeared out of place. After shutting the door again, she started to get ready for the day.

She had just slipped the top over her head when she heard her front door open.

"Elizabeth?"

Rushing out, she saw a furious and somewhat frightened Chris.

"What—"

He crossed the room in three long, determined strides and backed her up against a wall. A moment of panic registered before her brain kicked in again. *Chris. Not Jared.* She felt small pressed up against him like this, felt every muscle in his body against hers, but the fear wasn't there. And then she couldn't think anymore as Chris took her head in his hands, tilted it upward, and kissed her.

This was so unlike the kiss they'd shared previously. Before it had been soft and gentle, providing comfort. This kiss—this kiss had nothing to do with comfort. There was an edge to it. She could feel his anxiety seeping through the kiss itself.

Pushing away to hold her at arm's length, but not relinquishing his grip on her, he said, "What are you doing down here?"

She was so disconcerted from the kiss that it took her a moment to get her thoughts together. Before she could respond, his mouth was on hers again.

His lips were just as possessive as they had been before, but this time his hands roamed down her arms and back. Chris' touch sent heat through her body, and she felt almost dizzy from the sensation.

She didn't want to lose the feeling. Lifting her arms, she wrapped them around his neck. Suddenly Chris' body relaxed against hers, and he deepened the kiss as his hands continued to explore.

Something inside Chris had snapped when he'd come out of the shower and Elizabeth wasn't there. He could think of nothing but finding her as he'd raced down the stairs.

The moment he'd laid eyes on her, all reason went out the window. His body acted on instinct alone and had him pushing her up against the wall. He needed to feel her, to know she was all right.

Nothing he felt was the least bit gentlemanly. He wanted to devour her, to erase the dread he'd felt when he'd realized she was gone. He'd never felt that level of fear before, and he never wanted to again.

His hands slid down her lower back to cup her backside, pulling her against him. The feel of her soft curves pressed against him just fueled his desire.

When Chris lifted her up, it took little encouragement from him before she wrapped her legs around him.

Her lips were so soft against his, but they met his kisses with equal fervor. He could taste the orange juice she had with breakfast, but it held a minty undertone and the warm sweetness he remembered from the kiss last night.

Why did I ever think this was a bad idea?

Pressing her back against the wall, he slid his hand under her shirt. Her skin was just as soft as he imagined it to be. He took pride in her answering gasp. He explored her throat and neck with his mouth as her head fell back against the wall.

He was just inching his hand upward when he heard a knock on the open door behind him and a throat clearing. Chris took a deep breath and turned around, already knowing what he'd find. Jim was standing there with an uncomfortable look on his face.

"Sorry. The lady downstairs let me in. You said this was urgent, but I can come back if . . ."

"No," Chris said. He cleared his throat and let Elizabeth's legs slip back down to the floor. "It's fine." He took a step back from Elizabeth and noticed her face was flushed and her breathing was ragged.

As if on cue, Jan appeared behind Jim at the door. "Oh good, you found them." Then to Elizabeth she said, "I thought maybe you'd join me for coffee while the boys do their thing."

"Uh . . . sure," Elizabeth said, wringing her hands together.

Her eyes stayed fixed to the floor as she left, and then she turned back, looking at Chris once more before disappearing.

He didn't know how he felt about what had just happened between them. His body had wanted it, sure, but it didn't change anything. In fact, it made him feel like a cad. She needed a friend right now. She'd just had her personal space violated, and no one deserved that, especially her.

With a new determination, he turned to Jim. "Where do you want to start?"

It took a few seconds for Jim to catch up, but when he did, he was all business. "The perimeter."

They walked downstairs and he willed himself not to look at Jan's door when he went past, knowing she was in there.

The rest of the morning was full of distractions. Jim led him around the property, pointing out locations he felt needed lighting before they both headed back to the house for a walkthrough of every room on all three floors. They discussed sensors for the windows, new locks for the doors, and an alarm system for the main entry as well as each individual unit.

Some might have thought it was overkill, but he was just hoping it was enough. He never wanted to come home and see that look on Elizabeth's face again.

Jim handed him a sheet of paper. "This is a list of all the

recommendations I'm making. You can look them over, mark the ones you want to go with, and e-mail it back to me when you're ready."

Chris looked it over. Everything seemed pretty standard with a couple of exceptions, but they'd already discussed those. "You got a pen?"

It took all of twenty seconds for him to put a checkmark beside all the items and sign at the bottom.

He handed the paper back. "When can your guys start?"

Jim tucked the sheet back into a blue folder. "They'll be here first thing in the morning."

After they shook on it and Jim left, Chris lingered for as long as he could before walking back inside. For all his distractions, he was no better mentally than he'd been three hours ago.

He'd kiss her. Twice.

The first time he could almost justify. She'd been upset, and he'd gone in wanting to comfort her. It was completely innocent. At least that's what he tried to tell himself.

What had happened in her apartment this morning had made it clear that whatever it was could not happen again. He'd felt so out of control, desperate. He didn't like it. Logic had taken a backseat to his need to be as close to this woman as he could physically get.

And what would have happened if Jim hadn't appeared when he did? That was simple. He could have stripped her of every inch of her clothing and taken her against the wall.

He gripped his hair in frustration. He didn't like this—this out-of-control feeling. Women were trouble. They took and took until you couldn't give any more, and then they tossed you aside like yesterday's garbage.

But as those thoughts played on repeat in his mind, he knew they weren't always true. He could see how different Elizabeth was from Carol. Knew that they were cut from totally different cloth, but even if he dismissed his worries over getting hurt again, there was still her past. Her husband had only been gone for seven months and she had a lot on her plate.

She had baggage and so did he, plain and simple. The two of them were not a good idea.

The door to Jan's apartment opened and, as if sensing the direction of his thoughts, Elizabeth stepped forward, the doorframe surrounding her like a picture. "Hey," she said shyly.

He took a deep breath. "Hey." He tried for a friendly smile but wasn't sure he pulled it off.

"We saw your friend leave."

"Yeah, he's sending a couple of guys over tomorrow morning to start the installation. There's a lot to be done so it might take a couple of days."

She nodded. "Jan has a spare room. She said I could stay there until everything's ready. I thought—well, this way you wouldn't have to sleep on the couch."

He pushed himself off the wall. "Yeah. Yeah. That's a good idea."

Looking anywhere but at him, she said, "I'll just—get some of my things, then."

She turned to go, but he reached out to stop her. "I . . . I just wanted to say that I'm sorry about Carol yesterday. I don't know what's gotten into her."

"It's okay," she said.

"No, it's not."

She nodded, and he stepped back. Her body brushed by him on the way up the stairs. He wanted to stop her again, but he didn't. This was for the best. If he didn't gain some perspective soon, good or bad, rational or not, he was going to do something he'd regret.

CHAPTER 12

JAN WAITED DOWNSTAIRS FOR ELIZABETH, who was upstairs returning a call to her friend Stephanie.

She'd been staying with Jan for the last two days since the alarm installation was taking longer than expected. Windows weren't cooperating, and bushes and trees had to be trimmed. There was even some problem in the attic. Every delay seemed to put Chris more on edge. He'd taken to only going into work in the mornings and bringing a stack of paperwork home with him every afternoon.

In some ways, Jan was glad for the delay, even with the way Chris was acting. It had been a long time since she'd had someone living with her, and she'd missed the companionship. Elizabeth was a gem, the ideal roommate. And she was perfect for Chris. He was just being stubborn as usual and refused to see it.

Or maybe he does. Maybe that's the problem.

When her telephone rang, Jan smiled when she saw the caller ID.

"Hello. How are you? How's my boy?"

Jan laughed. "I'm well. And your boy? Well, let's just say he's being kept on his toes."

"It's his new assistant, isn't it?"

"You know about Elizabeth?"

"So that's her name." Marilyn chuckled. "I knew there was someone who'd piqued his interest, but he wasn't all that forthcoming with details."

"He's in denial."

"Obviously. What's she like?"

"She's perfect for him. Very sweet, but with a little bit of spunk, too."

"I've got an idea," Marilyn said. "Gage has a preseason game in Cinncy next Sunday. He's getting us all tickets, and I'm sure one more won't be a problem. It's an early game, and we were planning on having everyone over for a barbecue after. Do you think she'd come? I'd love to meet her."

"Just leave it to me," Jan said. "I'll make sure she's there."

"No," Chris said. "Absolutely not."

"You want to leave her here alone for the whole day? After what happened? Alarm system or not?"

Jan was one of the best women he knew, but right now he wanted to strangle her. She couldn't be serious. "You want me to invite Elizabeth to come to Gage's game? With my whole family?" He was just barely holding on to his sanity.

"Yes," Jan said, as if it made all the sense in the world. "Your mom and I have already talked about it, and she's having Gage get an extra ticket."

He groaned. Between the conversation he'd had with his mother last weekend and whatever Jan had told her, he was in for twenty questions. And that was just from his mom. There was no telling what he'd get from his brothers.

He knew what conclusions his family would jump to in their minds if he showed up with her. They would want to know everything about her, and she was not big on sharing. Not that he could blame her, given her history.

He rubbed his hand roughly over his head in frustration. With the struggle he'd had just keeping his distance, this was possibly the worst thing that could happen. He wanted to avoid thinking of Elizabeth that way, of remembering what it was like to hold her in his arms and feel her lips against his. Pushing them together on a family outing was the last thing he needed.

But he wasn't stupid. If Jan and his mother had already talked about it, it was a done deal. One way or another she would be joining them. He knew Jan was only being courteous, giving him the opportunity to extend the invitation. "Okay, fine. I'll ask her."

Jan gave him a hug. "See? That wasn't so hard, was it?"

He snorted, but hugged her back.

Two hours later, he knocked on Elizabeth's door. The men from the alarm company were finally finished, the alarms in place, but for some reason the idea of her back in her own apartment sent a rush of fear through his gut. She'd stayed with Jan while the workmen were there, and only came into work when Jan left to do her volunteer work. Everyone had agreed it wasn't good for anyone to be there alone until all the alarms were installed.

He'd like to say his fear had to do with her intruder, but he'd be lying. At work there were always ways to occupy himself, to stay focused on things other than his attraction to her. He'd made sure not to repeat his mistakes, so avoiding her was out of the question. Instead, he tried to act as though everything were normal and just ignore the elephant in the room. Here, however, there wasn't the buffer of work between them. Once the door closed, they would be alone. It was the reason he decided to remain out in the hall when he knocked on her door.

"Who is it?" she asked through the closed door.

"It's Chris. Can I . . . can I talk to you for a minute?"

When she opened her door, his best-laid plans almost went out the window, and he scrambled to calm his body down. She was wearing another one of her oversized dress shirt, yoga pant combos. He could see a hint of what lay beneath and his hands tingled, wanting firsthand knowledge of what their weight felt like against his palms.

"Hi." Her voice was all it took, and he knew he needed to get this over with before he went with his instincts.

He clenched his fists, willing his feet to remain where they were. "My brother has a game in Cincinnati next weekend. He's getting tickets for everyone, and I was wondering if you'd like to go."

"Game?" she said, clearly confused.

He'd told her nothing of his family, really. "Football. My brother plays for Tennessee."

It took her a moment, but then her face lit up. "Football? As in NFL football?"

"Yeah. He's their starting quarterback."

"I love football." She smiled.

He shifted, trying to make himself more comfortable. "You do?"

"Yes! I haven't been to a game since college, though."

"Oh. Well you'll love it, then. Gage always gets us really good seats."

"You could sit me in the nosebleeds and I wouldn't care!"

Her joy was infectious and, unfortunately, it didn't help his current situation. "So I'll let you know when we're leaving next week. It's an early game and about an hour's drive."

"Just tell me when and I'm there." She was beaming.

Ever since Chris had asked her to go to the football game, she'd felt like she was floating. She'd always loved football, but it was one of those things that she'd put on the backburner when she'd married Jared. The first time she'd watched a game after their marriage, Jared had forbade her from watching football in the house. It wasn't appropriate for a woman like her to watch a sport like football and yell like the rest of the fans, not even in front of the television in her own home.

Things were different now. Jared wasn't there to stop her, and Chris didn't seem to mind. He'd invited her after all. Plus, she was hoping this meant maybe she'd get some more time with him. Though he tried to be subtle about it, she knew he'd been careful not to be alone with her if he could help it.

At first, she'd considered that maybe he was regretting kissing her, but that didn't make sense. He'd kissed her twice. The first time had been wonderful, but the second—the second had been along the lines of feeling the earth move.

She'd spent the last week contemplating what exactly she should do about Chris and his reactions. After meeting his ex, she had a feeling she knew.

He was scared.

As big and tough as Chris was, she seemed to frighten him. And after seeing Carol, she could understand. She was obviously a user.

Now all she had to do was figure out what to do about it.

Just as she was shutting the computer down, her phone rang. "Daniels Custom Builders." She had stopped introducing herself as part of her hello after the call she'd received from Abigail. It wasn't a huge buffer, but every little bit helped.

A male voice she didn't recognize said, "Yes, I'm looking for Elizabeth Marshall. I was told I could reach her at this number."

She swallowed nervously. "May I ask who's calling?"

"My name is Detective Robert Stephens from the Springfield Police Department."

"Oh. Yes. Hello, Detective. I'm Elizabeth Marshall."

"Hello, Ms. Marshall. Is this a good time?" the detective asked.

Chris was suddenly standing in his doorway.

"Sure. How can I help you?"

"I just wanted let you know that the test results are in. Both the blood and the tissue are bovine. That's cow to you and me," he said with a little chuckle, trying to lighten the mood, no doubt. "Have you had any more incidences since this happened?"

"No, sir. Nothing new."

"Great. I want you to know I'm following up on the information you gave in your statements, and I'll get back to you if I have any follow-up questions. I'd also like to give you my direct number. If anything else happens, call me. Someone went to a lot of trouble to scare you. Hopefully that's all this is, but I don't want to take chances."

After she'd given him her number, he said, "There's a note in the report that there was no sign of a security system in place. I would highly suggest you look into that, ma'am."

"It's already done."

"Good, good. I'll let you go, then. Have a nice weekend, Ms. Marshall."

"Thank you. You, too, Detective."

Immediately after she hung up, Chris said, "What was it?"

"Cow."

He nodded. "Makes sense. There are plenty of farms around here. Easy access." She just stared blankly ahead. "Anything else?"

"No." She shook her head. "He just gave me his number and said to call him if anything else happened."

He came over and picked up one of his own business cards, wrote the detective's name and number on it, and put it in his wallet.

"Are you ready to go?"

"Yeah," she said, closing her purse. She quickly forwarded the phones to voice mail.

Chris walked her out to her car before getting into his own as he had every day since she'd returned to work. He'd never offered to drive together again, and she'd not brought it up. If he was scared of whatever was happening between them, she didn't want to make it worse. She was never alone, though. If Chris had to leave, Terry would come into the office to "make some calls" until Chris came back. Although she felt it was somewhat ridiculous, she appreciated the effort. Even if Chris hadn't kissed her again since that morning in her apartment, he was showing her he cared by making sure she was safe. It was new to her, but she found that she liked it.

Sunday morning Elizabeth and Jan piled into Chris' truck for the drive to Cincinnati. The two women were excitedly chatting away while he, on the other hand, was a nervous wreck.

He'd managed to keep things appropriate for the past week, making sure he was never truly alone with her. At the office, he stayed at his desk for the most part. And when she came in, he made sure his butt stayed firmly planted in his chair.

It had worked. He hadn't kissed her again even though the thought crossed his mind about a thousand times a day.

As much as his hormones were wreaking havoc with his mind, he knew there was no way his family would let Elizabeth's presence slide, especially his mom. He was already on alert due to their conversation two weeks ago, and there was little doubt that Jan had helped fuel the fire.

The problem was he couldn't deny it. He liked Elizabeth. He wanted her. He just wasn't sure those were good things. He had to keep reminding himself that eight months ago she was married. A relationship was not what she needed right now.

A relationship. Was he really contemplating getting involved in a relationship with her?

All too soon, his parents' house came into view. He parked in front and they all got out. His mom was out the door to greet them before they'd reached the front walkway.

"You made it," she said, pulling him in for a hug.

"Morning, Mom."

She smiled up at him before glancing over his shoulder. "Jan!" Marilyn quickly moved and gave her a warm hug. "It's good to see you."

"We really should get together more often."

"You're so right."

"So," Marilyn said, looking back over her shoulder at him. "Are you going to introduce us?"

"Oh! Of course. Sorry. Mom, this is my new neighbor and assistant, Elizabeth Marshall. Elizabeth, this is my mother, Marilyn Daniels."

Marilyn enveloped Elizabeth in a quick hug.

Her tense look almost had Chris stepping in when his mother leaned back and said, "I'm so glad you could join us today, Elizabeth."

"Thank you for inviting me."

A screen door opened and out came Chloe. Chris turned around to meet her bright smile. "Uncle Chris!" she squealed.

He bent down and picked up the four-year-old, and she hugged him. "And how are you today, Miss Chloe?"

She giggled. "We're going to the football game to see Uncle Gage play."

"I know. It's been a while since you've seen Uncle Gage, hasn't it?" She nodded in a way that reminded him of a bobblehead. "Well, I'm sure he misses you." Chloe glanced behind him and then ducked her head in his shoulder. "What's wrong?" he asked, looking behind him.

"Stranger," she whispered.

He looked back again and saw Elizabeth was still talking to his mother. Chris frowned. That didn't bode well.

Before he could dwell on the situation, he turned back to Chloe. "That's Elizabeth. She's living in the house with Jan and me now."

"Is she your girlfriend?"

"No, she's not." He couldn't even define what she was to him, let alone try to explain it to a four-year-old.

"Oh," Chloe said, seemingly disappointed.

Her reaction stung more than he would have liked to admit. Everyone seemed to have an opinion on his love life, or lack thereof. The sound of the screen door opening again had Chris looking over his niece's head to find Paul, his brother, strolling toward them with a smile on his face.

"I see you found your Uncle Chris."

The little girl twisted in his arms. "I did, Daddy."

He went straight for Elizabeth. "Hello. I'm Paul, and you are?"

His mom supplied the introduction. "This is Elizabeth Marshall. She's a friend of Chris'."

The implication was clear, and Paul turned with a raised eyebrow to look at him. "She moved into the second floor apartment," he said quickly.

"Ah," he said, clearly not convinced.

He'd known with every fiber of his being that if Elizabeth met his family they would not believe that she was just a friend. Unfortunately, there was nothing he could do about their assumption.

Soon Chloe wanted down so that she could meet Elizabeth, and he had to admit that, so far, his mother seemed to like her. That was more than could be said of Carol. His mother had never liked his ex-wife, not even when they'd been dating.

Just after eleven o'clock, everyone was ready to leave. Elizabeth had met everyone in his family except Gage, whom she would meet after the game, and Trent, his brother, who would be pulling up with minutes to spare if history was anything to go by.

Sure enough, with everyone already divided as evenly as possible between the two SUVs, two minutes before they were to leave for the stadium, Trent pulled up in a pickup truck not that much different than Chris'.

"Hey, family! Sorry I'm late," he said, waving to their mom, dad, and Jan in the other vehicle as he squeezed into the SUV with Paul, Chloe, Chris, and Elizabeth.

Once everyone was strapped in, Paul put his vehicle in gear and headed to the stadium.

Chloe said, "Uncle Trent, Uncle Trent. Guess what Daddy bought me?"

Trent glanced over at Paul. "What did your daddy get you, Princess?" Paul sent a quick glare over at Trent before returning his eyes to the road, which only made the brother's grin widen.

"I'm wearing Uncle Gage's jersey. See?" she said, squirming in her booster seat. Chloe was trying to pull the oversized shirt out from under the seat belt so that Trent could see the big number seven. "It has Uncle Gage's number and everything."

Trent twisted around in his seat to look back at his niece, and Chris knew exactly when he spotted Elizabeth. "Yeah, Princess. I like it. Uncle Gage will, too, I think."

"You think so?"

"Yeah. I do," Trent said to Chloe, but his eyes were on Elizabeth and she shifted.

"Hello there. I'm Trent. And you are?"

"Elizabeth."

"It's nice to meet you. And how do you come to be with us this fine day?"

Not liking the way his brother was looking at Elizabeth, Chris rolled his eyes and moved his arm to rest on the back of the seat behind her. There was no physical contact, but the implication was clear. "She moved into the second floor apartment at Jan's, and she's my new assistant."

"I see." Trent's expression clearly indicated he was not deterred by Chris' show. "Well, I'm glad you could come today. You can sit by me and I'll talk you through the game. Football is a lot more fun when you know what you're seeing." He winked.

Elizabeth's back straightened, and she got a spark of determination. "Oh, I don't know about that. Maybe it will be me talking *you* through the game."

Trent fell back dramatically. "Be still my heart. I think I'm in love!"

Chloe giggled at her uncle. Chris, however, was not amused. His fists tightened, and he had to bite the inside of his cheek to keep from responding.

From the front seat, Trent continued to flirt with Elizabeth all the way to the stadium. He took a little break when he went over to hug their mother, father, and Jan. After that, however, he was right back at Elizabeth's side, chatting away.

Chris said nothing. She wasn't his, not really, but the last thing he wanted was for his brother to flirt with her.

The game started and he hoped the flirting would stop. It didn't. What made matters worse was that Elizabeth seemed to be eating it up. She was smiling and laughing right along with him.

By the time halftime rolled around, he was seeing red.

"You know," his mom leaned in from her seat behind him and whispered, "if you'd stake your claim, your brother would back off."

Chris held tight to the arms of his chair and shook his head.

"Suit yourself," she said, sitting back.

It continued like that until it was time to leave. Tennessee had won the game by a field goal so Gage would be in a celebrating mood. Chris could only hope that didn't mean he'd have two brothers to fight off Elizabeth. One was enough.

CHAPTER 13

Elizabeth was having a wonderful time. There was lots of standing and shouting, just the way she liked it.

Trent had stayed close to her side the entire game. He poked fun at Gage or joked about how the other team couldn't seem to catch a pass, and yelled right along with her when a bad call had been made, or jumped up with her and cheered when there was an especially good play.

The only downside was that Chris had not participated in the celebration. Every time she'd glance over at him, he didn't seem happy. The rest of the family was getting into the game, while he just sat there looking as if someone had died. She didn't understand it. His family was great. They'd welcomed her, made her feel included. She hadn't felt this carefree since her parents had died in that horrible car crash almost four years ago.

It was only after Trent had lifted her off the ground in a celebratory hug at the end of the game that she understood. Chris didn't like his brother giving her so much attention.

She didn't understand. Chris hadn't made any attempts to kiss her again, nor had he acted as if he was open to discussing it. Maybe she was wrong. Maybe he just wasn't interested.

She liked Chris. More than liked him. And she loved kissing him. That was something she definitely wanted to do again.

But for whatever reason—a reason he wasn't sharing with her, apparently—he wasn't jumping at the chance to be with her. Meanwhile, Trent seemed more than happy with her company.

The seating arrangements in the SUV for the trip back to Marilyn and Mike's house were such that Trent could be in the back with Elizabeth. Chris didn't seem all that happy about it, but he didn't protest either, so she went with it. She was not going to force herself on a man who didn't want to be with her.

Once at the house, the brothers pulled out a large grill onto a spacious back deck and fired it up. She settled into a lounge chair and, of course, Trent sat in the one beside her.

Just as Chris' dad, Mike, was putting the meat on the grill, a sleek black sports car pulled up to the curb, and a young man who looked to be in his mid-twenties stepped out. She surmised that this was most likely Gage. The family resemblance was uncanny with his dark hair and broad shoulders.

Gage strolled with purpose toward the group lounging in the backyard, but went directly to his mother, picking her up off the ground and twirling her around. She swatted his arm when he finally put her down. "I don't know why you continue doing that to your old mother. You're going to give me a heart attack one of these days."

He laughed. "Nah. You're not old, Ma. Just seasoned." Gage winked.

Marilyn rolled her eyes.

"So," Trent said to his brother. "No entourage today?"

Gage shrugged, reached for a bottle of water, and downed it in what seemed to be one swallow.

"Well, I for one am glad you didn't bring one of those girls you seem to like to hang around with," his father said.

Gage ignored the comment and turned his attention to Elizabeth. "And who do we have here?"

After introductions were made, Gage strolled over to take a seat at the end of her lounger. "Well, that's a pity. We could use another pretty face in Nashville." She was floored by all the flirting. First Trent and now Gage. Chris was always so serious. It was hard to believe they were part of the same family.

Chris seemed less than amused as he pushed himself forcefully from his chair and excused himself, disappearing into the house. She just didn't understand him.

Fifteen minutes later, Chris emerged from the house and offered to help his father with the grilling.

The day continued on in that vein with the brothers flirting with her and Chris getting ticked off, disappearing into the house only to reappear fifteen to twenty minutes later. She tried not to let it ruin her day, but try as she might, she couldn't remain unaffected.

As they were getting ready to leave, Trent cornered her. "I was wondering if you'd like to go out to dinner with me on Saturday. I know this great Mexican place in Dayton."

She looked behind him to Chris, and Trent followed her line of sight before she could catch herself.

"Are you and Chris . . ."

"No," she said unable to keep the disappointment completely out of her voice. "No."

"Well then, there's no reason for you not to accept, is there? Or don't you like me?"

That made her laugh, which drew Chris' attention. She caught his stare and it sobered her. She turned her attention back to Trent and kept it there. "Okay. Sure. I haven't had Mexican in a long time."

Trent's smile was the kind that would have girls swooning. Unfortunately, she feared her heart was already attached to someone else.

"Excellent! I'll pick you up at five thirty."

She smiled. "I'll see you Saturday, then."

Before she knew what was happening, Trent leaned in and kissed her on the cheek. She blushed. "Till Saturday," he whispered before stepping away.

Okay, Chris thought. *This is my own stupid, moronic, idiotic fault.*

All the way home, he was fuming. Seeing Trent with his lips on Elizabeth had made him want to break something, preferably something attached to his brother. He'd never felt this way before, not even with Carol, and his head was spinning.

No one said a word during the hour-long drive home. Even Jan was oddly quiet.

It was a little before midnight when they pulled up to the house. Elizabeth and Jan got out first while he hung back. He wasn't ready to deal with whatever had happened between her and Trent.

From the cab of his truck, he watched the two women approach the door. Jan stopped, reached down, and picked up what looked to be a newspaper, and Elizabeth peered over Jan's shoulder to look at whatever it was. Suddenly both women stiffened, and Chris was out of the truck like lightning. He took the paper from Jan and looked at it.

The newspaper was dated seven months ago, and on the front page was a large picture of a woman dressed in designer clothes. Even with her head down and surrounded by police officers, the woman was still recognizable.

The headline read: MURDER OR SELF DEFENSE?

Whoever had left the newspaper had added a personal touch, outlining the word *Murder* in dark red ink, circling her face, and drawing an *X* through it.

Chris scanned the area, but the person who'd left the paper was probably long gone. "Let's get inside," he said, not wanting to take any chances.

After checking the alarm, he made the two women wait in the foyer while he checked the rest of the house and alarms. Everything appeared secure. At least that was something.

Before returning, he took out his cell phone.

"Hello?" a groggy voice answered.

"Detective Stephens?"

"Yes," he said, sounding more alert. "Who's this?"

"My name is Chris Daniels. I live in the building with Elizabeth Marshall. You told her to call if anything else happened."

"Yes, I did." He could hear shifting in the background and figured the detective was probably getting out of bed.

After Chris told him what happened, he said, "Someone is at the house now?"

"Yes. We're all here."

"I'll be there in twenty minutes."

Detective Stephens didn't stay long. He asked a bunch of questions such as where they'd been, and what time they'd left and returned home, which Chris answered. Elizabeth wasn't feeling up to dealing with people. In fact, what she wanted to do was hide in her bedroom for about a week.

"Ms. Marshall?"

She looked up at the detective from where she sat on Jan's couch with a cup of hot chocolate cupped in her hands. He was much older than she'd originally thought when she'd spoken with him over the phone. He had laugh lines around his mouth and eyes, and gray speckled through his light brown hair. "I've checked the surrounding area. Everything looks secure. I'm taking the paper with me and will have it dusted for prints, although getting a clean one off newspaper is tricky with the ink they use. I would suggest you have someone with you at all times when you go out, and make sure your doors are locked until we can find out who's behind this."

She just stared at him until she realized he was waiting for a response. "Sure."

"You don't have any idea who could be behind this?" He seemed doubtful.

Her shoulders sagged as she released a deep breath. "No. I mean, you read the article in the paper. People weren't all that happy about what happened, but I never expected anyone to track me down here. Why would they?"

"Mr. Daniels said you received a phone call last week from your mother-in-law."

She shook her head. "Abigail's angry, yes, but I can't see her doing this. She's a very straightforward kind of person. She'd just show up on my doorstep and slap me, or something."

"Grief can cause people to act out of character, Ms. Marshall."

She shook her head. "It's not her."

"Well," the detective said, straightening up, "I'm going to check it out anyway, just to be sure."

She nodded, not feeling like arguing a moot point.

When they were alone again, Jan sat beside her. "Is there anything I can do, dear?"

"No, but thanks. I think I'm just going to go up to bed now."

"You're more than welcome to stay here if you'd like."

"Thank you. Again. But I'd really like to sleep in my own bed." When it looked like Jan was going to argue, she said, "We have the alarm, and they didn't come inside this time. I'll be fine. Besides, you and Chris are right next door."

Jan patted her arm and stood. "Okay, then. You come get me if you need anything or if you change your mind."

"I will."

She returned her empty mug to the kitchen and hugged Jan good night before trudging her way up the single flight of stairs to her apartment. When she reached the landing, she noticed Chris standing in his doorway.

"You're sleeping up here?" he asked.

"Yeah."

He nodded, not seeming surprised. "My door is staying open tonight," he said and then turned and walked up the stairs, the door remaining open just as he'd said it would.

For some reason, everything felt different as she walked into her apartment, alone for the first time since that morning. It seemed like a lifetime ago.

Flashes of that night came back to her, and she could feel the blood covering her hands along with the porcelain from the vase she'd used to defend herself and ultimately put an end to her abuser.

With desperation, she ran to her bathroom and turned on the shower. She felt so dirty. The only thing driving her was the need to get clean. As she stepped in, she thought, *Will I ever get my life back?* She began to cry.

CHAPTER 14

CHRIS KNOCKED his alarm to the floor in the process of trying to turn it off before rubbing the sleep from his eyes and making his way to the bathroom. It was going to be a long day considering his lack of sleep and motivation. Morning had come too soon. Detective Stephens hadn't left until two in the morning, and getting to sleep after had been difficult. His mind just wouldn't shut down, and he was glad he didn't have to see any clients today.

Every time he closed his eyes, Elizabeth was there. Sometimes he thought of completely innocent things like her tapping her pen against her desk, as she was prone to do when she was deep in thought. Other times, usually right before he was about to drift off, his thoughts of her ran in a more erotic direction.

Last night they'd taken on the memory from last week of her walking out of his bedroom in nothing but his shirt and the blanket from his bed. Her bare legs teased him as they peeked beneath the thick fabric as if calling for him to unwrap her like a present, carry her back into his bedroom, and make her scream his name.

Thinking about all the ways he wanted to ravish her was not conducive to restful sleep. It was also rather uncomfortable.

After showering, he dressed in his work clothes and walked down the flight of stairs to his front door. It was still open, just as he'd left it the night before. Her door was closed, and he couldn't hear any movement inside. That was good. She needed her rest.

Chris paused at her door, trying to imagine what she'd look like curled up in her bed, fast asleep. The keys he carried to each of the apartments weighed heavy in his pocket, tempting him, but he pushed the impulse aside. The last thing she needed after the previous night was him creeping into her apartment and startling her.

He forced himself to keep walking until he stopped in front of Jan's door and knocked.

It took her a while to get to the door, and he heard her pause, checking through the newly installed peephole to see who was outside before opening her door. She was still in her nightclothes, which wasn't surprising considering it was only seven thirty in the morning. "Chris," she said, surprised. "Is everything all right?"

"Everything's fine as far as I can tell. I'm going to have a walk around outside before I leave just to be sure."

"Oh, okay. Good."

"I was wondering if you could bring Elizabeth to work this morning. I'd rather her not be alone."

"That's not a problem. I don't have any plans today."

"Thanks," he said. He turned to head out.

"Chris?" she said, and he turned around. "What if she doesn't want me to take her? She might not—"

"After last night, I'd rather not take any chances. Whatever you have to do—whatever you have to say . . ." He took a deep breath. "Someone went to a lot of trouble to get inside her apartment and then leave that newspaper where it was sure to be found. Until we know who's behind this, I don't want to take any chances."

Before Jan could respond, Chris disappeared out the front door.

He slid into the seat of his truck and let his head fall to the steering wheel. In all his years, Chris could never remember being this scared about anything or anyone. Maybe the cop was right. Maybe the person just wanted to frighten her, but the possibility that they could take it to the next level was there, nagging him.

The sun seemed too bright when Elizabeth rolled over and glanced at her alarm clock. She jumped out of bed. It was ten thirty in the morning, and she was late for work.

Why hasn't Chris called me? Knocked on my door? Something.

She raced through her morning routine, shoved a Pop-Tart in her mouth, grabbed her purse, and ran down the stairs as fast she could.

She was nearing the bottom when Jan opened her door and stepped out into the foyer. "Hi, Jan," she said in a rush. "Sorry to run, but I'm late for work."

"I know, dear. Chris wanted to let you sleep. There's no hurry."

She stopped in her tracks. "Oh." She wasn't sure how she felt about that. "Well, I don't want to take advantage."

Jan gave her a small smile, and locked the door to her apartment. "I know. But be that as it may, I'm glad for it. Now, let's get you to work."

"You're taking me?"

"Of course. You heard what the detective said. You are not to be alone, and I do believe driving to work by yourself would qualify as being alone. I mean, unless you have a man hiding in your trunk I don't know about," she said.

Elizabeth felt a little silly being dropped off to work by her landlady. Granted, she considered Jan a friend, but it was just weird.

When she walked in the front door to the office, she found Chris sitting at her desk with a phone in one ear and a stack of papers in front of him. He had a scowl on his face and bags under his eyes. Guilt washed over her.

Chris looked up, saw her, and gave her a half smile.

She went over to her desk and tucked her purse in the drawer, straightening just as Chris hung up the phone. "How'd you sleep?" he asked.

"All right. You should have woken me. I would have come in earlier."

"I know that," Chris said, vacating her chair. "You had a rough night. You needed your rest."

"And you didn't?" she asked incredulously.

"I'm fine."

"Chris," she said, touching the circles under his eyes.

He stepped back out of reach. "I'm fine," he insisted.

She dropped her hand, and an awkward silence surrounded them.

He cleared his throat. "There were a few calls this morning. I took care of most of them, but I left you Post-it notes with the ones that still need to be addressed. Also—" He paused as if debating whether to continue. "You received a personal call."

She felt a lead weight settle in the pit of her stomach. "Who?"

"Your mother-in-law."

"Oh."

"Apparently Detective Stephens contacted her first thing this morning." He left that hanging in the air for a moment before adding, "If your husband was anything like his mother, I have no idea how you put up with him for as long as you did. She's a vile woman."

A high-pitched laugh left her lips. For some reason, Chris calling her devil of a mother-in-law *vile* struck her as funny and nerve-racking at the same time. What in the world had she said to him?

"Sorry," she said, noting Chris' furrowed brow. Chris probably thought she was crazy. "It's just that I've felt that way for years, but everyone else seems to love her. It's refreshing to know I'm not the only one that feels that way."

Chris smiled. His whole face lit up as he joined in the joke. She felt a warm weight settle in her chest. "Well, don't you worry. After the conversation I had with her this morning, I doubt my opinion of her will ever change."

"Thank you." His words meant more than she could ever hope to explain. He was on her side. It felt good.

There was another long pause before he shifted his weight. "I'll be in my office if you need me. Terry's going to drop by in about an hour with lunch. Have you eaten?"

"I had a Pop-Tart on the way over," she said.

He grimaced. "That's not lunch. Or breakfast, for that matter. I'll have Terry add another sandwich and chips." With that, he turned and walked into his office.

She sighed, refocusing her attention on her desk. There were five notes arranged haphazardly on the right-hand side of her desk.

Scanning the notes quickly, she noticed one was from Stephanie. Feeling as if she'd wasted enough of her day already, she put the note from her friend aside and started working on returning the other calls first.

She had just hung up with a designer when Terry walked in. "Hey."

"Hey, pretty lady," Terry said, all smiles. "Boss man in?"

"Yeah, he's—"

"Hey." They both looked over to see Chris propped up against the doorjamb, his arms crossed over his chest.

For a moment, she forgot to breathe. His stance was so casual yet powerful at the same time. Chris' broad shoulders pulled against the fabric of his shirt, revealing the muscles in his arms. Muscles she had felt beneath her fingertips as they'd held her body against his. She suppressed a shiver at the memory.

He looked over at her and their eyes locked. Time seemed to stop, suspending them in the moment.

Then, just as abruptly as it started, Chris ended it by pushing off the doorframe and walking toward his foreman. "Thanks for picking up lunch."

"No problem. Gives me an excuse to get out of that heat for a while. I think we're supposed to reach the high nineties today. Add that to being on top of a roof and you might as well be in an oven."

They both laughed and the tension in Chris' shoulders seemed to ease. "Man, I don't miss that," he said, taking a seat at the mini conference table in the corner. "As much as I dislike paperwork, I'd trade it for humping shingles on a hot summer day in a heartbeat."

"Preaching to the choir," Terry said before taking a mammoth bite of his sandwich.

She slowly walked over to the table where the guys were sitting, picked up the bag with her food, and turned to go back to her desk to eat.

"Aren't you gonna eat with us?" Terry asked.

"Got in late today. I really should keep working."

He waved his hand dismissively in front of his face. "Work will wait. You should eat."

She looked over at Chris. His eyes met hers and held for a brief moment before he focused on his meal. "Okay. I guess I can spare a few minutes."

"Atta girl!" Terry said, and she laughed.

Chris was doing everything he could not to look at Elizabeth as she sat across from him and ate her lunch, but his gaze kept drifting. Everything the woman did was driving him wild! He felt as if his libido had gone into hyperdrive. If that wasn't enough, knowing someone was trying to get to her had him wanting to stake his claim in a very animalistic way. His current thoughts ran along the lines of her lying on his desk with her pants around her ankles, and him firmly situated between her legs. Just the thought was sending heat throughout his body and making it hard to concentrate.

This morning he'd missed her presence, but now that she was here, he wanted to be near her and as far away from her as possible at the same time.

When their lunches hit the trash, he asked Terry into his office and reluctantly closed the door. "I need to talk to you about something."

"Shoot."

He took a seat behind his desk and sighed. "It's about Elizabeth."

Terry smiled. "Did you finally get that stick out of your ass?"

"What?"

Terry paused and then laughed, shaking his head. "I guess that would be a no."

"Back to what I was saying," Chris said, giving his foreman a pointed look. "She's received some unwanted attention recently."

Terry looked shocked. "From the guys?"

"No. Why? Has someone said something? Done something?" he said, his voice rising in pitch.

"No." Terry sighed. "It's nothing like that so calm down before you give yourself a heart attack or something."

Chris took a deep breath, leaned back in his chair, and closed his eyes, trying to clear his head. *What is wrong with me?*

"So what is this unwanted attention?" Terry said, bringing Chris back to the present conversation.

"Someone has been trying to frighten her. So far it's only been at the house, but I don't want to take chances. The police are involved. I'm just worried, and so I wanted to ask if you'd look after her if I need to go to a jobsite."

Terry's face was sober as was his response. "Of course. Just let me know and I'll be here."

"Thank you."

He walked Terry out and shook his hand.

As Chris walked back into his office, he thought about all the hardships he and Terry had been through over the last three years. In the beginning, it had just been the two of them. They'd worked sunup to sundown some days. Weekends. Holidays. It didn't matter, and Terry had never complained.

He was the one person Chris had confided in, the one person who knew the whole story about what had happened with Carol. Not even Jan or his family knew he'd caught her in bed with his best friend, or that he'd found out shortly thereafter that it hadn't been her first go at infidelity. She'd been cheating on him nearly from the beginning of their marriage.

Often Terry would just listen, letting Chris get whatever it was off his chest. He wasn't one to pry, which was why when he did offer an opinion, Chris had learned to listen.

So why wasn't he sharing now?

With Elizabeth it felt different. She was—private. He didn't want to share what he was feeling for her with anyone. Not Terry. Not Jan. Not his mother. Certainly not his brothers.

He wanted her, but it wasn't right. Just not . . . yet.

The rest of the day went quickly. Just before five, he walked out of his office to find Elizabeth still on the phone.

"As long as I'm home by four, I should be fine. Oh. That's a great idea. Okay. I'll see you at nine, then. 'Bye." She didn't notice him until after she hung up the phone. "Oh!" she said, startled.

"Are you finished?" he asked, not really sure what to make of her conversation. It was obviously personal.

"Yes. Sorry." She gathered up her things and they left.

The ride home was quiet. Chris waited for her to bring up her phone conversation, but she never did. She'd obviously made plans for Saturday with a friend and his concern for her safety was there again in full force. He tried not to panic. When they arrived home, they parted ways, Elizabeth seeming just as distracted as he was.

He left the door open just as he had the previous night, but all remained quiet. As much as his body was craving sleep, his mind wouldn't shut off. It was downstairs with Elizabeth.

CHAPTER 15

For Elizabeth, Saturday morning arrived quickly. The week had been uneventful for the most part, with the only exception being two phone calls from her mother-in-law, Abigail Carter.

When she'd called the second time on Friday, Chris had taken the phone from her and told Abigail that this was an office and that she was disrupting his employee's ability to do her job and tying up his phone line with things that were not related to his business. He warned her that if she called there again, he would file harassment charges. She wondered if he could do that in reality, but either way, it was nice to have a man defend her for a change.

She wasn't sure, but she thought that second call from Abigail had led to the impromptu intervention last night. Jan had invited her and Chris to dinner, and as soon as the food was cleared away, they pounced.

Both Jan and Chris expressed their concerns regarding the scheduled shopping trip with Stephanie. When she'd refused a babysitter, both Jan and Chris made her promise to follow some rules to put their minds at ease, such as sticking to public places and parking close to the entrance.

Later, Chris reached into his pocket and pulled out what looked like a large lipstick tube. "Here," he'd said. "Keep this with you. Use it if you need to." He shoved his hands deep in his pockets. "I don't like that you're going alone tomorrow. I'd feel much better if you'd let Jan or I come with you."

"I'll be fine. Stephanie will be there except for the drive, and I've got my cell," she said. He still didn't look happy when he'd turned and walked upstairs to his apartment.

The object turned out to be pepper spray. She picked it up, familiarizing herself with its weight, before dropping it into her purse.

After putting the finishing touches on her appearance, she took a final look at her reflection. Since leaving Columbus and her old life, she rarely took so much time getting ready. She wasn't out to impress anyone but herself, but Stephanie was still from that world and she did care. Although her friend had never made her feel out of place as some of the others had, she felt it was only right to make sure she didn't embarrass her companion. She didn't have many friends.

As she pulled out of the driveway, she realized this was the first time she'd been in her car this week. It felt good to be alone with her thoughts. To say she hadn't been freaked out seeing that newspaper would be a lie. It chilled her down to her bones.

The thing was she was used to bad things happening to her. Jared used to lose his temper at least once a week. Some times were worse than others, but she'd rarely got off unscathed either way.

In the same vein, it was a rare week they did not have a dinner party or some sort of function to attend. Jared had been an up-and-coming lawyer in his firm, and people wanted to rub elbows with the new golden boy and his wife. The outside world wouldn't stop for domestic squabbles, so she'd eventually learned to suppress. Life went on. It was just the way of things.

It wasn't as if she didn't acknowledge what was going on around her. She did. But letting someone know how much they were hurting you wasn't going to make things get any better either. It hadn't with Jared, and it wouldn't with whoever this was. Letting someone see how vulnerable you were only made you an easier target.

Unfortunately, her two neighbors didn't understand that, especially Chris. He wanted her to tiptoe around her life instead of living it. She wouldn't do that. Not again. It wasn't some dirty little secret this time; the police were involved and she had the support of those around her. She was not crawling in a hole and hiding. She parked near the front of the mall just as she'd promised Jan and Chris.

Inside, she found Stephanie waiting for her at the entrance to the food court. "Liz!" Stephanie said, leaning in and giving her a kiss on each cheek.

She smiled and hugged her friend back. "How was New York?"

"It was fabulous, as always." Stephanie took her arm and walked her toward Saks. "I found this to-die-for red dress while I was there and I can't wait to wear it."

Even though Elizabeth was never one to beg for shopping trips, she still enjoyed it and loved getting new things just like anyone else. Jared had taken her to New York a few times with him on business, and she'd shopped. It wasn't so different except that the prices were higher, but there was also a vibe in New York that you didn't get in Ohio.

They walked into Saks and Stephanie immediately went to the women's dresses. "Now, enough about me. Tell me about this man you're going to dinner with tonight. Do you know where you're going?"

"All I know is that it's a Mexican restaurant in Dayton." She shrugged. She was equal parts looking forward to her date with Trent and wanting to cancel. It would be nice to go out again just to enjoy a meal, but the closer it got to the date, the more she felt as if she were cheating on Chris.

It was stupid. Logically, she knew that. They were not together, and from the way he'd been keeping his distance again, he didn't want to be with her.

So as much as her heart wasn't into tonight, she would go. Trent was a nice guy. She'd had fun with him at the game and the barbecue. At the very least, maybe they'd become friends.

Stephanie selected two dresses and held them out to her. "Mexican demands color, so what do you think of these two?" Both dresses hit Elizabeth mid-thigh. Each was cute and flirty. She hadn't done flirty in a long time. All her insecurities started to rear their ugly heads again, but she forced herself to try the dresses on anyway. *I can do this,* she thought with a deep breath.

The first, a strapless, multicolored dress, was quickly discarded. It probably looked great on someone with fewer curves than she, but on her it looked like she was about to walk down Hollywood Boulevard, not go on a first date.

The second, however, was nice. Still not what she was used to, but more . . . her.

The dress fell into place, floating over her thighs as it moved with her. It had a V-neck but was still modest.

When she emerged from the dressing room, Stephanie was waiting somewhat patiently. "Well?"

She held up the dress she liked. "The other one made me look like a streetwalker," she said, crinkling her nose.

Stephanie laughed. "Don't want that, now, do we?" she said, linking her arm once again with Elizabeth's. "I mean, we wouldn't want to give this new guy the wrong impression."

Stephanie didn't see anything wrong or awkward about her sleeping with her date. After all, she wasn't attached to anyone else, so why not?

That might be the modern way of thinking for most, but she wasn't into sleeping with every guy who crossed her path. Jared was the only man she'd ever slept with. She'd never been naked in front of another man, and given Jared's view of her body in general, she wasn't sure another man would ever get the chance.

As soon as that thought crossed her mind, she recalled her mental vision of Chris in the shower. That led her to the memory of what he'd done to her body and mind just by kissing her. Promptly, she squashed those thoughts. Daydreaming about Chris was not helping. Besides, he didn't want her, and she had a date with his brother to get ready for tonight.

His brother.

How was Chris going to react to her going out with Trent? She hadn't said anything about it and neither had Chris, so she doubted Trent had told his brother. It felt wrong to think it, but maybe, just maybe, this would give him the kick in the pants he needed. Something was there between them. She felt it every time they were in the same room together. But she wasn't going to force herself on anyone, especially someone who didn't want her.

Chris was a mess and he knew he was driving Jan crazy. As soon as Elizabeth's car was out of sight, he'd changed into old clothes and began working on anything he could think of. He'd started outside as the garden and flowerbeds needed weeding. Once he saw that Jan was up and about, he started mowing the grass. This kept him busy until eleven o'clock when he moved inside where it was a little harder to find things that needed his attention, but he found them.

After taking a shower and changing, he turned on the television. Nothing was on. Sure, there were a few games, but nothing held his interest. Normally he wasn't picky, but no matter what was happening on the screen, his mind continued to wander. He had to keep busy or he would go insane, so he pulled out a bid he'd brought home with him yesterday and began crunching numbers.

He knew it wasn't realistic to keep Elizabeth under lock and key all the time. She was a grown woman after all. But that didn't mean jack when he felt the need to protect her.

Hearing that she was going out alone to meet her friend had caused an irrational reaction in him. He'd been seconds away from storming up the stairs to her apartment. Luckily, Jan was able to calm him down somewhat and get him to agree to talk to her and explain their concerns over dinner.

She'd listened for the most part, and agreed to their suggestions. She'd even taken the pepper spray he'd given her, not that he'd given her a chance to refuse.

Even with all that, he was still anxious and would be until she was back at her apartment, safe.

At three forty-seven, he heard a car pull up the driveway and rushed to the window to confirm it was Elizabeth. The door to her red Honda Civic opened slowly and she stepped out into the bright afternoon sunshine. He was relieved to see she was in one piece.

As if sensing his stare, she shielded her eyes and looked up, and when she saw him, she gave him a small, nervous smile.

He didn't suppose he could blame her for that. After his overprotective reaction to her going out, she probably had no idea what she'd find waiting for her when she returned.

Moving away from the window, he chastised himself for his stupidity. How could he be so dumb? She had spent years with a husband who'd abused her, and although he'd never raised his hand to her and never would, she didn't know that.

He realized he needed to do better for her. No matter what he was feeling, she was not his and might never be. But even if one day she was, he couldn't allow his emotions to get out of hand; they would frighten her and that was the last thing he wanted.

Why was this so hard with her?

He took a deep breath before collapsing onto his couch. She was home. He could breathe again.

Not two hours later, Chris realized how wrong he'd been. The sound of another vehicle in the driveway roused him from his spot on the couch where he'd been attempting to watch a movie.

His brother's truck pulled up and parked beside his. He wasn't expecting Trent to stop by today. Then he stepped out dressed in black slacks and a dark blue button-down dress shirt. The last time Chris had seen his brother this dressed up was at their brother Paul's wedding.

What the . . .

Time seemed to stop as he heard her door open and close. Then her feet hit the steps with the click, click, click of heels as she walked down the steps. She wore a dress he'd never seen before, and she looked amazing in it.

Chris gripped the windowsill, his knuckles white, as he watched Trent walk to her and take her hand. His brother placed a soft kiss on the side of her cheek before saying something to her. Trent helped her up into the cab of his truck, walked to the other side, and got behind the wheel. Chris could do nothing but stare as they drove off.

In the back of his mind, he registered the sound of someone coming up the steps, but there was a disconnect in his brain. He couldn't move from the window, his gaze still locked on the horizon.

The footsteps stopped, and someone cleared their throat. He didn't respond. Seconds passed.

"She isn't going to wait forever, you know. If it's not Trent, it will be someone else."

Jan, thankfully, wasn't expecting a response out of him. She just turned and walked back down the stairs.

He couldn't take it anymore. He collapsed onto the couch, his head bouncing none too lightly on the back, leaving a slight throb in its wake. The thought of Elizabeth with anyone else left a sick feeling in his stomach.

TRENT PULLED into the parking lot of the Mexican restaurant. The ride into Dayton was relaxed. Their talk was casual, sticking mostly to what they'd each done earlier in the day. When they'd entered the city, however, conversation had died down, and she seemed content to sit back and enjoy the ride. So when she suddenly started laughing, it caught his attention.

"What?"

"The Crazy Burrito?"

"Strange name for a restaurant, isn't it?" He chuckled.

"It is," she said.

Trent maneuvered the truck into an empty spot, hopped out, and met her on the other side. "Good food. Good atmosphere. What more could you want?"

She smiled. "I'll hold you to that."

They were seated in a booth toward the rear of the restaurant. The place was nearly half full of patrons. It was an improvement since the last time he'd been here. *Word about this place must be spreading.*

While their server was off getting their drinks, he watched her. She was gorgeous. Last weekend she'd been dressed casually in shorts and a T-shirt. He'd found her stunning then, but tonight she took his breath away. He had no idea how Chris could live in the same house with her and not make a move. Was his brother blind or something?

Her hair fell softly around her face as she leaned over to look at her menu, and her dress showed just enough cleavage to make him want to see more. It was a complete tease.

She looked up and caught him staring. He just smiled, not the least bit ashamed. "Have you decided what you'd like to eat?" he asked, noticing their server coming their way.

Their server set their drinks down in front of them and quickly took their orders. Once they were alone, Trent decided it was time to get to know Elizabeth a little better. "If you don't mind me asking, why did you choose Springfield? Not exactly the first town I'd think of when relocating."

She took a sip before answering. "I wanted a small town but didn't want to leave Ohio. The why to Springfield specifically is simple . . . I love my apartment."

Her smile was polite, but he sensed that she was hiding something. Although he was curious, he reminded himself that this was their first date, and if he wanted a second, pushing her might not be in his best interests. His mother hadn't raised him to be rude.

"Jan and Charles spent a lot of time and money restoring that old house. They gutted the entire interior, putting in all new woodwork, walls, modern kitchens and baths. They always knew they wanted to rent out the top floors, so they went into the renovations with that in mind. Chris did most of the interior work, while I handled the outside. It really is a work of art."

"You did all the landscaping?"

"Yep." He smiled.

"It's beautiful. I love the rosebushes in the backyard."

"I'm glad you like them, but I can't take all the credit there. Jan loves her roses. She used to have her backyard lined with them at their old house. Did you know they were our neighbors growing up?" She nodded. "Anyway, she insisted I give her space for her roses at this new house even though it was impossible to have the layout and the multitude she had before."

"I've seen her outside fussing over them a few times. I'd say you did well. She seems happy."

He smiled. "I do my best. Jan's a special lady."

"Yes, she is."

The conversation drifted to some of Trent's childhood memories of Jan and his brothers, and before they knew it, their server appeared with their food.

"Wow. This is really good," she said, and took another bite.

"Told you," Trent said, stuffing his tortilla full of steak, onions, peppers, rice, and beans.

After sharing a dessert of fried ice cream, Trent asked if she'd like to take a walk in the park. Dayton was hosting one of its free summer concerts at Five Rivers. Even if the music wasn't appealing, it was a beautiful night, and he wasn't ready to take her home just yet.

The night air was warm as they walked side by side down the street and into the park, and he reached for her hand as they moved toward the music. The park was full of people, and he didn't want to lose her. Of course, there was the added bonus of physical contact, too.

She seemed to hesitate, but didn't pull away. It was only when they'd reached the edge of the pavilion and he'd moved behind her, wrapping his arms around her, that she stiffened and pulled away.

He dropped his arms and walked back to her side. "Is there something wrong?"

"What?"

The band had just started an upbeat song that was going to make conversation difficult, so he motioned with his head, once again reaching for her hand. She took it and followed him away from the crowd.

Once they were a safe distance away, he led them to a nearby bench and she sat down, smoothing her dress.

"Elizabeth, I don't want to be presumptuous, but I like you. I thought that you liked me, too."

She sighed, continuing to smooth out the nonexistent wrinkles. "I do like you, Trent."

He waited for her to continue. She didn't. "So what's the problem?"

She could have acted as if she had no clue what he was talking about, but thankfully she didn't. "I'm sorry. It just . . . I can't explain it, but it almost feels as if I'm . . . cheating."

Trent's shoulders stiffened as he sat up straighter. "I didn't think you were still married." He quickly glanced down at her left hand. No. No ring.

She pushed her hair back from her face and turned to him. "I'm not."

"Then I don't understand," he said.

She smiled shyly. "It doesn't make sense, I know."

"Elizabeth, if you feel that way then there has to be someone whom you feel you're wronging. If there isn't anyone else, then . . ." Trent let his words trail off into the night.

She didn't answer. Her gaze drifted absently across the lawn, not looking at anything specific as she continued to pick at the hem of her dress.

"There *is* someone."

She nodded, confirming his suspicions.

Trent was quiet as he thought about it. Then it hit him. "Chris."

She sighed and he knew he'd hit the nail on the head. For some reason, confirming that she was pining after his brother didn't give him any satisfaction. What he didn't understand was why she was out on a date with him.

Trent looked around them. Most of the people there were couples having a romantic evening under the stars, just as he'd hoped he and Elizabeth would be. Unfortunately, reality was not playing that game.

"Do you love him?" Why he asked he didn't know, but for some reason it seemed important.

She didn't answer at first. "I-I just . . ." She shook her head, leaving the words hanging in the night air.

Trent nodded. It might not be what he wanted to hear, but at least she was being honest.

He stood abruptly, trying to brush off the disappointment, and waited until she looked back up at him. "Just promise me you won't break his heart."

She swallowed hard, and he could see the tears in her eyes. "I promise."

The car ride home was filled with an awkward silence Elizabeth had no idea how to fill. Every time she thought of something to say, she thought better of it. Hindsight was twenty-twenty. She should never have agreed to this date given her feelings for Chris.

Trent's question kept replaying in her mind. *Do you love him?*

She had answered as honestly as she could, given that she didn't know what she felt for Chris. It was certainly strong. Stronger than what she'd felt for Jared. Even with him all hot and cold, he'd showed more care for her well-being than Jared ever had.

She wondered what that meant for her future. Although Chris had kissed her twice, he'd shown no interest in having a relationship with her. Every time she got close, he pulled away.

Of course, that could be because he knows you murdered your husband.

When they reached her place, Trent came around to help her out and walked her to the door, waiting patiently while she dug in her purse for her keys. "Thank you for a lovely evening, Trent. Dinner was great. I had a nice time."

"So did I." He smiled.

"I'm sorry," she said.

He held up his hand. "It's okay. You can't help the way you feel. I'm just glad you told me now and not after I made a fool out of myself by asking you out again."

She chuckled.

"Friends?"

She nodded. "I'd like that."

Trent gazed up at the sky for a moment before returning his attention to her. "If you really care for Chris, don't give up on him. He's a good guy."

"I know," she said. "It's . . . complicated."

He shrugged. "Life is complicated. You just have to decide what's important enough to fight for." Another awkward silence fell between them. "I should probably head home," he said, stepping back. "Good night, Elizabeth."

He got into his car, and she waved before inserting her key in the door and stepping inside. She waited in the foyer until she heard the truck engine start and then fade away before setting the main alarm and walking up the stairs.

She was so lost in her thoughts about Chris that she failed to see him sitting at the bottom of his steps, and she gasped. His shoulders were hunched over as if carrying a heavy weight, his face twisted in pain.

She took a step forward, reaching out to him.

Suddenly, Chris' expression hardened as he pushed himself up off the step and came toward her. She was caught unprepared and fell hard against the wall behind her.

By the time she found firm footing again, her heart was pounding in her chest. Panic set in from the feeling of his large body suddenly towering over her, pressing her into the wall. Chris' hands had surrounded her face, and he'd caged her in. She opened her mouth to protest when his lips crashed onto hers, silencing her.

His mouth was hard and demanding against her own. She only hesitated for a second before kissing him back, her conversation with Trent fresh in her mind.

Without warning, Chris pulled back. "Promise me you will never go out with him again."

She nodded, mute.

That seemed to be all it took as his mouth descended on hers once more. She felt that warmth spread through her body as she had every time he'd kissed her. This time she didn't hesitate to return his kiss. She rejoiced in the fact that for this moment at least, Chris wasn't pushing her away, and she was going to enjoy it.

His hands pressed against her sides again on their way down.

Then, before she could register what was happening, he was lifting her off the ground.

He groaned, burying his face in her neck. His hot breath felt good against her skin, and she felt her body reacting.

The next thing she knew, they were climbing. With each step, her anxiety grew. Could she do this? Is that what he wanted? Is it what she wanted?

Her body rigid, she held tightly to his broad shoulders. When they reached the top, she expected Chris to put her down. Instead, he only readjusted his hold on her, bringing her into closer contact with is body. He felt good, but she couldn't help but wonder what he was thinking. His hands were still holding her firmly. He had to feel all the flaws she hid beneath her clothes.

Chris planted a hard kiss on her lips before he started to walk again. She buried her face in his neck, and combed her fingers through his hair as she tried to calm herself.

She both heard and felt him kick a door closed as the muscles in his body shifted. Moments later, she was falling.

CHAPTER 17

SHE LANDED SOFTLY on top of his mattress, staring up into his eyes as he crawled toward her.

She watched him with wide, anxious eyes.

He paused.

In the hours she'd been gone, he'd felt miserable, an ache settling in his chest that he couldn't get rid of. When he'd seen her standing there, looking down at him in that dress, instinct had taken over.

It wasn't pretty, and he wasn't exactly proud of it, but the first thing to cross his mind had been to make her forget his brother. Trent was a great guy, and while he loved his brother and would fight tooth and nail to defend him at any other time—Elizabeth was an entirely different matter. In this one instance, he would fight Trent with everything he had in order to have her.

But no matter the need he had boiling inside him to take her, to make her forget Trent, he didn't want to hurt her. He knew her past, and the last thing he wanted was for her to fear him. She was too important. If he'd figured out nothing else in the hours she'd been gone, he'd figured out that much.

He closed his eyes, breathing deep and trying to calm himself.

His fingers brushed her hair away from her face. Two minutes ago, she'd been right there with him in the moment. Now she looked more like a scared rabbit, ready to dart into the nearest hole and hide. "Are you okay?"

Her response wasn't immediate, but eventually she nodded.

Needing to see her face better, he reached to turn on the light. But her whispered *please* caused him to pause.

"You don't want me to turn on the light?" She shook her head. "Why not?" Her eyes closed, but she didn't answer.

He closed his eyes and his head fell to her shoulder in defeat. He wanted her. Man, did he want her. But she had to want it, too.

With a deep breath, he pushed himself up on his arms and away from her.

It was the feel of her hand on his cheek that caused him to open his eyes again. "Please," she whispered, "don't stop."

"What's wrong?" His voice was a little harsher than maybe it should have been, but he was hanging on by a thread. The woman he'd been fantasizing about ever since she'd crossed his path was lying beneath him, her skirt riding up, revealing the creamy skin of her thighs. He wanted to feel that skin wrapped around his waist as he found ways to show her how he felt about her. Instead, he was trying to figure out why her words were telling him one thing and her body another.

"I'm just . . . nervous."

He scoffed. "You have nothing to be nervous about. Trust me."

There was a long pause before she nodded and said, "Okay."

Chris framed her face with his hands, watching her closely for any sign of doubt or indecision on her part. "You're sure?"

She nodded.

Pushing all his doubts and questions aside and all his worries that this was only going to complicate everything, he leaned down and kissed her once again, much gentler this time but full of barely controlled passion. She responded, wrapping her arms around him and pulling him closer. He did the same, lifting her off the bed in an effort to mold their bodies together.

Her lips were so soft, and he tried to convey all the emotion he was feeling through their kiss, but it was impossible. What he was feeling was too complicated. She was precious to him and yet at the same time he wanted her in a very primal way. The two were hard to reconcile in his mind and at that moment Chris wasn't trying.

As they kissed, he slid his hand down her neck to her collarbone and lower, following the outline of her dress. He felt the curve of her breast and traced the outline up one side and down the other until she was arching up.

She moaned, pressing herself into his touch. The feel of her beneath him was already amazing, and they were still wearing all their clothes. He wanted her, but for some reason now that he had her in his bed and willing, he was in no hurry. Not knowing if this would ever happen again, he wanted to savor every minute of it and commit it to his memory.

He sucked on the soft skin just below her ear, and she shifted her hips as she moved her hands over his shoulders and through his hair.

He gave a gentle squeeze to her nipple, and she gasped and dug her fingers into his back, giving him a sense of satisfaction he hadn't felt in, well, ever. He needed to see her.

Leaving her breast momentarily, he slid the strap of her dress off her shoulder, trailing kisses over the newly uncovered skin, first one side and then the other. The dress clung to her cleavage, not wanting to reveal what was beneath.

Seeming as anxious as he was to remove the obstacle keeping him from his goal, she rolled over, and he unzipped her dress, pushing it down as far as it would go. The fabric fell loose, and he quickly pushed it down out of his way to reveal the most perfect breasts he'd ever seen.

Without rational thought, he leaned down, sucking a nipple into his mouth. She responded by burying her fingers into his hair and holding him to her. He'd been dreaming about this since he'd first laid eyes on her. The reality was so much better.

Elizabeth floated in a world of sensation. Downstairs, when Chris had first kissed her, it had been raw, aggressive. Now he was treating her as if she might break. It was such a contrast, just like him. Chris could be hard and demanding, but he had also been there for her as no other man had.

Her brain was barely functioning as he used his teeth to draw her nipple into his mouth. Everything she felt was so different, new, better than she remembered.

She held her breath as his mouth left her breasts and moved down her body. He moved her dress out of the way as he continued lower.

Suddenly her dress was gone, and Chris was kneeling between her legs, looking down at her. The only thing left of her clothing was a pair of black panties.

Even with the lights off, she felt bare, and insecurity reared its ugly head as she frantically reached out for the blanket to cover herself. With clothes, she'd learned to hide her flaws. There was no masking them laid out like this.

Chris grabbed her wrists, stopping her. Their eyes met and he leaned in, covering her. "Are you cold?" he asked, placing a soft kiss just below her ear.

"No." She shook her head.

He buried his face in her hair, brushing it out of his way before going back to work on her neck. "Then why are you trying to cover yourself?" When she didn't answer, he lifted his head and looked her in the eyes. "You're beautiful, Elizabeth. You have nothing to be ashamed of."

"But—"

"No buts. Your curves are what dreams are made of. I want to worship every inch of you, and then do it again, and again."

Chris looked so earnest as he hovered above her. The doubts were still there, but she wanted to believe he was being truthful.

Pushing that nagging voice away, she planted a quick kiss on his lips and then lay back down on the pillow, giving him what she hoped was a sultry smile. "If that's the case, you're wearing way too many clothes."

Chris belly laughed, quickly removing his shirt and unbuckling his jeans, and pushed them down his legs. Then he threw them in the corner, leaving him only in his underwear.

He was back on top of her. "Better?"

"Better." She gasped as he kissed her again.

Chris could not remember the last time sex had been this much fun. They laughed and joked with each other, but it didn't take away from his need to be with her. In fact, it was only increasing it.

She always seemed to have her guard up. It was nice to see her enjoy herself and be happy.

The kiss he'd initiated had quickly gone from playful to heated. Lips and teeth were coming together, desperate to connect. Tongues were seeking, exploring. Hands were moving, caressing. Everywhere she touched him was charged with an energy that pulsed through him, demanding more.

Soon his good intentions of going slow were out the window as he removed the final bit of clothing between them and reached into the drawer beside his bed for a condom. He was thankful he'd never thrown them out in one of his rare deep cleans, and hoped they were still good.

Reaching between them, he made sure she was ready before guiding himself inside. Feeling her was, hands down, the best sensation Chris had ever experienced. Words failed him as he began to move.

Her sounds and her body moving in time with his was something he never wanted to forget and hoped he'd get to experience again in the near future. She felt right beneath him, every curve molding to his body as if it was made to be there, pressing against him.

Every moan, every gasp, spurred him on. She was beautiful laid out on his bed like this. His only wish was to have his lamp on so he could see every inch of her without the shadows. He made a note of that for later. He needed to know why she had been so fearful.

She gripped his shoulders as her breathing picked up and he sucked one of her nipples into his mouth as he reached down to where their bodies were joined. Not two minutes later, her head was pressed back into the pillow, her mouth opening wide as she screamed his name.

Seeing her find her release, he quickly followed.

Falling forward, he tried to keep his weight off her as much as possible, but it was difficult because her arms were wrapped tight around his waist. She seemed to be clinging to him for dear life.

He placed small kisses along her face and neck, hoping to calm her. She only clung tighter, and he wondered just what was going through her mind.

He knew more about her marriage than most. Given the way she had reacted to being nearly naked in front of him, he figured her husband hadn't been all that generous with compliments about her body. Now he was wondering about how he'd treated her after they'd made love. Had he just tossed her aside? The thought made his blood boil, and he knew he had to calm himself. She needed to feel cared for, not deal with his anger issues toward her dead husband.

Eventually, he knew he needed to move, and as he pulled away, she clung to him for a second longer, but then reluctantly released him. He didn't want to leave her, but he needed to clean up.

Hoping to soften the blow, he kissed her forehead and whispered, "I'll be right back."

She nodded, but didn't look at him.

Elizabeth watched him walk into the bathroom. She couldn't believe they'd had sex, but she wouldn't change it for the world. He'd made her feel special, wanted.

She put her fingers to her lips, still feeling the aftereffects of his kisses. Chris had been attentive and made sure she'd enjoyed their time together just as much as he had.

The light went off in the bathroom and Chris, in all his naked glory, walked confidently toward her. He slipped under the covers, lifting one side. "Join me?"

It was strange. She was more nervous about spending the night with him than she had been about the sex.

As soon as she was under the blankets, he reached for her. She tucked her head in the crook of his arm and closed her eyes.

"I care about you, you know," he whispered.

"I know."

"I'm sorry I reacted the way I did tonight. The thought of you going out with my brother . . . well, I didn't handle it well."

She chuckled. "I noticed."

All was quiet for a few minutes before he said, "I meant it, though. I don't want you seeing him again. I just . . . the thought of you with him . . . it drove me crazy. Him kissing you . . ." He tightened his grip.

"Nothing happened," she said. "Trent and I are just friends."

He nodded but held her closer still as if making sure she was really there.

Neither of them said anything more, and she began to relax. It felt good to be in his arms.

CHAPTER 18

As conscious thought leaked back into Chris' brain, he felt a warm presence beside him. Elizabeth. The memory of what they'd done last night flooded his mind, and all he could think about was doing it again.

Opening his eyes, he found her sprawled out on her stomach, arms over her head, legs stretched apart. The sheet was tangled around her waist and legs, leaving her upper body uncovered. The sunlight was streaming in through the large window across the room, playing on her skin. It was breathtaking.

Before he could second-guess his actions, he slid down the bed halfway so that his mouth was in line with the small of her back.

He hadn't been exaggerating last night when he'd told Elizabeth that her body was what dreams were made of. She was no stick figure model. She had curves in all the right places. Her breasts were perfect. And her hips were the kind that just made you want to grab hold and never let go.

Slowly, he removed the sheet, unveiling the perfection beneath. When she didn't stir, he mentally gave himself a pat on the back.

Then he positioned himself in between her open legs and leaned down to place kisses on her backside. Other than a barely-there moan, there was no reaction.

He continued with soft kisses up her spine until he reached her neck. There he paused, but her breathing was still slow and even, so he continued with his plan, slipping his hand between her legs as he sucked on her neck.

She was suddenly awake. She never opened her eyes, but her breathing changed. Her body pressed down into his touch. "Chris!" She gasped as he continued, not relenting.

He felt her body tighten seconds before she screamed. When she calmed down, he removed his fingers, rolled her over, and gave her a deep kiss. "Good morning."

She wrapped her arms around his neck. "Good morning," she said with a sigh.

"How did you sleep?"

She laughed. "Like the dead."

"Hmm." He nuzzled into her neck again. He really liked it there; liked her reactions. "Are you hungry?" he asked in between kisses.

"Uh-huh." She gasped as he nipped and sucked on her skin, and he laughed, loving her reaction.

Forcing himself up, he got out of bed and pulled her with him, wrapping his arms around her, somehow fearing if he didn't keep a physical connection with her, she would become self-conscious again. He was hard as a rock, but he wanted this morning to be about her. She needed to feel comfortable. The last thing he wanted was for her to change her mind and think last night had been a mistake.

She sighed and returned his embrace.

"Why don't you head on into the bathroom while I make us some eggs?" He smiled against her hair. "I'm feeling the need for lots of protein this morning."

She chuckled.

He released her, and immediately saw the reaction he'd been fearing. She glanced down at her naked body and reached for the sheet to cover herself.

As much as he wanted to, he didn't stop her. Instead, he waited for her to tie the thin fabric around her body before leaning in to give her a soft peck on the lips. "You don't need to cover yourself in front of me, you know." He took her hand not holding the sheet against her body and brought it between them, letting her feel firsthand what the sight of her did to him. "I would gladly look at your naked body all day if I could. Well, maybe I'd want to do more than look." He smiled.

Her eyes were wide as she stood staring at where her hand was on his body. He saw her swallow and, thinking that maybe he'd pushed enough for now, released her.

She hesitated a moment before clutching the sheet with both hands and walking quickly across his bedroom. Her hips swayed seductively all the way, although he doubted it was a conscious action.

Nevertheless, he had to stifle a groan at the sight. She was a temptress even if she didn't know it. He quickly dressed and left to cook breakfast as he'd promised.

She realized the moment the door shut that she had forgotten her clothes in the other room. It was stupid really—he'd seen her naked last night and again this morning—but she waited until she heard him leave before going back out to get her dress.

She debated taking a shower, not knowing how he'd feel about her invading his space like that, using his soap and shampoo. A memory of the first and only time she'd used Jared's shampoo came to the forefront of her mind. She'd never made that mistake again.

Closing her eyes, she took a deep breath and reminded herself for what felt like the millionth time that Chris was *not* Jared. Her gaze drifted to the door that led to his bedroom where this morning he'd woken her up with an amazing orgasm. She'd expected him to roll her over and take her then, but he didn't. Instead, he left his arousal unfulfilled.

The continued contrast between Chris and Jared left her head spinning. Jared was all she knew. She'd learned his rules and had walked the line as closely as she could. Now she felt like a fish out of water.

Her mind went once again to Chris' unselfishness this morning. Would he really care if she took a shower and used his things?

The conclusion came to her almost instantly. No.

Without second-guessing herself, she grabbed a towel out of the linen closet, and turned on the water.

After her shower, she slipped her dress back on, and went in search of Chris.

She found him standing over the stove in a pair of faded blue jeans and nothing else. He looked like something out of a magazine. He didn't see her at first, so she was able to take a few moments to admire him.

She must have made some kind of noise because he whipped his head around, and when he saw her, he smiled. "The eggs are almost done. Can you get the juice from the fridge?"

"Sure."

She didn't realize how hungry she was. She ate the eggs and toast Chris had prepared and still didn't feel full. As if reading her mind, Chris stood with his plate. "More?"

"That's okay," she said, not wanting to seem like a pig, especially if he was planning to see her naked again anytime soon.

"You sure?"

When she didn't answer, he went back to the stove, turned the burner back on, and cracked more eggs. "What are you doing?"

"Making more. I'm still hungry and so are you."

"How did you know?

He sighed. "I have no idea what kind of lies that husband of yours put in your head, but there is nothing wrong with your body. You're hungry and you need to eat. End of story."

She felt a little embarrassed. He'd read her so well. And he was right, she did have to stop letting what Jared said affect her so much. Chris seemed to have no problem with the way she looked, so why should she?

When the new batch of eggs was done, he took her plate and filled it without another word. She didn't protest.

"Do you have plans for the day?" he asked as they put the dishes into the washer.

"Not really. I just need to go to the store for some food at some point. And, of course, Jan is expecting us for dinner this afternoon."

He turned and looked at the clock. Ten. They still had plenty of time. "I need to stop by the office and pick up some paperwork. I was wondering if you'd like to come with me. We can stop by the store to get your groceries on the way back."

She smiled. "I'd like that."

"Good," he said, pulling her into his arms for a quick kiss.

Twenty minutes and a lot more kissing later, they were leaving after she ducked down to her apartment and changed into a pair of jean shorts and a T-shirt. For once, she'd not thrown a loose-fitting dress shirt or jacket over her outfit. After dressing, and seeing how it outlined all her curves, she'd almost changed, but one look at Chris' expression and she was glad she didn't. He looked as if he was about to throw her over his shoulder and march them right back up to his bedroom and keep her there.

The stop off at the office was quick. Chris had left the drawings he'd been working on last week and wanted to check them out again. It was the project from his friend Bryan. The new drawings had been finalized, and they'd already broken ground even though the homeowners were still nailing down the details on the interior. He hoped their indecision wouldn't push back construction any more than it already had.

When they arrived at the supermarket, he followed along as she went down each aisle, placing things in her cart. He enjoyed watching her there just as much as he did in the office. The view from behind wasn't all that bad either.

It was after twelve by the time they returned home, and he insisted on carrying her bags into the house, which was ironic considering their first meeting was in a very similar and yet completely different situation.

She was in front of him as they walked back out to his truck for another load. They'd been talking about her love of all things chocolate when she stopped.

He stepped around in front of her, and when she looked up at him, he saw the fear in her eyes. "What is it?" he asked. She nodded toward her car.

It took him a moment to see it, but there, tucked underneath the windshield wipers, was a white envelope.

"Go in the house."

"What?" she said, startled.

"The house." He didn't wait for her to respond. Instead, he positioned himself behind her and guided her forward. Once in the foyer, he went directly to Jan's door and gave two hard knocks.

Jan took one look at them and her face paled. "What happened?"

"Can we come in?"

"Of course," Jan said, moving out of their way.

Chris quickly went to Elizabeth, taking her face in his hands. "I want you to stay here. I'll be back." He leaned in to press his forehead to hers. Before she could protest, he walked out the door.

Even though Chris was fairly sure there was no physical danger, he didn't want to take any chances. He scanned the area quickly, making sure he didn't see anyone lingering in the tree line, before checking to make sure nothing was connected to the envelope that would trigger something far more dangerous.

Seeing nothing, he took a deep breath and reached for his cell. After the last time, he'd put the detective's number in his directory.

"Detective Stephens."

He swiftly informed the detective of what they'd found. After a few additional questions, and conformation that Chris did have gloves handy, he was instructed to carefully remove the envelope and check its contents.

As soon as he had it in his hand, he knew there were pictures inside. Trying not to damage the envelope any more than was necessary, he opened it to peer inside.

The first picture was a side view of Elizabeth and Trent from last night. They were standing in a crowd with him standing behind her and his arms wrapped around her waist.

Although the sight of his brother with his arms surrounding her sent a spark of jealousy through him, his fear overshadowed everything. Someone had followed her last night.

Quickly, he flipped through the rest of the pictures. There were ones of them walking into the restaurant, down the street, through the park. More still of them sitting on a park bench, Trent leaning into her as if he was moments away from touching her.

"You still with me, Mr. Daniels?"

"Yeah. I'm still here. It's pictures taken last night when Elizabeth was out with my brother, Trent."

"Do you have a large plastic bag you can put everything in? We may get lucky and snag a print."

"I'm sure Jan has something," he said absently, still staring at the picture of Elizabeth sitting on the bench next to his brother.

"Good. I'll get there as soon as I can, but it will probably be a good hour or two. Any chance your brother is around?"

"I can call him."

"You do that. I'm gonna want to talk to him, too."

After the detective hung up, he glanced back at the house before he dialed his brother.

"Hey! Didn't expect to hear from you today."

"Trent, did you notice anyone following you last night?" he said, cutting to the chase.

"What?"

"Someone was following you last night, taking pictures. I have them in my hands. Now I ask again, did you notice anyone following you last night?"

"No," Trent said, his voice hard. "Why would someone be following me?"

He leaned back against her car and released a breath that was anything but calming. "They weren't following you. They were following Elizabeth. It's a long story."

"Then I suggest you start talking."

A little over an hour later, Trent arrived. He was dressed in khaki shorts and a polo shirt with *Daniels Landscape Design* embroidered over his heart.

As soon as he noticed her across the room, he walked over. "You okay?"

"Yes."

His face scrunched up and he looked doubtful, reminding her of Chris who was standing only a few feet away.

"Can I get you anything to drink, Trent? Looks like you've been out working in this hot sun this morning. Water?" Jan asked.

"Yes, please," he said. "Thanks."

They'd just sat down when the buzzer sounded, alerting them that Detective Stephens had arrived, and she tried to collect herself. Chris leaned in and placed a soft kiss behind her ear. "You look lovely."

Just the absurdity of that statement, all things considered, made her laugh. Of course, the fact that his breath lingered on her neck a little longer than it should have probably added to her sudden mood change.

Everyone stood as Detective Stephens entered the apartment. As the only one in the room the detective had never met before, Trent introduced himself.

After Jan made sure he was given something to drink, Detective Stephens grabbed a dining room chair and swung it around so that he could straddle it, facing Elizabeth. "How are you holding up, Ms. Marshall?"

"Fine." It was an automatic response, and she felt Chris cringe beside her.

The detective nodded and turned to Chris. "You have the pictures?"

Chris stretched to reach the envelope, safely secured in a large ziplock baggie, and handed it to the detective.

From inside his jacket pocket, Detective Stephens produced a pair of rubber gloves. He placed them over his hands before opening the bag and removing its contents. He looked through the pictures one by one, taking his time. "Date?" he asked once he was finished.

"Yes," Trent confirmed. Chris stiffened beside her and on impulse, she took his hand.

The good detective missed nothing and raised his eyebrow.

Thankfully, Trent quickly said, "It was a first date, a getting-to-know-you type thing. By the end, we agreed to just be friends."

"Is that right?" Detective Stephens asked, looking at her.

"That's right," she confirmed.

"Did either of you notice anyone following you? Acting suspicious? Anything?"

"No," she said.

"I didn't see anyone either, but it was getting dark by the time we left the restaurant. There are a lot of places to hide downtown if that's what you're looking to do."

"Yes, it does look like most of these were taken from a distance."

"Do you have any leads?" Chris asked.

"We've checked out Mr. Carter's family and a few of his colleagues. So far, all of them check out. We're still working on it. There were a lot of people who weren't happy with what happened."

There were a few more questions back and forth between Trent and the detective, but Chris was only half listening. His focus was on Elizabeth.

"You sure you're all right?" he whispered.

She nodded, but he wasn't sure he believed her.

Turning his attention back to the detective, he asked, "Is there anything we can do about Abigail Carter?"

"Do?"

"She called again Friday harassing Elizabeth at work. I told her not to call again or I'd file charges. Any suggestions? I can't exactly change my office number."

"How often is she calling?"

"Three times this week."

"If she calls again, let me know right away. I'll see what I can do."

After a few more words of caution from the detective, Trent and Jan walked him out.

The moment they were alone, Chris had his arms around her.

"I'm fine. Really."

"You always say you're fine, even when you're not."

"I'm sorry."

He pulled back enough to look into her eyes, but didn't release her. "Don't be sorry, just be honest." She nodded, and he hugged her once again. Having someone to lean on felt really good.

Two hours later, Elizabeth was surrounded by Chris' family. The only one missing was Gage. Being a pro football player, he couldn't walk away from a game just because someone had taken pictures of her and his brother on their date last night.

She honestly didn't understand why his family had dropped whatever plans they had for the day and showed up on their doorstep. Sure, Trent was in the pictures, too, but this was about her, not him. So when Chris ran upstairs to grab a soda for his dad and Paul, she followed him and voiced her confusion.

He seemed equally confused by her question. "Why wouldn't they?"

"Because they don't know me."

He pulled her close, giving her a kiss that made her toes curl. When he released her, they were both breathing hard.

"Because you're important to me."

He picked up the drinks and walked back downstairs, leaving her just as clueless as she was before. The only difference was that now she was wishing they would all go home so she could have Chris to herself.

Once they were all sitting in Jan's living room, Paul took charge. "The local PD are involved?"

"Yes," Chris said.

"Good. Why don't you fill us in on what's going on?"

Chris touched Elizabeth's shoulder. "Do you mind?"

So many emotions passed through her at that moment: relief, terror, anger at whoever was doing this to her. She was trying to start over, and now Chris' family was going to know about her past. Her gaze drifted up to Chris', and he gave her what she thought was an encouraging smile. "Please."

Sentence by sentence, she listened to Chris share her dirty laundry with his family. He didn't tell them everything, just the basic facts. She wondered if they'd all start looking at her differently now that they knew she'd killed her husband.

To her surprise, Paul was the first one to comment. "I remember that. It was big news in Columbus."

She didn't respond other than to nod and shift uncomfortably.

Marilyn came over, knelt down in front of Elizabeth, and pulled her into a hug. "I am so sorry that happened to you."

All the months she had endured the hateful comments of her former friends and Jared's colleagues, she'd never cried in front of others. Ironically it wasn't the hate that broke her, it was the kindness.

She clung to Marilyn while she cried, letting all the months of hurt, the pain of the years of abuse from Jared, pour out of her.

She felt the couch shift beside her. When she opened her eyes, she found Chris. He had become her rock. How would she deal with it if one day he decided she wasn't worth all the grief? That thought brought on another round of tears.

His family stayed a little while longer, finally leaving around six, and the house felt strangely empty with them gone.

"Are you sure you're okay, dear? I had no idea you'd gone through so much and now this," Jan said, hugging Elizabeth.

It was a sad commentary on his life that he was jealous of Jan's show of motherly affection toward Elizabeth. Chris wanted to be the one holding her, comforting her.

The moment he could do it without being rude, he led Elizabeth up the stairs. "Do you want to get some clothes from your place?"

She looked up at him, and a blush covered her cheeks. "Am I staying with you again tonight?"

"I'd like you to."

Her blush deepened and she nodded.

He waited just inside her apartment, and when she came out of her bedroom, she was carrying a duffel bag.

"It's just overnight." He smirked.

She ignored his comment and said, "Do you mind if I use your shower?"

Visions of her in the shower, water running down her body, filled his mind. He reached for her, plastering her against him before placing a hard kiss on her lips. "Only if I get to join you."

She tucked her head shyly into his chest. "You want to shower with me?"

He tilted her head up so he could look into her eyes. "Well, I was hoping to do more than just shower," he said, running a hand suggestively down the length of her body.

She swallowed hard, obviously nervous, and he was reminded of this morning and how she'd covered her body. But before he could offer any more reassurances, she said, "I think that could be arranged."

CHAPTER 19

ELIZABETH ARCHED her back and stretched, feeling the pull of muscles she never knew she had.

Last night had been what dreams were made of. Well, really sexy dreams anyway.

As promised, Chris had joined her in the shower and they'd stayed under the spray until the water began to cool, only to continue what turned out to be the best and longest foreplay of her life in his bed. She'd never felt sexier or more beautiful in her life.

Joining with Chris was more than just the physical. Sure, she found him attractive, hot, sexy, and every other term for *drop-dead gorgeous* you could think of. She wasn't sure any woman with eyes wouldn't. His dark hair, deep brown eyes, broad shoulders . . . she could go on and on, but when he was inside her, she felt connected to him in a way she'd never felt before. And then after, he'd held her again until she'd fallen asleep.

Reluctantly, she threw off the covers and strolled into the bathroom, smiling the entire way.

When she picked up her duffel bag, her fingers ghosted over the baby doll she'd tucked into her bag last night. She pulled it out, enjoying the feel of the silk and wondering what Chris would have thought of her surprise. It had been an impulse purchase, and she'd never had the courage to wear it before, even alone, but for some reason she'd wanted to try with Chris.

They'd never gotten that far. Clothes hadn't been on either of their minds for the rest of the night.

"What have you got there?" Chris' voice startled her, and she dropped the nightie.

"Uh . . ."

He pushed his large frame away from the door and walked over to her. He bent down and picked up the silky material from where it had fallen on the floor and held it up by the straps. Chris' eyes met hers, and instead of commenting, he neatly folded the baby doll and put it back in her duffel bag.

Then he stepped closer, pulling her into his arms, his lips going directly to her neck, and he placed a kiss just under her jaw. "I'll try not to be too impatient tonight so you can wear it for me. I'm sure the color will look amazing against your skin. Plus," he said, continuing to kiss her, "it will give me the opportunity to take it off you."

She released a huge breath. She'd taken a chance last night putting it in there and although she knew Chris was nothing like Jared, she couldn't help but compare the two. Jared had been her first and only lover before Chris, and seeing her in anything like the silk nightie in question was not on his list of desirable things to do. It was another of those things she'd tried once and never again.

He gave her a quick kiss. "Are you done? Breakfast is almost ready."

She blushed. If only he knew how much time she'd wasted on her daydreams. "Can you give me five more minutes?"

He kissed her again before stepping back. "You can have all the time you want. I'm the boss, remember?" He smiled. "I'll sign your tardy slip."

She laughed. It felt so good to be like this. But as he walked away, her insecurities crept in, and she wondered how long it would last before he realized she wasn't what he really wanted.

If someone had told Chris that his Monday would have ended up the way it did, he wouldn't have left his bed this morning.

Before he'd left for work, it couldn't have been more perfect. He woke up with Elizabeth naked in his bed and would have been content to just lie there with her all day.

Why couldn't he go back to that?

It was now just after eleven, and he was standing in front of his office, staring down Abigail Carter. She'd shown up ten minutes ago ranting, raving, and refusing to leave.

Apparently Detective Stephens had called her regarding an alibi for Saturday evening, and Mrs. Carter was not pleased someone she felt was beneath her, namely Elizabeth, was disturbing her world. Again.

It didn't matter that Elizabeth had not contacted her or that Abigail had been the one to track her down in the first place. To Abigail Carter, she was perfectly within her rights to call and disturb the life of the woman who'd "murdered her little boy."

Chris tried very hard to rein in his temper on that one. She was delusional if she thought her "little boy" was innocent in all this, but she made Elizabeth out to be a gold digger who'd manipulated her son into marrying her.

When Chris couldn't get the woman to leave immediately, he had Elizabeth call Detective Stephens while he waited outside with Abigail. It was over ninety degrees already, but there was no way he was letting that woman stay inside with Elizabeth.

As if things couldn't get any worse, his mom pulled up just as Detective Stephens did.

"Hello, Christopher." Then she noticed the detective. "Well hello, Detective."

With the distraction, Abigail tried to sneak back into the office, but Chris quickly stepped in front of her. "I don't think so."

She huffed and walked back down the sidewalk.

Chris strolled over and properly greeted his mother, giving her a quick hug. "Not that I'm not glad to see you, but what are you doing here?"

"Well, I just thought . . ." Glancing over her son's shoulder at Abigail, she lowered her voice. "I just thought with everything that Elizabeth might need some cheering up, so I baked some brownies. Chocolate always makes things better."

Chris smiled. He had no idea where this thing with Elizabeth was going, but it made him happy to know that his family liked and accepted her.

"I'm sure she'll love it. Thanks."

As his mom went inside with the brownies, he walked over to where Detective Stephens was glaring down at Abigail. "Explain to me again why I shouldn't haul you down to the station."

"I've done nothing wrong," she insisted. "I have every right to see my daughter-in-law."

"Mrs. Carter, you're walking a very fine line. Why exactly are you here to see Ms. Marshall?"

"Marshall? She doesn't even have the decency to keep my son's name!"

The two men just stared at her as she teetered on the verge of hysterics.

Then she suddenly seemed to compose herself. It was an amazing transformation. He'd seen Carol do something similar, but not with as much grace. One second she looked as if she were going to spout snakes from her head, and the next, she was back to being the well-mannered society lady, full of composure and not a hair out of place.

Thankfully, Stephens wasn't fooled. "I think that what name Ms. Marshall goes by is nothing you should be concerned with. I'll ask you again, why exactly are you here?"

"I told you. I wanted to see my daughter-in-law." Her voice was now dripping with false sweetness.

"Well, considering I received a phone call from Ms. Marshall regarding your unexpected visit, I would conclude that her employer does not wish for you to interrupt his place of business, and he's perfectly within his rights to ask you to leave. I might also point out that this is private property, and he could have you arrested for trespassing."

Abigail glared at Chris briefly before returning her attention to the detective. "My apologies, Detective Stephens." Then, without further ado, Abigail Carter pushed her shoulders back and walked between them. "Good day, gentlemen."

She got into her Lincoln and drove away.

"I don't trust her," Chris said.

"Not as far as I can throw her," Stephens agreed.

"So what do we do?"

"Not much we can do yet. So far her alibis have checked out, and although showing up here was ballsy on her part, all you could get her on was the trespassing, and I'm not even sure that would stick given the right lawyer."

Chris nodded. "Thank you for coming."

The detective paused as he got into his car. "Let me know if she shows up again. Maybe I'll bring a uniform and scare her a bit, just for kicks."

Chris was still chuckling as he walked back into the office. He would pay to see Abigail Carter in handcuffs.

Elizabeth jumped when the door opened, thinking for sure Abigail had somehow gotten past Chris and was coming after her. That woman was a force of nature.

It was Marilyn Daniels.

"Hello," she said, concern in her eyes as she pulled up a chair and set a covered container in front of Elizabeth before pulling her into a hug. "How are you and who is that nasty woman outside?" Removing the plastic lid she declared, "I brought chocolate!"

She laughed as Marilyn picked up a brownie and handed it to her. "Thank you."

"Not a problem. Chocolate is the solution to all the world's problems."

The brownie was filled with delicious chocolate chunks and after a few bites, she did feel better. Maybe there was something to that chocolate euphoria thing after all, and after a few minutes of indulging, she explained the situation to Marilyn.

"I should probably feel sorry for the woman losing her son, but considering the circumstances, I don't," Marilyn said matter-of-factly.

Just then Chris walked in. "Is she gone?" Elizabeth asked.

"Yeah. For now, at least." He pulled up a chair and for a few minutes, they forgot all about Abigail Carter.

Finally, Marilyn stood and said, "Well I should probably get going. I promised your dad I'd go with him this afternoon to find a new pair of sneakers. I don't know what it is, but that man usually hates shopping."

"Maybe he just wants your lovely company, Mom," Chris said, standing to give her a kiss on the cheek.

She swatted his arm. "You're as bad as your brothers, you know that? I don't know where you boys get it from."

Chris laughed. "Does the saying 'the apple doesn't fall far from the tree' ring any bells?"

"Walk me to my car, Chris?"

He should have known what his mother had up her sleeve the minute she asked him to walk her to her car. Instead, she caught him by surprise. Maybe he could chalk it all up to Abigail Carter's unexpected visit this morning, but he doubted it. It was more likely due to the cloud he was still floating on from waking up with Elizabeth in his bed for the second morning in a row.

"I'll expect the two of you to be on time for dinner this Sunday. One o'clock sharp."

"Wh-what?"

"Don't play dumb with me. You cannot tell me there's nothing going on between you two." When he didn't deny it, she said, "Now that that's settled, I'll see you Sunday. Don't do anything I wouldn't do." She slid behind the wheel.

Chris laughed, shaking his head. "Apple. Tree."

Marilyn laughed right along with him as she started her car and pulled onto the street.

When he walked back into the office, Elizabeth gave him a message from Terry asking that he call right away.

Apparently, Carol had shown up on a jobsite this morning. She'd gone with the pretense of bringing the guys water, but had shown up wearing a denim miniskirt and white dress shirt tied up right below her breasts. Needless to say, his guys were distracted by her presence and that was before she "accidentally" spilled water down her front.

He wasn't sure what he was going to do about Carol. He knew what she wanted, but that wasn't going to happen. She'd burned him once, and it was never happening again.

Plus, he had Elizabeth now. Well—sort of. They hadn't exactly discussed it.

Glancing out his office door to the woman on his mind, he watched as she tucked a strand of hair behind her ear. Memories of last night filled his mind, and suddenly sitting in his chair was no longer comfortable.

He tried to change the direction of his thoughts, but now that he knew what it was like to have Elizabeth in his bed, he wasn't sure he ever wanted her out of it. She was smart, beautiful, and cared about others. Her body was to die for. There was nothing about her that he didn't love.

He didn't know exactly when it happened or if it was even one moment, but there was no denying it. He loved Elizabeth Marshall.

As he watched her, he wondered how she felt about him. He knew she enjoyed his company, but he had no idea what, if anything, she wanted from him. How would she react if he told her he loved her?

Even though she was nothing like Carol, his old insecurities were still there. And if he thought what Carol did hurt him, Elizabeth had the power to ruin him.

CHAPTER 20

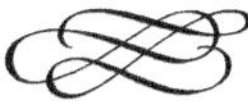

THE REST of the week passed without incident. Elizabeth continued to sleep upstairs with Chris. After those first two nights, it had just sort of happened without discussion.

When they'd gotten home on Monday night, the baby doll had been forgotten. After the stress of the day, they'd worked together to make a simple dinner before climbing into bed and just holding each other. She thought it would have been weird to stay in Chris' bed when they hadn't had sex, but in some ways that night had felt more intimate than the previous two.

They did finally break out the baby doll on Saturday night and it was even better than she could have imagined. He'd complimented her and kissed every inch of her as he'd slowly removed it. It had been a sweet torture that led to the most intense orgasm of her life.

It was now Sunday afternoon and they were on their way to Chris' parents. Even though she'd been there before and met his entire family, this time it felt different. They hadn't been together then. Now they were. Sort of.

She had no idea what she was to him. That wasn't entirely true. He'd said she was important to him, but this was all so new to her. Did he feel the same way she did? She knew that he was more important to her than anyone had ever been. He held her heart in his hands, and she knew that if he chose to, he could crush her to the point she wasn't sure she'd recover. The intensity of her feelings for him scared her.

Over the last week, they had spent most of their time together, and at work he was never far away. When they came home, they'd stop by her apartment for whatever she would need before disappearing upstairs to his place. They'd make dinner, watch television, and then make love. It didn't really matter to her what they did. She just enjoyed being with him.

"You okay?" he asked.

"Yeah," she said, attempting a smile. "I guess I'm just a little nervous."

He frowned. "What are you nervous about? You've met everyone before."

"I know. It's just . . . things are different now."

He didn't deny it. "They are. But my mother wouldn't have invited you if she didn't want you there. It's going to be fine."

She nodded.

"Gage has a game today, so after we eat we'll all huddle around the television and watch." He gave her a small smile. "You should like that."

She laughed. "I'd never turn down watching football, though it's sort of neat actually knowing one of the players."

"Gage was always a standout player, and his high school coach encouraged my parents to send him to camps whenever possible, given his potential. It's paid off, though. Now he's one of the best in the league."

"He's the youngest in the family, right?"

Chris nodded. "Yes. It's Paul, me, Trent, and then Gage. There's a five-year gap between Trent and Gage. We always tease him about that."

Over the last week, Chris had been laughing and joking around more. She loved it.

"How far apart are you and Paul?"

"Two years. It's almost the same between me and Trent."

"I can't imagine having three little boys in the house all under the age of six. Your mother is a brave woman."

"She is." He smiled, obviously proud of his mom. "She's amazing. She also didn't take crap from any of us."

"So tell me more about your brothers. I know some about Trent." Chris snorted and she ignored him. She already knew he was trying to forget that she'd been out on a date with him. "I know nearly nothing about the other two. Are either of them married? I mean, I know Paul has a little girl . . ." She let her voice trail off, hoping he'd pick up the conversation.

"Paul's wife was killed by a drunk driver two years ago. Chloe is his world. There isn't anything he wouldn't do for her."

"Oh, that's horrible."

"It was. He's better now. Having Chloe helped. He had to stay strong for her."

"And Gage? Is there a woman in his life?"

Chris laughed. It wasn't a nice, full of fun and humor laugh, but more of a sarcastic one. "Women would be more accurate."

She gave him a puzzled look.

He sighed. "Gage is what you'd call a player. What he does and who he is . . . I don't want to make him sound like a horrible person or anything, but his relationships, if you can call them that, never last long."

"Oh. I see."

"He's a good guy, but women throw themselves at him all the time because he's a star and they want a piece of him. He just doesn't say no."

She wasn't sure what to think of this new information. Gage barely spoke to her when she'd met him at the barbecue. Of course, Trent had been monopolizing most of her attention. Maybe there was some unwritten rule with the brothers that they wouldn't encroach on each other's territory. That certainly seemed to be the case with Trent when he'd found out her feelings for Chris.

He continued to share stories about his brothers as they drove, and she thought about how flattered she was that she'd been included in their family get-together.

He wasn't sure when his mother had told him to bring Elizabeth with him to dinner, but knowing she was being included gave him a sense of pride. She was his, at least for now, and he was going to enjoy it.

He parked and helped her out. She'd insisted on dressing up, wanting to make a good impression, and she looked positively beautiful.

When she'd told him this morning she needed to get ready in her apartment, he'd been slightly disappointed. Watching her get dressed was one of the highlights of his day. The way her body would bend and stretch as she put her clothes on . . .

On Thursday he'd nearly thrown her on the bed and forgotten about work when she bent over to pick up her blouse she'd dropped on the floor. She'd just put on a pair of black stockings that hugged the tops of her thighs in a sheer circle of lace. He knew she'd not meant to tease him, that just wasn't Elizabeth, but he couldn't help the way he'd reacted. He'd come up behind her, grabbed her hips, and ground himself into her backside. It had led to an intense make-out session, making them fifteen minutes late for work. She was slowly relaxing when it came to how he viewed her body, and he was loving the new, more confident Elizabeth.

Chris knew immediately when he'd gone downstairs to pick her up why she'd wanted to get dressed alone. She once again had sheer black stockings gracing her legs. Even now, after being in his truck with her for an hour, talking about his family, he still wanted to pull up her dress and find out exactly what she was hiding underneath. Not a good idea. He cleared his throat, trying to concentrate on something besides her body.

"You ready?"

She took a deep breath. "As ready as I'll ever be."

Taking her hand, he walked into the house, pulling her after him.

The smell of meat and spices filled the air as they walked through the hallway toward the kitchen. His mother was at the stove, Chloe was sitting with Paul attempting to put icing on a cake, and his father and Trent were busy setting the table.

Chloe was the first one to notice their arrival. "Uncle Chris!" she squealed, causing everyone else to turn.

He hugged his niece. "What are you doing, Princess?"

"Daddy and I are icing the cake for Grandma," she said seriously. Then her attention turned to Elizabeth.

"Do you remember Elizabeth? She was at the barbecue we had after Uncle Gage's game."

When Chloe didn't say anything, Elizabeth asked, "What kind of cake is it?"

Her face scrunched up in frustration. "Chocolate chip."

"Ooh, I love chocolate. Did you and your daddy make it?"

She shook her head. "Grandma did. Daddy and I are just helping put the icing on top." She smiled with pride.

"It looks really good. I can't wait to try it," Elizabeth said. Chris was so glad she was getting along with Chloe.

"Have to wait until after we eat."

Everyone laughed and Paul said, "That's right, Chloe. We all have to wait until after we eat."

"Chris, Trent, help me carry everything to the table and we can get started."

Dinner was fun. As usual, everyone shared what was currently going on in their lives—the PG version of it, anyway, given there were little ears at the table. Chloe had just started her second year of preschool and spent a good ten minutes talking about a new friend she'd made.

Elizabeth fitted in as if she'd been there all along. She joined in conversations and laughed and joked with the rest of them.

As was tradition, the men took over cleanup. After some convincing, Mom, Chloe, and Elizabeth went into the living room to relax.

"So . . ." Trent said as Chris took a stack of dishes to the sink.

When he turned back around, both his brothers were looking at him. "So . . . what?"

Chris' father smirked, walked over with another set of dishes, and patted him on the back. "I like her."

"Thanks," he said.

"So is it official now?" Trent asked. "You finally decided to man up?"

"I don't know what you're talking about."

They all laughed.

"Okay. Yes. We're . . . together. Happy?"

"Oh, come on, Chris. No details?" Trent teased.

"Not on your life, little brother."

At three thirty, everyone was sitting around the living room ready for the game to start. Chris' arm brushed against her, careful not to get too close to her, given their audience. If they were at home, he'd have his arms around her or maybe she'd be sitting in his lap. Neither position he was envisioning was appropriate at the moment.

At half time, Tennessee was up by fourteen points, and Gage was having a great game.

One by one, everyone left the room. His mom and dad disappeared to get some snacks, Trent said he had to make a phone call, and Paul went to help Chloe in the bathroom. They were alone, and he couldn't stop himself from taking advantage.

He nuzzled into her neck and pushed her hair to the side, grazing his lips behind her ear.

"What are you doing?" She gasped.

"Kissing you," he said. "You have no idea what I want to do to you when we get home. I've been dying to see what you have on under that dress all day."

That's when Trent walked back in the room, clipping his phone back to his belt, and they broke apart.

By the time they'd left, Elizabeth was a mess. All during the second half, Chris had continued to tease her.

From the outside, she was sure it had looked completely innocent. He would lean over to whisper something in her ear, lingering just a little too long and blowing on the base of her neck. Or run the tips of his fingers up the underside of her arm. Or rest his hand right alongside her leg, playing with the fabric of her dress, reminding her of what he'd said at half time.

They got back and she looked up at the second floor where her apartment was. Her apartment. It didn't even feel that way anymore. *How is that possible?* After only a week, she felt more at home at Chris' than she ever had in hers.

But she knew why. Chris was what made the difference. It didn't matter if it was her place or his as long as he was there with her.

They barely made it up to his place before his kisses turned urgent, lavishing her neck, and he was unbuttoning her clothes as he went. He gathered her dress and pushed it up around her hips, groaning as he felt the lace tops of her thigh-highs. "I knew it. I knew you were wearing these."

Before long, she was standing in front of him in only her bra and panties. She would have felt self-conscious if not for the way he looked at her.

He tugged on the hem of her panties, pulling them down her legs. "Take off your bra," he commanded.

She was literally shaking with excitement as she complied, letting it drop to the floor.

He knelt before her and trailed his hands up her legs, lifting her right over his shoulder before placing a soft kiss on the inside of her thigh. No one had ever touched her this way, and she knew that if she had any say in it, no one but Chris ever would again. She loved him. Loved how he made her feel. Then all thoughts ceased as he kissed her most intimate spot.

She closed her eyes and just enjoyed the feel of him between her legs.

CHAPTER 21

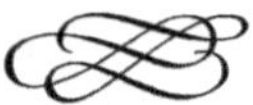

Terry showed up at the office just after ten because Chris had to meet with a few clients that he couldn't put off any longer. He was nervous about leaving Elizabeth even though he trusted Terry completely. It just wasn't the same as him being there.

His first stop was a breeze. The clients were thrilled and could do nothing but rave about the guys and the work they were doing. Chris wished everyone was like that.

The second took more time, and afterward he called the office to see how things were going. He could hear the smile in Elizabeth's voice and wondered if she was blushing. He'd spent a good amount of time that morning making sure she wouldn't forget him today.

"How's your morning going?" she asked.

"Two down, one to go. How are things in the office?"

"Terry's watching me like a hawk," she said conspiratorially.

He laughed. "Good. He knows I'll have his head if he doesn't."

"Chris, I'm fine. Some pictures and an old newspaper won't hurt me."

That sobered him up quickly. "Don't make light of it, Elizabeth. I know you've been through a lot, but you can't just dismiss those things or the fact that someone was in your apartment. Have you forgotten that?"

"No. And I'm not. Making light of it, I mean. It's just . . ." She took a deep breath. "I don't want to be scared all the time. And when you're around, I'm not. I know that makes me sound needy, but . . ."

He knew exactly what she meant and the urge to tell her he loved her was on the tip of his tongue. The only thing that stopped him was that he wanted to look into her eyes the first time he said those words. He had no idea how she'd react, and that scared him. He knew how he felt, and he wanted to tell her. He just had to find the right time.

"I should let you go," she said.

"I'll be back to pick you up and take you home."

"Drive safe."

"I will."

The urge to say I love you surged again, but he just hung up the phone and got back to work.

Two hours later, he was finishing up with his third client when his stomach growled. Had he really forgotten to eat lunch?

He pulled into a drive-thru and loaded up on more calories than he usually ate in a day, let alone a meal, but it was the quickest alternative.

He had pulled up to the window to get his food when he spied Carol across the street, and he grimaced, remembering her visit to his jobsite last week. He still needed to confront her about her behavior. To be honest, the only thing he'd made a priority lately was Elizabeth.

Just as the teenager handed him his bag of food, Carol slid behind the wheel of her car and pulled out. In a split-second decision, Chris followed her.

What was it they said about a watched clock? Elizabeth was finding that out firsthand after checking the clock again.

She hadn't been exaggerating when she'd told Chris that Terry was watching her like a hawk. He'd brought in a bunch of papers that looked like architectural specs, and he'd been poring over them all day, making notes. Chris did that as well, but he always stayed in his office. Terry was out in the main room with her and every time she'd get a call, he'd look up, listen, and then go back to his papers. It made her wonder how much Chris had told him about her situation.

It was three o'clock when she heard a vehicle out front, and her heart kicked up, hoping Chris was back. Unable to help herself, she jumped up and looked out the window.

Her hopes were quickly dashed. Instead of Chris' black pickup truck, it was a silver Lexus, and she hurried back to her desk, readying herself for what she assumed was a potential client.

"Everything okay?" Terry asked.

That's when the door opened, and a well-dressed man stepped into the office. He looked around before spotting her, and she knew immediately that this wasn't a client.

"Elizabeth Carter?"

"Marshall."

"Excuse me?"

"I go by Marshall now, not Carter," she said. "What can I do for you?"

She saw Terry move out of the corner of her eye, but she ignored him. She knew better than most that you never turned your back on men like this.

The man reached into his pocket and pulled out an envelope along with a single sheet of paper.

"What is it?" she said, taking it.

She read over the paper quickly. She'd seen many of these in her past. A lead weight settled in her stomach, and she felt as if she were going to be sick.

With emotionless professionalism, he said, "Good day, Mrs. Carter." Then he turned on his heel and left.

Terry waited for the door to close before coming over to her desk. "What is it?"

With trepidation, she lay the documents down and looked up. "I've just been served."

"What?" Terry asked.

"My in-laws," she said absently, handing him the papers. A lawsuit would mean so much more than just going before a judge. The press would get word of it, and her name and picture would be splashed across the front page like before. Just the thought of going through all that again made her sick.

A pang of longing to feel Chris' arms around her ached in her chest, but he wasn't here.

"They're suing you?" Terry said incredulously.

She nodded.

If Terry didn't know before that she'd killed her husband, he certainly did now.

Chris wished for the millionth time that Paul were there. His brother was much better at tailing people than he was.

He followed Carol through downtown, trying to stay far enough back that she wouldn't see him but close enough that he wouldn't lose her. It was a lot harder than it looked in the movies.

She made a few stops but nothing that lasted longer than ten minutes. He wasn't sure what had compelled him to tail her, but Paul had once told him it was instinct that led to solving cases, and for some reason his gut was telling him to find out what Carol was up to.

Just as he was about to give up and head back to the office, she turned and drove out of town. It didn't take him long to figure out where she was going. With a sinking feeling, he followed her straight to his house. He slowed down and pulled over, hoping she hadn't seen him yet.

He'd expected her to drive up to the house, but she didn't. She pulled off to the side of the road just beyond the house, stopped, and then backed up. It wasn't until he saw her do this that he realized there was a small clearing almost directly across from the driveway, perfect for a car to slip into. And with the surrounding trees, unless you were paying close attention, you wouldn't even notice.

He debated confronting her right then, but he decided against it. Now that he knew she was there, he wanted to watch her. He was also going to call Paul and get his opinion.

He waited until a car drove by, hoping it would distract her as he put his truck in reverse.

The drive back into town took longer than he would have liked. Traffic was relatively easy to navigate in Springfield, but the closer it got to five o'clock the more congested it got. It also didn't help that he had to stop for a train. He thumped the steering wheel with the heel of his hand. All he wanted was to get back to Elizabeth.

When he arrived at the office, he breathed a sigh of relief, parked his car, and practically skipped up the sidewalk. Nothing that happened in the last hour could dampen the joy he felt knowing he was about to see her. Before he could make it inside, she flew out the door and flung herself into his arms.

He pulled her close, relishing the feel and smell of her. "I missed you," he said.

"I missed you, too."

It was only then he realized she was crying. "What's wrong, baby? Are you hurt?"

She shook her head and clung to him tighter.

He managed to get her back inside and into her chair.

"I'm glad you're back," Terry said, startling him.

"What happened?"

Terry handed Chris the papers, and he scanned them quickly. Abigail Carter couldn't harass Elizabeth in person, so she'd found another way.

Knowing that words would be useless at this point, he didn't comment. Letting the papers drop to the floor, he pulled her into his arms and cradled her to his chest as her tears soaked his shirt.

CHAPTER 22

IT WAS a while before Elizabeth had calmed down enough for them to leave. Chris hated seeing her like this. She was such a wonderful woman, and although he understood that Mrs. Carter had lost her son, he had a hard time feeling sympathy for the woman when she was intent on causing Elizabeth pain.

After seeing her in distress, he'd completely forgotten about Carol until he was almost to the house. He pulled into the driveway, but as he put his truck in park, he took extra time to scan behind him through the rearview mirror. Sure enough, her car was still parked across the road, barely visible among the foliage.

He helped Elizabeth out of the truck and into the house, and once inside, he steered her to Jan's place instead of going upstairs.

Jan opened the door with a smile that quickly disappeared. "Oh no. What happened?" She ushered them into her living room and over to the couch, where he sat down and pulled Elizabeth against his side.

Chris held on to her as she told Jan about her visitor today. Even though he'd heard it before, had seen the papers himself, the rush of anger was still just as strong as it had been earlier.

"I'm so sorry, dear," Jan said, gathering her into a hug.

He felt the loss of their connection and all he wanted was to hold her and never let go, but he had some things to do. "Jan, is it okay if she stays here with you for a while? I need to make a couple of phone calls."

"You go on ahead."

He quickly took his leave and ran up to his apartment. Keeping the lights off, he dug in the back of his dresser drawer until he found the old pair of binoculars he'd bought that one time his father had gotten the brilliant idea for them all to go camping together. While Trent and Chris both worked outside, and Paul and Gage were used to dealing with the elements, none of them enjoyed camping. Then again, that might have been because his father refused to let them take more than the bare minimum, insisting that they hunt for whatever else they required. Needless to say, it had never happened again. It went down with his dad's other attempts at male bonding including a weekend on a ranch "wrangling cattle" and trying to rebuild an old Ford Mustang.

That was five years ago, and he hadn't used the binoculars since that weekend, but he was grateful for them now.

Sticking to the shadows, he walked over to his window facing the road. With the moon high in the sky, it wasn't hard to see her car. And with the aid of the binoculars, he could clearly see Carol using a pair of her own to spy on him. He watched her lower her binoculars and take a bite of a sandwich before going back to her watch. She was clearly there for the long haul; he just wasn't sure what she was waiting for exactly.

He retrieved the phone from his pocket and dialed his brother.

"Detective Daniels." Paul was ever the professional, and Chris wondered if his brother ever looked at his caller ID because he always answered the same.

"Hey, Paul, it's me. You got a minute?"

"Always."

He told Paul about the wrongful death suit against Elizabeth while he watched Carol.

"It will probably get thrown out if she was cleared of any wrongdoing criminally. From what I read, it was a pretty open and shut case. She had several defensive wounds."

Chris felt sick as he thought of what Elizabeth had endured at the hands of her husband. It wasn't right, and it wasn't fair. He wished he could kill the bastard all over again.

Paul said, "She should have a good lawyer though, just in case. The Carters have money and connections."

"I'll talk to her about it. Could you recommend someone?"

"If she doesn't have one already, let me know. I've got some friends with the Columbus PD. I'm sure they could recommend someone."

"Thank you, Paul."

"Anytime. If you haven't already, you should let Detective Stephens know as well. If the Carters aren't involved with the items she's been receiving, then there isn't much he can do, but it is suspicious that they've filed a lawsuit now."

"I agree. I'll call him in a minute, but there's something else I need to talk about."

"Okay, shoot."

"Carol is here, waiting in her car."

"I didn't think you had anything to do with her anymore," his brother said, sounding confused.

"I don't." Then Chris realized that what he'd said probably didn't come across just right. "She's not in the driveway. She's parked across the road in a small clearing and watching the house with binoculars."

"What? How long as this been going on?"

"No idea. I saw her today and something told me to follow her. We ended up here."

"And what time was that?" Paul was in full cop mode.

"About four o'clock."

Paul sighed, frustration leaking through the phone. "Call Detective Stephens. Tell him what you told me, even the part about Carol. We've been thinking the Carters are behind this because they're the obvious suspects, but if Carol knows you're seeing Elizabeth, then she's just as likely, especially if she's staking out your house."

Chris hung up a few minutes later, and immediately dialed Detective Stephens and filled him in on the day's activities. He wasn't happy. "I'll be there within the hour. Stay in the house until I get there."

When he made his way back downstairs to Jan's, Elizabeth was curled up on the couch with a mug in one hand and a phone in the other. She looked up when he walked in, and he was happy to see she wasn't crying. She even managed a small smile for him as he placed a kiss on the top of her head before going in the kitchen to find Jan. He found her standing at the kitchen counter.

"Hey, who's on the phone?"

"Oh, you're back," Jan said, looking over her shoulder. "She's talking to her friend, Stephanie, I think."

He nodded before taking a closer look at what Jan was doing. "Wait. You're baking?"

Jan actually blushed. He'd never seen her blush before. "I figured we might be having company and that they might enjoy a little snack."

"Uh-huh." Chris didn't press the issue. Jan was like his mother; she liked to take care of people, so that wasn't what was throwing him. It was the blush. Why exactly was she blushing?

"Did you want some coffee? I made a pot."

"Sure."

After Chris had disappeared upstairs, Jan tried to ply Elizabeth with all sorts of drinks and food. She reminded Elizabeth of her own grandmother with whom she'd spent summers as a child. Grandma Marshall had believed food could cure whatever ailed you.

She had settled on a cup of hot chocolate with marshmallows. She knew she'd been indulging too much lately, but given the day she'd had today, she needed the chocolate. Jan had then declared the need for cookies and had been holed up in the kitchen ever since.

Knowing Jan was just in the other room was comforting, but she wanted Chris. On some level it bothered her that she'd become so dependent on him in such a short amount of time, but she couldn't help the way she felt. She had given Jared everything, and he'd still demanded more. With Chris she felt she could be herself. He didn't try to change her, or tell her she wasn't good enough or thin enough, or that her outfit just wasn't stylish enough.

Looking back at it now, she wondered how she'd stayed with Jared for so long. In college, he'd swept her off her feet. She'd come from a modest upbringing, and he was flash and sophistication. He was already in law school, showing lots of promise, which only added to the appeal. He'd wined and dined her through her last two years of school and then proposed. Back then, she'd felt she was living a fairy tale. It hadn't taken long for the bubble to burst.

She forced herself to stop thinking about the man who used to control her, and called Stephanie to see if she'd heard anything. Stephanie still ran in the same circles, and if the Carters were building a case against her, surely she would have heard.

"I just can't believe they're doing this to you, Liz."

"So you heard?"

"Of course I did. Trudy Shultz was going on and on about it over lunch today."

"I figured it was too much to hope."

"So how are you dealing with it?"

"I don't really know yet. The lawyer just delivered the papers today. I'll have to find an attorney and see what my options are."

"Well, you know I'm here. I can always ask Don for a recommendation for you. It's not his field, but you know how they all know each other around here. Columbus isn't that big of a town."

"I know." That had been part of the problem. Everyone knew Jared, whether by reputation or personally. If the police had decided to charge her in Jared's death, she would have had to look outside the capital city for representation. No one would have touched her with a ten-foot pole. She wasn't sure any of them would take her on now.

The conversation then shifted to a dinner party Stephanie and her husband, Don, were hosting this coming weekend, and she was more than glad for the change in topic. She heard all about the fancy invitations Don had insisted on even though everyone on the guest list was already aware of the party. It was something that, unless you ran around in certain social circles, you just didn't understand. Then again, she still didn't.

The door opened and Chris walked in, looking as handsome as ever. He strolled over to her and placed a soft kiss on her hair. She closed her eyes to enjoy the feel and smell of him so close. She couldn't wait to get him upstairs.

He ran his fingers across her cheek before he walked into the kitchen, leaving her alone again, and she felt lighter now that he was there.

Only then did she remember her phone call and turned her attention back to Stephanie, who talked about her lunches, dinner parties, and charity functions. It was exactly what Elizabeth's life had been, minus the time spent as a punching bag.

Chris returned from the kitchen and sat beside her, and she immediately shifted closer to him. He wrapped his arms around her, nearly pulling her into his lap.

When the buzzer to the outside door sounded, he got up to answer it, and Elizabeth wrapped up the phone call with Stephanie, telling her she'd call her in a couple of days. Chris might have thought he was being discreet by going upstairs, but she knew he'd called the detective. She just didn't know what exactly Stephens could do since it was not against the law to file a civil suit against someone. Just as she hit the end button on her phone, Chris came back in, followed by Detective Stephens.

She stood, offering her hand. "Good evening, Detective."

"Evening, Ms. Marshall." He walked over to the seating area. "Mr. Daniels here tells me your in-laws have gotten creative."

She went over what had happened that afternoon and showed him the paperwork. He looked it over studiously before handing it back to her.

"I'm not really sure what you can do," she said. "It's not like this is against the law, so I'm sorry you had to drive all the way here for this."

"That isn't why I came, ma'am, but I figured since I was here and this does have to do with the case in a roundabout way, I decided it would be good to at least take a look." Jan brought in a tray of cookies and coffee for everyone. "Why thank you, ma'am." The detective smiled, and Jan blushed.

"So why did you come?"

Chris cleared his throat, and all eyes were on him, but he was only looking at Elizabeth. "While I was out today, I saw Carol and decided to follow her."

She didn't like the direction this was going. "You followed her?"

He nodded. "I would have been back at the office sooner if I hadn't, but it turned out to be a good thing."

"Why was that a good thing?" she whispered, her mouth suddenly dry.

"Carol ended up here, across the street from the house, and the last time I checked, she was still there."

"She's still there," Detective Stephens said.

Her eyes went wide. "But why?"

"That good for nothing . . ." Jan muttered under her breath. Elizabeth knew Jan was not a fan of Chris' ex, but she'd never heard her say anything bad about her.

"That's what I'm here to find out. I wanted to come in and talk with you first, but on my way out I'm going to stop and have a little chat with your voyeur."

The detective asked Chris a few more questions before getting up to leave, and Jan jumped up to show Detective Stephens to the door.

Once they were alone, Chris leaned back against the couch and turned to face her. "I don't want you to think I've been keeping things from you. It's just you were so upset this afternoon and there really wasn't a lot of time."

While she was a little disappointed he hadn't told her right away, she did understand. She'd been an emotional wreck when she'd seen him. "Don't worry about it."

He released a heavy sigh and pulled her into a hug. "Thank you."

She hugged him back, but it still wasn't close enough. She crawled into his lap and straddled him, something she would've never had the courage to do a month ago.

He must have read her mind and pulled her against him, kissing her, and soon they were both panting. He trailed his lips down her neck as he cupped her from behind.

She couldn't seem to get close enough. "I need you," she whimpered.

Chris made a low sound of approval in his chest. He grabbed her hand and pulled her after him, out the door, and up the stairs. Chris was going to make love to her and make her forget, for just a little while, everything that was going wrong in her life by celebrating the one thing that felt right.

CHAPTER 23

ON MONDAY MORNING they'd left the house to find all four of Elizabeth's tires slashed. Then on Tuesday, when they'd arrived home from work, her car was covered with egg goo that had baked on for several hours in the heat. It was stupid, childish stuff, but Elizabeth felt it beginning to fray her nerves.

When Detective Stephens stopped by the office on Wednesday with an update, he commented that the egg and tire incidents felt different to him. The break-in and the newspaper had the lingering feel of hate and vengeance. These new attacks were more like high school pranks.

The first person to come to mind was Carol. She wanted Chris back and was determined to make it happen, one way or another. When she mentioned this to the detective, Chris almost spilled his coffee all over the front of his shirt from laughing. It bothered Elizabeth that Carol seemed to think she could get him back, but his reaction made her smile.

After the detective spoke to both of them about the damage to her car, Chris offered the use of his office so that she and the detective could talk in private. Stephens also wanted her to go over her relationship with her husband from the beginning again.

Detective Stephens was silent as she went over the ups and downs of her relationship and then marriage to Jared Carter until she reached the part about her leaving him.

"Did you know who the other woman was?"

"No idea. I didn't get that far. At the time, I didn't care."

"How did you find out about the affair?" he said, shifting.

"I went to visit him at his office. He wasn't expecting me. I knocked, walked in without waiting, and found him sitting at his desk in a rather compromising position."

"And you didn't see the woman?"

"No." She shook her head. "She was underneath the desk, and I didn't stick around to find out."

The detective made some notes on his small notepad. "Is there anything else you remember about the woman? Perfume? Hair color?"

"No. I'm sorry. Like I said, I didn't see her, and I was so furious that I just stormed out."

"Do you recall any changes in his behavior over your marriage? Did he start staying out late where he hadn't before, or maybe taking long business trips?"

"No. Jared rarely went out of town on business. His cases were all in town or the surrounding counties. He did work late a lot, though. Sometimes he'd stay at his condo instead of coming home."

"When did that start?"

"A few months before my parents died, I think. I'm really not sure. He had a high-profile case, lots of overtime. It was a long time ago, and he handled those types of things. I wasn't involved. Is it important?"

"If this woman felt she belonged to him in some way . . . it could be that he was supporting her financially, or it was just an emotional connection. Either way, you killing him took that away from her."

"Oh."

"Do you think whoever is doing this is a woman?"

"It's hard to say for sure, and I don't want to rule anyone out, but it is a distinct possibility."

Before he left, Detective Stephens recommended a few locals for legal representation since Elizabeth was having trouble finding someone in Columbus. It appeared that the Carters were using their influence once again. Both Chris and Paul offered to help, but she'd felt the need to try to do this on her own. It wasn't working out the way she'd hoped.

The detective also advised Chris to have cameras installed on the outside of the house. The property was too far out in the country for a neighbor to notice anything suspicious.

After the detective left, Chris said, "You okay?"

"Yeah. I just wish it would all go away. I want to live my life and be happy. Is that too much to ask?"

Chris pulled her closer to him. "No, it's not," he said, giving her the softest kiss.

"Thank you," she whispered.

He smiled, resting his forehead against hers. "You're welcome."

Chris stood in his kitchen, heating up some leftover lasagna. It had been a long week, and he was ready for the weekend.

Elizabeth had finally found an attorney to represent her. He was from Dayton and didn't mind traveling to Columbus. Of course, the fact that she had no problem paying helped.

At no point in time did Chris ever think to question her financial status. When she'd moved into the house, she said she was looking for a job. He'd just always assumed that was because she needed one. She didn't. Not at all.

He knew something wasn't right when the lawyer offered to travel the thirty minutes to Springfield to meet her instead of her having to drive into Dayton. Lawyers just didn't do that for your average client, and he said as much to her.

She'd fidgeted a little and then begrudgingly admitted that she was worth more money than he would probably see in his lifetime. Jared Carter's family had money, which she'd inherited upon marriage. Add that to his success as a lawyer, even one as young as he was, and it totaled quite the sum.

Chris was still reeling from the information. He'd never met anyone before who was independently wealthy. The fact that it was Elizabeth made him feel small somehow. Why was she with him, working for him? It didn't make any sense.

The sound of footsteps on the stairs alerted him to her presence. "Hey," she said, walking toward him.

She had changed into a pair of blue jeans and a dark green T-shirt that showed off her breasts perfectly. He swallowed, suddenly nervous. Chris knew she was the same woman who'd been sharing his bed for the past two weeks, but finding out how much money she had in her bank account made him feel insignificant all of a sudden. What could he really offer her?

That night when Elizabeth walked out of his bathroom in her latest temptation, he wrapped her in his arms and held her. She was the perfect woman. He was far from a perfect man. She deserved better. He just hoped she didn't realize it and walk out the door.

It had been three days, three long days since they'd made love. Her body was humming, and there was no relief in sight.

On Friday night, once she'd changed out of her work clothes, they polished off the lasagna and watched a movie on the couch. Any other time, Chris would have been all over her. She'd yet to see an ending to one of the movies they'd watched together, not that she was complaining.

Instead of ravishing her as he normally did, he'd just held her. Sure, he'd kissed her neck and shoulder, showing her affection, but that was as far as he took it. Then she thought maybe they'd get somewhere in the bedroom. She'd even worn one of her more revealing nighties. She watched as his eyes widened when she'd walked toward him, but instead of getting what she wanted, all he did was hold her again. He was holding back, and she didn't know why.

The rest of the weekend went much the same. He'd kiss her and hold her, but that was it. She was starting to wonder if he'd changed his mind. Had her life finally become too much for him to handle? Was he trying to let her down easy? She tried not to think about it as she prepared herself to meet with her lawyer, Mr. Frederick.

Again, Chris had offered his office. She felt as if she was taking advantage, but he'd insisted. "Here is a much better alternative than the house. Besides, you're safer here with me, just in case."

It was hard to argue because he was right. Jan wasn't always at the house; she came and went throughout the day. Plus, she wasn't sure how she'd feel about a man she'd never met before being in her apartment.

Mr. Frederick arrived at one o'clock on the dot. She remembered what Jared had always said about being punctual and how it said something about a lawyer's attention to detail.

Her attorney looked to be in his fifties. His hair was perfectly trimmed, suit tailored to fit his tall, lean body, and the way he carried himself told the world that he was in charge. He made her nervous.

Chris seemed to sense her anxiety and came to stand beside her.

She was grateful for his support, and it helped settle her nerves. "Mr. Frederick?"

"Ms. Marshall?"

"Hello. Thank you for coming," she said, shaking his outstretched hand. "This is Christopher Daniels."

"Ah, yes," Mr. Frederick said. "You're Ms. Marshall's employer."

"I am," Chris said.

Elizabeth didn't miss the fact that Chris also took a step closer to her, placing a hand on her lower back.

Mr. Frederick didn't appear to have missed it either. "I see." Then he turned his attention to her. "It's a pleasure to meet you both."

"Likewise," she said, still not feeling totally steady. Chris was helping, but this man reminded her too much of Jared. Older, yes, but he still had that cocky confidence her husband wielded in large doses.

"Is there somewhere we can talk?" he asked.

"Yes. Right in there," she said, pointing toward Chris' office.

Chris waited until Mr. Frederick was several feet away before whispering, "Are you all right?"

She nodded.

"Do you want me to stay with you?"

"Yes." She glanced at the floor before meeting his eyes again. "Are you sure you're ready to hear about my life with Jared?"

"You want me there, I'm there." He tilted his head toward the office, and without another word, they walked in together.

The meeting was long. If she'd thought Detective Stephens asked a lot of questions, then she was sorely mistaken. Every time she tried to skim over a detail, Mr. Frederick would stop her, asking extremely invasive questions. He asked about their time in college, dating, their wedding and honeymoon . . . even their sex life was fair game.

She didn't miss Chris' reaction to each and every element she shared with Mr. Frederick. Talking about her past was difficult, and her tears flowed freely through most of the questioning. They'd had to stop a few times for her to compose herself. In the middle of talking about a particularly aggressive sexual encounter she'd had with Jared after one of their fights, Mr. Frederick stopped her. She was grateful as she was finding it hard to force the words out.

"Maybe you should wait outside, Mr. Daniels," her attorney stated in a calm, detached voice.

Elizabeth looked at Chris. His breathing was ragged and his nostrils were flared. She grabbed his hand and gave it a reassuring squeeze. She'd been so intent on answering Mr. Frederick's questions that she'd forgotten about how the details of her life might affect Chris.

"I'm not going anywhere," Chris said through clenched teeth. He gave her an approximation of a smile. Retelling her story was hard, but it was part of her past and something she'd already dealt with, whereas Chris was learning these details for the first time.

Mr. Frederick sighed. "Then you're going to have to calm yourself down. It is quite apparent that you and Ms. Marshall are in a relationship of some sort, and I could not care in the slightest. However, if I'm going to represent her properly at this hearing, I must know the details of her married life, and unfortunately that includes all the nasty details you may not wish to hear. Do you want the judge to dismiss this case?"

"Of course I do," Chris said indignantly.

Mr. Frederick's professional demeanor slipped for just a moment. "Look, I understand what you're going through. If someone had treated my wife or daughter like that, I'd want to string him up by his neck." Then he sat back in his chair and smirked. "Legally speaking, of course. Now, let's finish this so that I can make the Carters wish they'd never heard of Elizabeth Marshall."

Elizabeth was quiet on the ride home. She'd pulled inside herself again, and he didn't like seeing her like that.

Luckily, Jan was out when they arrived back at the house, so they were able to go straight upstairs. Elizabeth sat on the couch while he made them grilled cheese sandwiches. He was still reeling inside from the details of her marriage. He'd known it was bad, but what her husband had done was beyond anything he'd imagined. Wife or not, the man had raped her over and over again.

He brought the sandwiches over to her, and placed the plate in her lap before taking a seat beside her.

"I'm sorry," she said.

"What?" He was sure he hadn't heard her right.

She turned to look at him, tears streaming down her face. "I'm sorry. I know . . . I know you didn't want to hear all that today."

Their sandwiches were quickly forgotten as he pulled her into his arms. She clung to him, burying her face in his neck. He held her, gently rubbing her back, until she calmed down.

Finally, the tears receded, and she pulled back. His hands glided up her arms and neck until he reached her beautiful, tear-stained face.

He waited until she'd opened her eyes before speaking. "Let's get one thing straight. You are never to apologize for that animal or for the things he did. Ever." He watched as she worked it out in her head.

"Okay," she whispered.

His thumbs brushed the tears from her cheeks as he kissed her. "You are an amazing woman, Elizabeth Marshall."

"I'm not."

"You are." He placed another quick kiss on her lips before sitting back and picking up his sandwich. "Which is why you need to eat."

She laughed, picked up her sandwich, and took a small bite.

They watched an old movie on cable. He wasn't a huge fan of black and white movies, but she enjoyed them, and most of the time they weren't that horrible. Of course, before this past week, he'd spent most of their movie time trying to devise creative ways to distract her.

Tonight, however, he'd been trying to pay attention, so he wasn't expecting her to start a conversation. "What was your marriage with Carol like?"

"What?"

"You found out all about my marriage today. I guess I'm curious about yours. Was she always like she is now?"

"No." He sighed. "Are you sure you want to know this?"

She nodded and turned to face him on the couch.

"When I first met her she was a waitress at a sports bar in Dayton. She was all smiles and bubbly personality. Me and some of the guys I worked with would go in there after work for dinner and to unwind. We were young and single. It was a good place to relax after a long day building houses."

"You asked her out."

"Yeah. She'd waited on us a few times and seemed interested. We dated for almost a year before I asked her to marry me. At the time, she took my breath away. Looking back now, however, I don't think my brain had a lot to do with that train of thought."

"So she was good in bed."

He looked up, not knowing how she would react. Instead of being upset, however, she was smiling. He chuckled. "Yeah. I was twenty-six when I proposed. What can I say?"

"What happened?"

"The short of it? I found her in bed with my best friend."

Elizabeth gasped, her hand covering her mouth in shock. "Oh, I'm sorry."

He laughed. "Why are you apologizing?"

She cringed. "Sorry. I just . . . it's a habit, I guess."

He let it go when he saw her smile. The last thing he wanted was to bring back her tears, so he decided to finish his own sorry tale instead. "I filed for divorce the next day. Before it was final, I found out she'd slept with at least five others while we were married."

Suddenly, he found himself enveloped in her arms. *She* was hugging *him.*

It was different, but he liked it.

CHAPTER 24

AFTER HER MEETING with Mr. Frederick, life as Chris knew it changed. The lawyer had insisted that the best defense was a good offense, and even though this wasn't a trial, it meant getting the press on her side. Keeping them out of it altogether wasn't an option. The Carters were too high profile.

They'd arrived at the office the following week to a full parking lot of reporters. Never in a million years would he have thought this many people would be interested in her case.

Elizabeth wasn't surprised. "There are less than I expected, actually. Then again, it's still early."

"Less?"

"Yes," she said, taking a seat behind her desk just as she normally would.

Chris glanced back at the door, remembering the sea of reporters and cameras outside. He'd seen stations from Columbus, Dayton, and Cincinnati. How much worse could it get?

Mr. Frederick called the office not ten minutes later and agreed with Elizabeth's assessment. He also gave the two of them instructions on how to act when they were anywhere their picture could be taken. There could be no intimate contact. No hugging. No kissing. Chris couldn't even put his arm around her or hold her hand. The two of them had to act as if there was nothing between them except friendship.

Despite their protests, Mr. Frederick pointed out how it could be used against her in the courtroom. Besides, Chris could still touch her inside the office and at home. It was just in public he'd have to restrain himself.

"No comment" became the phrase of the day as she fielded a steady stream of phone calls from various reporters. It made things slightly chaotic, but he figured once it was over they could go back to the peace and quiet of their home.

He had no idea how wrong he was. When they pulled up to the house, they had to weave through several van loads of reporters and cameramen screaming questions and taking pictures.

Luckily, Jan was waiting on the other side of the door to let them in quickly. He'd never been so thankful to be home in his life.

They both followed the same routine they had for the last week. They hadn't made love in over a week, and it was killing him. It was his fault, of course. She had made every effort to entice him. Each night she'd come to bed draped in lace and silk, and every night he just—couldn't.

He couldn't explain how he was feeling, not to her, not to himself. He loved her. He wanted her. At the same time, he felt wholly unworthy of her.

That night as they were lying in bed, holding each other, he heard her sniffling. He rolled her over to face him and saw lines of tears on her face. "Baby, tell me what's wrong."

She looked up at him with so much pain in her wide eyes. "You don't want me anymore."

"I do." He hoped she could hear the conviction in his voice. It hadn't been a question and his heart nearly broke in two. She was everything to him. There was no way he could not want her. He tried to wipe the tears from her cheeks, but she pushed his hands away.

"No, you don't."

"Why do you think that?"

"You never touch me anymore."

"Yes—"

"No, you don't. Not like you used to. I miss feeling you touching me, inside me."

Chris felt like he was going to cry. "I'm so sorry. I never meant for you to feel that way. I do want you. You have no idea how much."

"Then why won't you make love to me anymore?"

He sighed and rubbed his hands over his face, stalling. He hated talking about his insecurities, his failures. But he also couldn't let her think this was her fault. "I'm just a blue collar guy. I own my own business, sure, but I love to work with my hands, building things. I'm never going to be more than a builder."

She looked up at him in confusion and said, "I know. What does that have to do with anything?"

He took a deep breath and plunged in with both feet. "How could I ever be enough for you?"

Suddenly, her eyes softened. "You think you're not good enough for me?" She chuckled.

"I don't think it's funny," he said a little offended.

"Oh, Chris," she said, throwing her arms around his neck. "For five years I was married to a man who constantly tried to change me because he thought I wasn't good enough. It nearly broke me. Why would I do that to the man I love?"

His eyes grew wide as her words registered, and the dam broke. All the emotions he'd firmly pushed down bubbled to the surface and surpassed all logical thought.

He kissed her hard and fast and then held her as he stared into her eyes with all the love he had for her. "I love you," he said and kissed her again, longer this time. "You have no idea how much."

"Oh, Chris!" He began kissing and nipping at her neck just the way she liked it, and she arched her back into his touch, craving what she'd been denied for the last week. His hands were everywhere as he made up for lost time. Her body was singing by the time their bodies joined together as they murmured words of love. She'd never felt more cherished. Chris was both rough and gentle at the same time, and she found release three times before he finally let go, burying his head in her neck and moaning his pleasure. They didn't move for a long time as they held each other. She enjoyed the weight of him, pressing her into the mattress.

He mumbled something she couldn't make out. "What?"

Finally, Chris turned his head to the side so that she could see him. There were tears in his eyes. "Don't ever leave me."

"Never," she said. "Never."

<h1 style="text-align:center">CHAPTER 25</h1>

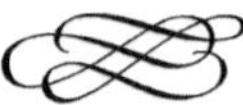

ELIZABETH TOOK a shower while Chris slept, and she hoped to finish before he woke.

Last night had been more than she could have ever hoped. Not only had they both confessed their love for one another in both words and actions, they had talked about a future together.

He wanted her to move in with him. Officially. Even though she hadn't slept in her apartment for three weeks, hearing him say that he wanted her there with him always, made her insides do little flip-flops.

When Chris had asked her to never leave him, her heart nearly broke. After hearing him talk about his ex-wife, she knew his first marriage was the cause of his insecurity. Chris was so strong and confident most of the time that it hurt her to see him so vulnerable. His opening up like that only made her love him more.

She turned off the water, swiftly dried, and tiptoed into his bedroom. She smiled. *Their* bedroom.

Chris was still asleep, so she threw on one of his T-shirts and hurried into the kitchen. He'd been so good to her, making their breakfast every morning, being there for her every minute she needed

180

him throughout this whole ordeal. She wanted to do something nice for him, even if it was only breakfast in bed.

She was just about finished when a commotion outside caught her attention, and she turned the burner off and went to the window to see what was going on.

The first wave of the reporters had moved on to bigger and better stories. There were still a few lingering, trying to get that one picture they could turn into a front-page story.

Parked in the driveway was a black Mercedes with dark tinted windows.

The door opened, and Stephanie stepped out.

Elizabeth panicked and ran back into the bedroom to get some clothes. She couldn't answer the door in only Chris' shirt. Scrambling to put on a pair of jeans, she tripped on the end of the rug and landed face first on the floor.

"Ouch!" She rolled over and rubbed the side of her face. She really hoped it didn't bruise. That was all she needed.

"Are you okay?" Chris asked in a groggy voice.

"Yeah," she said, looking up from the floor. "Sorry I woke you up."

"I needed to get up anyway."

He pushed the covers off, revealing his naked body, and she swallowed, nearly forgetting her earlier panic.

"What are you hungry for this morning?" he asked.

"Oh," she said, shaking her head. "I . . . made breakfast for you. Sorry. I . . ." Then she remembered why she'd been scrambling around for clothes in the first place.

"What's wrong?" he asked, helping her up.

"Stephanie's here," she blurted. "I-I need to get dressed and go downstairs. She doesn't know . . . about us."

"She's your friend, right?"

"Yes."

"Then take your time and get dressed. I'll go down and bring her up here. If you've made breakfast for us, I'm sure there's enough for three." He gave her a quick kiss before he pulled on a pair of blue jeans and disappeared out the door.

She was so stunned, she didn't move for a moment. Stephanie was going to find out about Chris. About Chris and her . . . as a couple. For some reason, she wasn't all that sure she wanted that to happen and wondered if it was because she knew Chris would never fit into Stephanie's world. Her old world. Just as Chris had known he wouldn't.

She heard movement on the stairs and knew she was running out of time. Whatever unease she felt about Stephanie meeting Chris didn't matter. She could only hope it went well.

Chris rubbed the sleep from his face as he marched down the stairs to get Elizabeth's friend. He'd met Stephanie briefly in Columbus, but that was as Elizabeth's boss. The woman had struck him as someone who cared too much about appearances. He didn't really understand why Elizabeth would want to be friends with her. His girl was nothing like that.

His girl.

A hopeless grin spread over his face. They'd confessed their love for each other last night. She was moving in with him permanently, and he wasn't letting her go.

When he opened the door, he came face-to-face with a woman who could have stepped off the cover of a fashion magazine had she been a few years younger. Her blond hair was swept back away from her face, and she was dressed in a cream-colored suit that looked more expensive than his truck.

"Oh," she said with a look of confusion. "I'm looking for Elizabeth Marshall. Is she available?"

Her speech was formal, and it was obvious she didn't recognize him.

He opened the door wider, allowing her in. "She's upstairs. Follow me."

The clipped sound of her designer heels hitting the wooden stairs echoed off the walls as they walked up one flight.

When they reached the second floor, Stephanie said, "Thanks." She turned to knock on Elizabeth's door.

"She doesn't live there."

"Yes, she does. She lives on the second floor," she said with conviction.

He shook his head and opened the door to his apartment. "Not anymore." Just saying that felt good.

He continued up the stairs to his place, and after a brief moment, she followed.

He walked straight into the kitchen, opening the oven to see what Elizabeth had made for breakfast. Scrambled eggs, hash browns, and sausage. He removed the three overflowing plates, and turned off the heat.

"Coffee?" he asked, reaching up to get mugs.

"Yes, please," Stephanie said, glancing at the kitchen table. It came with four chairs, but only seated three comfortably.

His apartment was smaller than Elizabeth's since it had originally been the attic, but it was perfect for him. From the expression on Stephanie's face, Chris could tell that she didn't approve.

He filled both coffee mugs and brought Stephanie hers along with cream and sugar. "Have a seat. She'll be out in a few." He motioned to the kitchen table.

He walked back over to the counter, took out a third mug, and filled it with hot chocolate mix. He'd learned that Elizabeth really didn't like coffee much and only drank it when she didn't have a choice.

Just as he finished, Elizabeth emerged from the bedroom fully dressed with her hair and makeup done. She'd gone the extra mile for Stephanie's benefit, and it irked him.

She took a seat across from her friend while he brought the food to the table and sat between them. As he started to dig in, he realized neither woman was eating. He looked pointedly at Elizabeth. She hadn't been this hesitant about eating since that first time he'd made her breakfast and she'd been afraid to ask for seconds.

When he finally caught her eye, he glanced down at the food, hoping she'd take the hint.

"Oh, there's plenty of food, Stephanie, if you're hungry," she said.

Stephanie took a large sip of her coffee before wrinkling her nose. "No, thanks. If I ate that, it would go straight to my hips."

Chris just shrugged and loaded his plate. If the lady didn't want to eat, that meant more for him.

He'd polished off several bites before he realized Elizabeth's plate was still empty. "Aren't you eating?" he asked Elizabeth.

"Oh. Yes. Of course." She scooped one spoonful of eggs onto her plate followed by a single serving of hash browns and one piece of sausage.

Chris frowned. He didn't like that she wasn't eating, and he knew it had everything to do with their early morning guest.

"Oh, Liz," Stephanie said. "I've been trying to reach you for two days. Now I know why." She smiled. "I was worried with everything going on, so I decided to drive out here this morning and check on you."

"Sorry."

Why is Elizabeth apologizing? Okay, he needed to relax. It was not out of the ordinary for her to worry about her friend. *Stephanie just rubs me the wrong way, and I'm letting everything about her irritate me.*

Taking a deep breath, he quickly finished his breakfast and left them alone. If he couldn't bring himself to be nice to her for Elizabeth's sake, then he'd just try to make himself scarce when she was around.

Elizabeth watched as Chris walked into the bedroom.

Stephanie raised a professionally shaped eyebrow and glanced at the door Chris had just disappeared behind. "So . . ."

Elizabeth blushed. "Yes."

Her friend leaned forward. "Well, he's nice to look at. If you had to pick someone for a little extracurricular activity, he definitely isn't a bad way to spend some free time."

Of course, Stephanie would assume that Chris was just a roll in the hay, a little fun. Chris had just pointed out last night how different he was from the world she'd come from, and Elizabeth hadn't given Stephanie any reason to think differently.

"It isn't like that. We're . . ." She had trouble finding the right words to express just what Chris was to her. *Love of her life* came to mind, but she wasn't sure her friend would understand.

Stephanie and Don had an arrangement that was mutually beneficial to both partners, discretion being the only rule. She didn't really believe in love, and it was how she viewed all relationships whether they were between husbands and wives or friends.

Elizabeth decided to just stick to the facts. "He asked me to move in with him, and I said yes."

Her friend's eyes widened as she looked around the apartment. "So you're really going to live *here*?"

She shrugged. She wasn't ashamed of Chris, and she wasn't going to pretend to be. "Yes," she said. "We're here most of the time anyway."

Stephanie stared at her as if she'd lost her mind. Then she laughed. It wasn't a sarcastic, *you've got to be kidding me* laugh either. This was a laugh that made you want to join in, so she did.

Stephanie lifted her coffee mug in toast. "You are one of a kind, Liz Marshall. One of a kind."

Chris stayed in the bedroom for most of the two hours Stephanie was there.

He took his time getting ready, taking a long shower. He looked around the bathroom and could see Elizabeth's mark in so many places, from her makeup sitting on the counter to her hairbrush and curling iron tangled with his electric shaver. Seeing their stuff mingled made him smile. This really was her home now.

As he moved back into the bedroom, he overheard their conversation. Most of it revolved around the upcoming court hearing. Chris still didn't get their friendship, although he guessed he didn't really have to. He wasn't a tyrant. She could be friends with whomever she wanted.

When he heard them saying goodbye he came out. He noticed Stephanie's demeanor had completely changed. She now looked at him with the kind of appreciation that made him slightly uncomfortable. Chris knew most women found him attractive, but her look made him feel naked.

"Hopefully we'll meet again, Chris Daniels," she said.

Chris chose to ignore the words that came out a little too friendly. "Have a safe drive back to Columbus."

Stephanie just smiled and winked at him before turning back and giving Elizabeth a hug. "I'll see you in a few weeks. Call me if there's anything I can do, okay?"

"I will. Thanks."

The women disappeared down the stairs, and Chris decided to clean up the kitchen.

He was drying his hands when Elizabeth put her arms around him. "Thank you," she said, placing a kiss between his shoulder blades.

He tossed the dish towel aside and twisted in her arms. She was more dressed up than usual, but she was still his. "For what?" he asked before he kissed her.

He leaned back against the counter, still holding her close. "For letting her stay. We could have gone downstairs to my apartment. I wouldn't have minded."

He shook his head. "No. You live here now."

She smiled and hugged him tight. His cheek rested on top of her head. "I love you," she said and he smiled. Those words sounded so good coming from her.

He kissed her soundly this time, and there was no hesitation in her response as she pulled him closer.

In one quick motion, he picked her up and carried her into the bedroom.

Laying her on the bed, he hovered over her and looked down in amazement. "I love you, Elizabeth Marshall." His words were reverent as he tried to convey just how much she meant to him with those three little words.

Tears pooled in her eyes, and she reached for him again. He spent the rest of the day making sure she had no doubt in her mind how special she was to him.

CHAPTER 26

DETECTIVE ROBERT STEPHENS sat behind his desk, looking at the evidence in front of him. He'd been over it more times than he could count and had gotten nowhere.

He was a small-town detective and, to be honest, he shouldn't have been devoting so much time to a case that had gone cold, but something about Elizabeth Marshall's situation had gotten under his skin.

Her husband's death had been high profile. Even before he'd met her, he'd heard about it. It was hard not to with all the media coverage.

What he didn't understand was why someone had waited seven months after the fact to finally act. And just as odd, just as suddenly as things had started, they'd stopped when the Carters brought the civil suit against her.

Abigail Carter was the easy out; she'd just decided to pursue a legal option. But the blood on the wall of Ms. Marshall's apartment felt too personal to him. Not that Mrs. Carter wasn't personally involved; she most definitely was. Jared Carter was her son after all. But he couldn't see her getting her hands dirty like that. No, this felt like a crime of passion. Something a scorned lover would do.

It was too bad Ms. Marshall had no idea who'd been under her husband's desk that day. He'd contacted the detective who'd handled Jared Carter's case, but since the woman had no bearing on the death itself, he didn't have any information on her.

There was also the possibility that the press parked outside Ms. Marshall's residence had deterred the culprit from continuing. If that was the case, then as soon as the media moved on to bigger and better things, it would start up again. It was also likely to escalate quickly, and that was something he'd like to avoid.

The vandalism was something he had to take into consideration. Although his gut told him the two were unrelated, he couldn't rule it out. Especially since it all started after Ms. Marshall had moved to Springfield.

Maybe he was looking at this all wrong. Maybe it had nothing to do with her husband. He doubted it, but a good detective never completely dismissed suspects until there was indisputable evidence of their innocence or a more viable suspect emerged.

Time seemed to pass in a blur for Elizabeth. Her relationship with Chris was beyond amazing. He made a point to show her every day how much he loved her. It was so new and different that sometimes she found it overwhelming.

In an attempt to prepare her for the hearing, her attorney had sent her a steady stream of material to review. The Carters were pulling out all the stops. They'd held two press conferences over the last week trying to drum up public sympathy. Unfortunately, it was working despite the press release Mr. Frederick had sent to the news media. It was understandable. They'd lost their son and played the sympathy card while leaving out many important details. Details Mr. Fredrick constantly reminded the media of.

Detective Stephens had also been a regular visitor. The first time was two weeks ago. He'd sat them both down, looked them straight in the eye, and demanded to know exactly what their relationship was.

"Who needs to know?" It was awkward at first, and Chris' response was defensive.

Thankfully, the detective didn't seem offended by the outburst. "Since it's obvious that you two *are* in a relationship, I'm sure I'm not the only one who's noticed. And since the incidences involving Ms. Marshall didn't start until she moved to Springfield, it's just as likely it's someone who's unhappy about that as it is someone from her past. I'm not discarding my original course of thought on the matter, but I don't want to discount other possibilities either."

What he wanted was a list of all the people she'd met since moving to Springfield, both new and old. He also wanted a list of everyone Chris had talked to about her.

It turned out to be a very long list once they'd put them together. She had almost forgotten about them going to Columbus all those months ago and meeting Bryan, Karen, and the various others who'd attended the meeting. Detective Stephens asked if anyone of these people stood out, and she brought up her confrontation with Karen.

Stephens called every few days to see if they'd remembered anyone else. Even though Detective Stephens was only doing his job, he was starting to get on Elizabeth's nerves.

After one particularly grueling conversation, she was near tears. It wasn't just the detective, but everything. The press had taken to shouting crass comments at her as she walked in and out of the office, and with her court appearance only days away, her lawyer called and made her go over her statement verbally twice. It was exhausting.

The latest call from Detective Stephens was the last straw. She wanted to cry.

"Come here." Chris pulled her into his arms, and for the longest time he just held her. "Is there anything I can do to make it better?"

She shook her head. "No. I just have to get through it. There's nothing you can do."

Chris reached across the desk and forwarded the phones to voice mail.

"What are you doing?"

He kissed her and said, "Taking care of you." Walking backward,

Chris led her into his office and shut the door. He sat down, pulling her with him. "Do you want to talk about it?"

"No." It made no rational sense to her, but suddenly she just wanted the kind of forgetfulness that only Chris could give her. "Love me," she said.

He groaned. "Are you sure?"

"Yes. Please." She moaned and pressed herself against him.

Chris grabbed the back of her head and kissed her hard and fast before pulling back enough to looking into her eyes. "You have no idea how many times I've wanted to make love to you in my office."

"Really?" She grinned.

"Oh, yeah," he said.

His lips were soft and sure as he laid her back, never breaking contact. It reminded her of their first kiss in front of the house. He'd been comforting her then, too.

Chris followed her down, lying on top of her while supporting his weight on the couch.

He released her hair and combed through her curls before unbuttoning her blouse. When she'd gotten dressed this morning, Chris had commented that she looked like a librarian in her white button-down blouse and black pencil skirt. She'd been tempted to change, but he'd assured her that he liked it—a lot.

Then he'd proceeded to show her just how much he liked it by nearly undressing her in the middle of the kitchen. She had to fix her hair, makeup, and clothing for the second time, but she didn't complain. Chris made her feel like a sex goddess—beautiful and desirable and his.

His mouth blazed a hot path down her neck and collarbone to her breasts.

He took his time pushing her bra out of the way, releasing her breasts. To him her body was perfection. She was soft in all the places a woman was supposed to be.

Taking a nipple into his mouth, he worked on her skirt. As much as he loved her in it, he'd like her just that much more out of it.

He also knew what was hiding underneath. She wore the sexiest undergarments. They were all silk and lace and feminine. Chris usually had to leave the room while she was getting dressed or else they'd end up in bed again. This morning during their heated make-out session in the kitchen, he'd gotten a glimpse of her white lace panties, and he couldn't wait to take them off her.

Her hips rose from the couch as he ran his hand up the inside of her thighs. She gripped his hair, holding him to her breast. It was amazing seeing and feeling her body respond to him. He'd never enjoyed foreplay, or sex, this much in his life. Everything with Elizabeth was intensified, and he couldn't get enough of her.

Her skirt was bunched up around her hips, his lower half pressing against her thigh as he reached the junction of her legs. By the time he stood to remove his pants, her entire body was flushed a pretty pink and her chest was heaving with her labored breathing.

"Beautiful," he whispered and he lay back on top of her.

Removing the last barrier between them, Chris entered her and they both moaned before he kissed her again.

It was a slow joining. There was nothing rushed. The outside world didn't exist. It was just them. Together.

After he reached down to where they were connected, it didn't take long for her to fall, and her tears welled up as the emotions of the day finally found their own release.

Chris buried his head in her shoulder, holding her as tightly as he could while he continued moving toward his own fast-approaching climax. She was everything to him and he'd take her past, her present, and her future as long as he got her.

She caressed his back, making him feel loved and cared for, like he mattered to her. He turned his head to the side, brushing the tears from her cheeks.

"So did that live up to your office sex fantasy?"

He laughed. "It was one of them."

Her eyes widened. "*One* of them?"

"Yes." He kissed her. "The other involves you bent over my desk."

"Mmm," she said. "As much as I hate to say this, we have work to do."

"Do we have to?"

She laughed. It was a wonderful sound. "Yes. Now get off me," she said, pushing against him.

"Okay, okay."

She kept her hair down. Knowing that she would have that disheveled look for the rest of the day made him grin like a schoolboy. She gave a final tug on her skirt.

"Elizabeth?"

"Hmm?" She stopped and turned.

"I love you."

Her smile could have lit an entire city block.

CHAPTER 27

THE DAY HAD FINALLY ARRIVED. Elizabeth couldn't believe she was on her way to Columbus to face a judge who would decide if she would pay damages to Jared's family. It was like something out of *The Twilight Zone.*

Late last night, Paul had shown up with his backpack and informed her that he would be going with them tomorrow. Until then, she figured she would be going to Columbus by herself. She should have known better.

Chris was very protective of her. Whenever the reporters had gotten too close, he'd used his body as a shield. And whenever she was upset or hurting, he'd tried to make it better. He really was her knight in shining armor. So she shouldn't have been surprised that he was coming, too, but she was.

Chris had spoken to Mr. Frederick, who had told him he should not be in the courtroom if he couldn't hide his emotional reactions to whatever was said. The solution? Paul was going to sit in the courthouse with Chris to help keep him calm if need be. She'd tried to argue that she'd be fine on her own with Mr. Fredrick there, but it was no use with Chris and Paul so determined. Neither would budge.

"You all right?" Chris asked, sitting in the back with her while Paul drove. They were only a few miles outside Columbus and traffic was starting to pick up. Thank goodness they didn't have to be at the courthouse until ten.

"I'm fine. Just thinking."

"About today?"

"Last night, actually."

He pressed his lips together in deep concentration. "Are you still upset that I'm coming with you today?"

She smirked, an impish gleam in her eye. "No, I was wondering how your mother dealt with four boys who were single-minded when they wanted something."

Paul must have heard her because he began chuckling in the front seat. "Mom learned pretty fast that if she gave us an inch we'd take a mile, so it was pretty hard to get anything past her. That and she learned to pick her battles." His voice softened. "Someone is after you, sweetheart. The two of us not coming with you wasn't an argument you were ever going to win."

"I know," she conceded. "I just don't want to relive all this again. I feel helpless."

Before Chris could answer, Paul spoke up. "You aren't helpless, Elizabeth. Think about it this way. Do you think of police officers as helpless? Of course not. But most of us have partners, especially in situations where we know there is danger. This is no different."

She thought about that for a moment. "You're right. I just . . ."

"You were a victim all those years you lived with your husband, and don't want to be ever again. I understand. But that doesn't mean you shouldn't ask for help when you need it. We all need help sometimes."

"Thanks."

"Anytime. Besides," he said, glancing back at her in the rearview mirror and winking, "you're my little brother's girl."

She blushed while the two brothers laughed. She looked up at Chris, who was smiling. Maybe this day wouldn't be so bad after all. Paul had insisted on driving. He'd told her and Chris that it was to give them some time to relax on the way there, but that was a lie. Over the last few days, he'd been talking almost daily to Detective Stephens. In fact, it was his idea for Paul to accompany them.

At first the detective had seemed reluctant to share information with Paul, but eventually, as he kept hitting brick walls, he'd relented. The two had managed to narrow down the list to three women, two of whom lived in Columbus.

The first person on their short list was Abigail Carter. She had the most obvious reason to go after the woman who killed her son. She also had the means to make things happen without actually doing it herself, making an alibi a moot point.

Carol was next on the list. As much as Paul didn't think she would go as far as breaking into the house, he had to agree that they couldn't rule her out after they'd caught her stalking Chris.

The third was the woman Jared had been having an affair with. She'd been smart enough to keep it discreet. No one at Jared's firm seemed to know anything. Or if they did, they weren't talking.

They pulled up to the hotel. While her lawyer was hoping for this to be a one-day ordeal, he couldn't promise and suggested that they get a room just in case things ran over into the next day. She just wanted it to be over. Chris turned to her. "I'll be right back, okay?"

"I know."

Then he kissed her. "I love you," he said and was out of the car.

Releasing a heavy sigh, she sat back in her seat.

"You okay?" Paul asked.

She met his eyes in the rearview mirror. "Not at all." Then she smiled. "I just want to get this over with."

"It'll be fine. You'll see."

Chris' chest hurt. He didn't like being separated from Elizabeth even for the few minutes it would take him to check in to their hotel and take their bags up to their room. Sure, she had Paul with her, and he was grateful, but it wasn't the same. He'd watched her struggle these last weeks. Today would be worse than all those combined.

After getting out of the car, he'd rushed inside the hotel, eager to get back to her.

Once he went upstairs to the room, he placed their bags against the far wall and took a quick look around.

He'd just turned to leave when there was a knock at the door. When he opened it, his heart fell.

"Carol? What are you doing here?"

She was in a dress that left little to the imagination. Three years ago, it would have driven him wild, but now he was just repulsed, and he wondered what he'd ever seen in her.

"Aren't you going to invite me in, Christopher?"

"Hadn't planned on it, no."

"Oh, come on. I just want to talk."

"You aren't dressed for talking," he said bluntly. He'd learned a long time ago that beating around the bush with her got him absolutely nowhere.

She looked down at her clothing. "Don't you like it?"

"Not really. Then again, I don't have to like it, now do I?"

"Don't be like that. The one thing that I could always say about you is that you were never rude. What's that woman done to you?"

"That's none of your concern."

"So you admit it." Her tone changed from sweet and flirty to that of a jealous lover again, and she poked him in the chest as she said, "You admit that you're with that tramp."

Does she not understand we aren't together anymore? "You'll not speak about her that way," he said through gritted teeth. "She is the most decent person I've ever met."

Carol seemed undeterred by his display and slipped past him into the room, walking straight to the bed and sitting down.

Chris leaned his body back against the wall, letting his head fall back. *Could this morning get any worse?* He took two deep breaths. "What do you want, Carol?"

"You," she said without pretense.

"Not going to happen."

She looked like she'd just been slapped. "You . . . you'd rather stay with a *murderer* than me?"

He laughed. "She didn't murder her husband, but if that's the way you want to look at it, then so be it."

"I bet I could change your mind," she said, toying with the low dip of her top, trying to entice him. That might have worked once upon a time, but she had nothing on Elizabeth.

"You really think you can change my mind through sex? Have you forgotten that our marriage ended because I found you in bed with my best friend?"

Anger flared in her eyes. "You bastard! I would never have cheated on you if you could have pulled yourself away from your hammer and nails long enough to pay me a little attention."

"That's rich. You cheat and somehow it's my fault. I can't say I'm surprised, though. You never were one to take responsibility for your actions."

She lunged at him, arms flaying. "I hate you! I hate you! I hate you, Christopher Daniels! I wish I'd never met you!"

It didn't take much to contain her. She was wild and out of control, but she also had no fighting skills. He'd grown up with three brothers. Knowing how to gain the upper hand in a fight was sort of a prerequisite.

With her hands safely behind her back, he walked her out into the hall and down to the elevators where he pressed the down button.

"What are you doing?"

"Helping you leave."

"I hate you."

"You said that already," he said as the elevator doors opened and he "escorted" her inside.

She glared at him as he stepped away. "I should have done more than slash her tires and egg her car. You were mine! Mi—"

Chris grinned as the elevator doors closed.

He quickly turned on his heel and crossed to the stairwell. The confrontation with Carol was unexpected. It had also kept him away from Elizabeth long enough.

When he reached the bottom, he scanned the lobby for any sign of Carol before crossing to the double doors leading outside. He spotted the car and quickly crossed the street.

"What took you so long?" Paul asked as he got in.

"An unexpected delay," he said. "Let's go."

CHAPTER 28

ELIZABETH WALKED with Chris and Paul into the lobby of the brand new courthouse. It was quite different from the old building, very modern with large glass windows everywhere. Jared would have liked it.

She frowned as her thoughts drifted to her husband. He was her past. And even though he was ultimately the reason she was here today, she didn't want to think about him. He couldn't hurt her now and neither could his family.

Someone touched her arm and she jumped.

"Sorry," Paul said.

"It's fine," she said, giving him a small smile.

"Everything okay?"

She shrugged one shoulder. "Just . . . remembering."

"Ah. Yes," Paul said. "Your husband was a lawyer."

She sighed. "Exactly. And most of those memories I'd rather not relive."

"I understand," Paul said as he scanned the crowd, his height giving him a good vantage point. Without warning, he gripped her arm and said, "Walk."

"What's wrong?"

Chris was on her other side, and he seemed equally as alert. "Your in-laws just arrived."

"Oh," she said before coming to a full stop and digging in her heels. "I won't run." Her voice was determined. She wasn't scared of Abigail Carter.

"I understand and admire your strength," Paul said. "It would be better if we didn't have a scene in the lobby. Mrs. Carter looks like she's out for blood."

She still felt like avoiding Abigail equated to running, but as she started to calm down, she realized Paul and Chris were probably right.

"Do you see Mr. Frederick?" she asked, trying not to let her emotions take over.

"There he is." Chris pointed to her attorney weaving his way through the crowd.

"Good morning, Ms. Marshall."

"Good morning."

After a few introductions, Mr. Frederick led them upstairs to a sparsely decorated conference room with a large table and four chairs. It still had that new smell to it.

Mr. Frederick said, "Now, Ms. Marshall, I know we've gone over everything, but I wanted to know if you had any questions before we go before the judge."

"No," she said. "I can't think of anything. I just want this over with."

"I completely understand." Then he looked over at Chris. "You'll be in the courtroom?"

"Yes."

"Am I going to have a problem with you getting out of hand?"

"No."

"How about you?" he asked Paul.

"I'm a cop. I doubt anything will surprise me. I've dealt with their kind before."

"Very well, then. Shall we?"

They stood and followed Mr. Frederick back out into the hallway and toward the elevators.

The minute they stepped into the hallway containing the various courtrooms, Elizabeth locked eyes with Abigail. Her blue eyes were cold and full of hate, reminding Elizabeth of Jared, and pricked her spine, but she refused to look away.

I'm not running.

Paul and her attorney flanked her on either side while Chris stood at her back as they walked past the Carters to the courtroom entrance. After a cursory search of her purse and Mr. Frederick's briefcase, they walked in.

The courtroom wasn't huge. A massive wooden bench stood at the front of the room, dwarfing every other piece of furniture. In front of that were two tables, each with three chairs. Behind the tables were four rows of chairs. Court was in session, so they took seats on the back row to wait their turn.

Judge Olivia Connor sat erect in her plush leather chair as she listened to the arguments in the case before her. Her dark hair was pulled away from her face in a tight bun, giving the impression that she was all business.

Her ruling was swift, and from what Elizabeth could gather, fair. It gave her hope that this judge wouldn't be swayed by the status of the Carters.

"Carter versus Carter?" the bailiff announced.

She and Mr. Frederick made their way to the table. Seconds later, Mr. and Mrs. Carter walked into the courtroom with Shawn Haines, a senior partner in Jared's old firm. She was acquainted with the man and knew he was good. He rarely lost a case because he was willing to do just about anything to win.

She turned worried eyes to her lawyer, but he just patted her arm and gave her an encouraging smile. It didn't settle her nerves.

The judge waited until both parties were seated before looking down at the folder in front of her. "John and Abigail Carter?" she asked, looking over at her in-laws.

"Yes, Your Honor."

She nodded and turned her attention to Elizabeth. "Elizabeth Carter?"

"Yes, Your Honor, but it's Marshall now."

Abigail started to protest, drawing the attention of the court, but Shawn placed his hand on her arm, and she quieted down.

"Is Marshall your legal name now?" the judge asked.

"Yes, Your Honor."

Mr. Frederick shifted through the papers in front of him and stood. "I have the decree right here."

The bailiff took the document and handed it to the judge. She looked it over and made a note. "Very well, then. Everything looks to be in order. Mr. Haines, would you like to present your client's case against Ms. Marshall?"

"Yes, Your Honor."

It took every ounce of discipline she had in her not to jump out of her chair and defend herself as Shawn presented "the facts." He painted her as a money-hungry gold digger, but the biggest blow came at the end when he said, "And in a moment of rage, Ms. Marshall attacked her husband with a glass vase, killing him. The Carters are only asking that the woman who murdered their son not benefit from his death. They are asking that all his property and monetary assets be returned to them."

"Thank you, Mr. Haines." The judge turned to her table. "Mr. Frederick?"

"Thank you, Your Honor." Mr. Frederick pulled out a thick folder and gave it to the bailiff. The judge opened the folder and skimmed its contents. "If you look at page three, you'll see that the doctors confirmed Ms. Marshall had fresh defensive wounds. There was also evidence of older wounds. The DA concluded it was self-defense and did not press charges."

"Mr. Haines do you have anything to add to the evidence Mr. Frederick has presented?"

"Jared Carter was not a violent man, Your Honor."

"Mr. Haines, I asked if you had any additional evidence, not your opinion."

He hesitated before answering. "No, Your Honor."

"We will recess for lunch and resume at one o'clock."

As soon as Judge Connor was out of sight, Abigail came after her. "You worthless piece of low-rent trash. I *begged* Jared not to marry you, but he wouldn't listen. You blinded him. Made him think you were a proper *lady*, worthy to be by his side, but you never were. You could never hold a candle to my boy!"

John Carter stood behind Abigail, holding her back as best he could while the two lawyers stood in the middle.

Chris and Paul appeared out of nowhere. "Mr. Frederick, why don't you, Chris, and Elizabeth go ahead? I'll meet you downstairs."

She let her attorney lead and tried to ignore the hateful things Abigail was shouting at her. It wasn't until they were in the hall that she breathed a sigh of relief. She wanted to collapse in Chris' arms, but she knew she couldn't. Not there.

"I need to make a call. If you want to freshen up, Ms. Marshall, the restrooms are right over there," Mr. Frederick said, pointing across the hall.

She glanced at Chris and then to her attorney. "Yes. Thank you."

"I'll be right here," Chris said.

She walked the short distance down the sleek hallway to the women's restroom. Everything in there was just as modern looking as the rest of the building. Setting her purse on the counter, she found her brush to tame some hairs that had decided to rebel.

"Are you okay?" a familiar voice said.

She turned and smiled. "Stephanie! Yeah. I'm fine."

"Good," Stephanie said, surprising Elizabeth by pulling her into a hug. "Do you have lunch plans? I was hoping we could grab something."

"I don't know," she said, thinking of Chris and Paul. She couldn't just leave them, and she got the distinct impression from Chris that he didn't really like being around Stephanie.

"Come on. The restaurant is just around the corner, and it will get your mind off this whole business for an hour."

"Okay." She sighed. "Give me a minute?"

"Sure."

She went back into the hall expecting to find Chris. When she didn't, she peeked into the courtroom, looking for Paul. What she didn't expect was to find him lying on the floor, rubbing his jaw and smiling while guards surrounded Abigail and moved as a group to escort the woman out with her husband and lawyer trailing after her.

Chris was helping his brother up. "Hey," Paul said, seeing her first.

"Hey, yourself. You all right?"

Paul laughed. "Yeah, I'm good. I think that woman must carry bricks in her purse or something."

"She *hit* you?"

Just then, Stephanie poked her head into the courtroom. "Everything okay?"

"Who's this?" Paul asked.

"Paul, this is my friend, Stephanie. Stephanie, this is Paul Daniels, Chris' brother."

"It's nice to meet you, Mr. Daniels. You're just as handsome as your brother."

"Sorry to interrupt, but we need to get a statement from the two of you," the bailiff said.

Paul glanced back and forth between the two women. "We won't be long."

Chris hesitated.

"It'll be fine. Stephanie wanted to get some lunch anyway," she said.

"What restaurant? We'll meet you there."

"Luigi's. It's just around the corner. You can't miss it," Stephanie said.

He nodded.

"Chris, let's go," Paul yelled from across the room. He was holding the door open, waiting.

Reluctantly, Chris reached out and quickly squeezed her hand before turning toward his brother.

"Come on," Stephanie said, taking her arm. "I'm starving."

After one last look at Chris, she followed Stephanie into the hallway. She could see Mr. Frederick in an intense phone conversation. She knew she should probably say something to him before leaving, but she didn't want to interrupt him, and Stephanie was already moving her in the opposite direction.

Instead of taking the elevator, Stephanie led her down a large glass staircase. It gave her the sense of floating since she could see everyone below through the distorted glass.

When they reached the bottom, Stephanie marched them both out a side door. "I got here a little late," she said. "There were a few reporters lingering out front, so I thought this way might be best."

Elizabeth paused, looking back over her shoulder at the large glass building. *The restaurant is right around the corner*, she rationalized. It wasn't as if she was going far, and she had her cell phone on her just in case.

"You coming?" Stephanie asked, looking back.

"Yeah," she said, picking up the pace.

CHAPTER 29

Jan finally tired of pacing a hole in her living room floor and decided to go out. It wasn't doing her any good to sit there, waiting like a nervous Nelly. Chris and Elizabeth said they would call when they knew something.

She pulled into Bartlett's Drug, walked directly to the one-hour photo, and dropped off her pictures. Chris had been bugging her for the last few years to get a digital camera, but her old one worked just fine, and she didn't see the need to spend that kind of money on something she could do without.

Jan thanked the photo tech and walked back to the pharmacy to drop off her prescriptions.

Gary, the pharmacist, greeted her by name and took the empty bottles. "It's going to be a good half hour, Jan. We're a little backed up this morning."

"That's okay, Gary. I'm in no rush."

She walked back up to the front of the store and grabbed a shopping cart. She liked Bartlett's because they stocked a few grocery items as well. When all she needed were a few items, it was sometimes easier just to come here rather than fight the lines at the big stores.

Maybe she was showing her age, but she missed the small locally owned grocery stores where you knew everyone and they knew you.

She had just picked up her photos and was flipping through them when someone bumped her cart. She blushed furiously as she came face-to-face with Robert Stephens. Jan might be old, but she wasn't dead. He was very attractive for his age.

"Oh! I'm so sorry, Detective. I wasn't looking where I was going."

He smiled. "Mrs. Weaver. It's good to see you."

"It's good to see you, too. Are you here doing some shopping as well?"

"Just needed a few things before I head to the station. Are those pictures?" he asked.

"Yes." She nodded, eager for an excuse to step a little closer. Jan had been dropping hints all over the place and the good detective just wasn't getting it.

She shuffled through the pictures from the barbecue at Marilyn's and showed him one of Chris with all the brothers.

"Quite the family resemblance, isn't there? There's no doubt these four are related," he said.

Jan smiled, enjoying the relaxed atmosphere for once. Every other time she'd seen him, it had been all business. "They were a handful growing up. Their mother is a saint." She laughed.

When she reached the last picture, she felt a twinge of regret. She didn't want him to leave. For just these few minutes, she'd forgotten about her anxiety, and she could already feel it creeping back in.

"Well," she said, putting the pictures away, "I guess you'll need get go—"

"Wait."

She looked up at him.

"May I see those photos again?"

"Sure," Jan said, handing him the pictures.

He flipped one over. "These were developed here?"

"Yes. Is something wrong, Robert?"

He held up one of the photos. "You see the watermark on the back here?" She nodded. "The pictures left on Ms. Marshall's car have the exact same watermark. I've been checking with every photo place between here and Dayton trying to find a match."

"So whoever was stalking Elizabeth and Trent had the pictures developed here?"

"I need to find a manager."

Jan followed him as he strode to the front desk.

When the manager emerged, he flashed his badge and the picture. "Do all your pictures have this watermark?"

"Yes, sir, they do. Is there a problem?"

"How long do you keep your security tapes?"

"The hard copies are kept here at the store for a month, and then we send them to be archived and then to storage. Why?"

"I think I'm going to need to see those tapes."

It was a quarter to one, and Chris was worried. Okay, he was beyond worried. Something felt off. He'd already given his statement, and was waiting on Paul to finish giving his. Things were taking much longer than he'd thought they would. He had a death grip on his cell phone as he checked the clock once again. Only a minute had passed since the last time. Maybe it was because Elizabeth wasn't there where he could see her, touch her. No matter what it was, something just felt wrong.

He was about to dial her cell when his phone rang. "Elizabeth?"

"No. It's Detective Stephens. I'm guessing she's not with you."

"No."

"I thought you were going to court with her today."

"I did. There was an incident with Abigail Carter and Paul, and I had to stay behind to file statements. I was hoping we'd be done by now."

"You need to find her."

Chris stayed on the phone while he went to find Paul. "What did you find out?"

"Stephanie Manning's the one who's been stalking her."

"Her friend Stephanie?" Chris said, halting in his tracks just before the door.

"Yes," he said. "We got lucky. She had those pictures developed at a drugstore near your house. They have her on tape, dropping off and picking up the pictures on the night in question. She's our girl."

Chris' stomach churned. Elizabeth considered Stephanie a friend so she wouldn't be on her guard. "Elizabeth's having lunch with her right now." He pushed his way through the closed door that would lead him to his brother.

At his entrance, Paul looked up and stopped mid-sentence, abandoning his statement. "What is it?"

"I'll alert the Columbus PD," Detective Stephens said. "Do you know where they were going?"

"Luigi's. Stephanie said it was nearby."

"I'll see if they can send a patrolman. They can at least pick her up and hold her for questioning."

Chris was already on his way out, knowing that Paul would follow. He was halfway to the elevator when he asked, "Anything else?"

"If you happen to find Mrs. Manning first, don't let her know you're on to her. We don't know what she's capable of."

"Where is this place?" Elizabeth asked as they turned left down an alley.

"Not too much farther. It's this little out-of-the-way place. Not too many people know about it yet, which is perfect. The food's great, and the atmosphere is to die for," Stephanie said.

It was the middle of the day so there was plenty of light in the alley, but other than the two of them, it was completely deserted, which seemed odd to her.

Stephanie stopped so abruptly Elizabeth ran into her back. "Oh. Sorry."

"No harm done." Stephanie smiled, straightening her suit jacket. "You ready?"

She looked at the door in front of them. There were no signs indicating a restaurant or commercial venture of any kind. "Here?"

Stephanie nodded. "This is the back entrance, of course. I figured it would be better for you to keep a low profile today. Plus, I know the owners, so it won't be a problem." With a flourish, Stephanie opened the metal door. "After you."

She cautiously took a step inside. There was enough light to see, but just barely. To her right was a concrete staircase that seemed to go on forever. In front of her was a short hall that ended at what looked to be a freight elevator. She didn't see the entrance, back or front, to a restaurant.

"Where—"

She felt a sharp pain as something hit the back of her head, and then nothing as her world went black.

Slowly, Elizabeth began to register the sounds around her again. There wasn't much, just the mild hum of electricity. She tried to open her eyes, but the second the light hit them, she was in incredible pain.

Where am I?

"Welcome back."

"Stephanie?"

She laughed. "Who else would it be?"

Elizabeth tried to sit up, but that was when she realized her hands were tied behind her back. She could feel something hard and cold digging into her wrists. She took her time sitting up and propping herself against the hard wall. Just as slowly, she tested her eyes again. The sun was bright. There were windows everywhere with a magnificent view over the city. A familiar view.

She suddenly realized where they were—Jared's downtown apartment. His firm was right across the street. But why were they there?

"I thought you were my friend. Why are you doing this? Did the Carters—"

Stephanie slapped her hard across the face, and her head whipped around with the force of the blow. It was mild compared to what she'd experienced with Jared, but he'd rarely gone for her face. He tended to stick to the areas that were easily covered by clothing.

She felt cold inside. This was someone she trusted. The friend who'd stuck by her when everyone else had turned their backs. Jared had lost all but her outward loyalty long before she'd left him. Stephanie's betrayal hit her harder than anything Jared could have ever done to her.

Emptiness settled in her stomach, making her feel nauseous. Her former friend walked across the room, ignoring her. She noticed the place was still exactly the same as she remembered it. When she'd moved to Springfield, she'd handed it over to a property management company here in town. She still owned the place, but they were to lease it for her and take care of any maintenance. From the looks of things, no one had moved in yet.

She also realized that meant no one was likely to find them. Chris and Paul thought they were at the restaurant. It was possible they wouldn't finish at the courthouse in time to come looking for her, and wouldn't realize something was wrong until she didn't show up again at one.

Looking around, she didn't see anything that could really help her. The minimal furnishings and sleek modern design Jared favored didn't leave many options she could use to escape.

Panic started to rear its head, but she tried to breathe through it. If she wanted any chance of getting out of this, she had to keep her wits about her.

Ripping fabric brought her attention back to Stephanie, who had a pile of what looked to be clothing in front of her, and she was slowly shredding it.

She was about to ask Stephanie what she was doing, but thought better of it. She'd learned from experience that it was often best to be invisible in these types of situations.

Her mind raced, trying to figure out exactly what was going on and why Stephanie was doing this. If she could figure that out, maybe she could find a way to use it to her advantage. She didn't have a lot of options.

It made no sense. Stephanie had always been the one person Elizabeth could talk to. The one person Jared never had a problem with; in fact, he encouraged it. They were here in the downtown apartment, and Stephanie had a key.

The wheels in her head came to a complete halt as all the puzzle pieces fitted together. She knew it was probably better to keep her mouth shut, but she needed confirmation. "It was you. You were the one underneath Jared's desk. You were the one he was having an affair with."

Stephanie gave her a sinister smile. "You always were a slow learner. Jared said you'd never figure it out, and if you hadn't busted into his office that day, you never would have."

Knowing Stephanie had been the other woman hurt. It also explained a lot. The one person she'd thought of as her true friend in her former life was the one who committed the ultimate betrayal. "How long?" she asked, feeling cold again despite the hot sun streaming in through the windows.

Stephanie just laughed, never pausing in her continued destruction of the material in front of her. "You were a toy, Elizabeth. A pawn. Only you thought you were anything more. Jared certainly never did. He needed a wife to parade in front of his colleagues that he could keep in line, and you fit the bill; meek and moldable."

She thought back to all those nights he'd spent in this apartment. All the nights he'd worked late.

The click of heels brought her attention back to Stephanie who was walking toward her, material in hand. It was then she recognized what Stephanie had been ripping up. Her dresses. She remembered that not-quite-right feeling when she'd looked in her closet after the break-in. Now she understood. What wasn't making sense was why she'd taken her clothes.

Stephanie knelt down so that she was at her eye level, and ran her manicured fingernail from Elizabeth's temple to her jaw. "I'm going to enjoy killing you."

Elizabeth's eyes widened as a jolt of fear surged through her. Her gaze darted around frantically looking for anything that could help her. She could tell by the look in Stephanie's eyes that her time was running out. She didn't want to die.

Stephanie laughed and stood. "I wonder how your little boy toy will feel when he finds you've taken a nosedive from your dead husband's condo. Do you think he'll be sad?" Stephanie pouted mockingly.

She was stunned. How had she never seen this side of Stephanie? How had she not known she was psychotic?

"Chris will never believe that I jumped. Neither will the police."

"Sure they will. I'm not stupid, you know. That's why I'm setting the scene. You're going to leave a suicide note and everything." Stephanie continued to laugh as she moved around the condo, preparing for Elizabeth's fake suicide.

Reality set in. Stephanie could actually pull this off. She could kill her. Whether she got away with it or not was irrelevant.

The words Chris had spoken to her the night they declared their love came back to her with complete clarity. *"Don't ever leave me."* His desperation had cut straight to her heart, then and now. She couldn't leave him. She'd promised. With a sudden desperation, she looked around the room again, trying to find an escape, a weapon, anything. She was a survivor, and she was going to find a way to survive this.

CHAPTER 30

GIVING his statement had taken much longer than Paul had expected. Being an out-of-state cop seemed to complicate things for some reason. By the time Chris burst into the room, it was almost one o'clock.

He followed Chris back out into the hall without questioning what was going on. Chris was acting like a man on a mission, and for now, Paul was content to follow him.

The hallway was full of people, just as it had been earlier. He watched his brother's eyes scan the crowd and knew he was looking for Elizabeth. There was no sign of her or her lawyer.

He turned on his phone and realized he had ten messages. The first was from Detective Stephens telling him what he'd found out about Stephanie Manning. He now understood why Chris was acting frantic.

Just as he was about to suggest to Chris that they go downstairs and locate a police officer, he saw Elizabeth's lawyer exit the elevator followed by two uniformed officers. None of them looked happy.

Chris noticed them, too. "Is she with you?" he asked.

"No."

"She has to still be with Stephanie," Chris said.

"Agreed." Paul turned to the officers. "Ms. Manning said they were going to a restaurant near here called Luigi's. Do you know it?"

The two men wrinkled their brows before the one on the left answered. "There's no restaurant by that name near here. Nearest one I know of is near campus and that's a good five miles."

Chris let off a string of curses.

Paul rubbed a hand over his head. "This isn't good. She's with Stephanie."

"We've got to find her."

Paul turned to the officers. "Can we get a look at the security cameras? We know they were in the building less than an hour ago."

"The judge will be back soon, and I need to tell her what's going on," Mr. Frederick said.

"You do that," Paul said. "Also, see if the judge will agree to hold Mr. and Mrs. Carter for us. We don't know if they're involved."

The ride down to the basement took too long in Chris' opinion. Elizabeth was somewhere with a woman who had stalked her, broken into her apartment, and thrown blood all over her bedroom wall. This same woman had sat beside him last week and only pretended to be her best friend while they ate breakfast. The woman obviously had a screw or two loose.

Thankfully, with the two officers beside them, they made it through the security check without too much difficulty. The security room was big with wall-to-wall monitors. It didn't take more than a minute to pull up the footage of Elizabeth with Stephanie Manning walking through the building and out a side door.

Chris' chest constricted. He needed to find her.

"Do you have any cameras outside?" Paul asked.

"Only on the front of the building."

"There are some outside cameras on the other buildings around here, but accessing them will take time."

"Time we don't have," Chris said, already moving toward the door.

"Where do you think you're going?" Paul said.

"I need to talk to the Carters. They live here. They run in the same circles as Stephanie. Maybe they have some idea where they've gone."

"They may not talk to you."

The look in Paul's eyes said it all. Chris was grasping at straws, and he knew it. "I can't lose her, Paul. I just can't." Without another word, Paul clasped his brother on the shoulder and they both trekked back upstairs to see if they could wheedle any information out of the Carters.

When they walked into the courtroom, things were not looking good. "Give me one good reason, Mr. Frederick, why I shouldn't hold your client in contempt."

"I'm sorry to interrupt, Your Honor," Paul said, coming forward. "I think I can shed some light on this if you would allow me."

"And you are?"

"Detective Paul Daniels of the Indianapolis Police Department. I've been working with Detective Stephens of the Springfield PD, investigating crimes committed against Ms. Marshall. She's been receiving threats recently."

The judge glanced down at the papers in front of her again. "Springfield is where Ms. Marshall currently resides?"

"Yes."

"And why is the Indianapolis PD involved?"

"They aren't. My brother, Chris, lives in the apartment above Ms. Marshall. I became involved at his request about a month ago."

"I see," the judge said. "Please proceed, then."

Paul kept to the facts as he filled the judge in, but it still took time, time that Chris knew they didn't have. The judge motioned to the bailiff and handed him a note.

"We have reason to believe that the Carters may have some idea as to where Ms. Marshall is."

"Like I'd tell you anything even if I knew," Abigail said.

The judge narrowed her eyes. "Mrs. Carter! I will not tell you again to watch your tone in my courtroom. And I might add that if you do know something about Ms. Marshall's whereabouts and fail to share it, you could be charged as an accessory to kidnapping if something happens to Ms. Marshall."

That and the two police officers who stepped into the room seemed to bring her up short as she looked desperately to her husband and lawyer.

Mr. Haines finally said, "Try Jared's old condo. It's only about three blocks from here."

The lawyer swiftly wrote down the address, and Chris grabbed it out of his hand and ran for the door, Paul and the two police officers hot on his heels.

"Hey!" Paul yelled, running down the hall after him. "Where do you think you're going?" He held the door to the elevator open, detaining Chris inside.

"Get out of my way, Paul."

"You can't just go storming over there half-cocked. You need to leave this to the police."

Chris took a deep breath and looked his brother straight in the eye. "What would you do if it were Melissa?" He knew it was a low blow bringing Paul's wife into this, but Chris didn't have time to argue. Instead of stepping back and letting Chris go, Paul jumped inside the elevator with him, along with the two police officers. "What are you—"

Paul cut him off as they began their descent to the lobby. "You asked what I would do, and you're right. But I'm not letting you go alone. You're my brother. If things get dicey, keep your head down."

Elizabeth wasn't having much luck in freeing herself. The only positive was that Stephanie seemed preoccupied with whatever she was doing and wasn't paying her any attention.

All that changed in an instant. "Okay, then. Are you ready? I don't want to keep you tied up," Stephanie said, cackling at her own joke.

Elizabeth tried to make it difficult as Stephanie pulled her to her feet and then pushed her onto the balcony outside. She tripped over a chair and landed hard on her right arm.

"Oh, don't worry," Stephanie said. "A few more bumps and bruises won't matter when they scrape your body off the pavement."

She grabbed Elizabeth by the hair, pulling her to her feet, and brought her to the cast iron railing. At thirty stories up, taking a fall from this height would be more than enough to kill her.

Elizabeth gasped when the cast iron dug into her waist as Stephanie moved behind her, pressing her against the railing. She could hear the bustle of the city around her, and feel the heat from the sun beating down on her. The tall concrete and brick buildings of the city she'd called home for nine years surrounded her. She wondered if this was really it. *Will this be the last thing I ever see, feel?*

A sharp point at her wrists brought her thoughts back into focus. She wasn't dead yet, and she wasn't giving up.

"Say goodbye, Liz. You never were good enough," she said, slicing the bands around her wrists.

The moment she felt the bands snap, Elizabeth used the momentum to push both her palms against Stephanie. It was enough to give her a little room to move. She twisted around and shoved Stephanie hard, pushing away from the railing.

She made a run for the door, but only made it a few feet before Stephanie charged her, causing them both to lose their balance. Before she knew what was happening, she felt the railing pressing against her side as Stephanie's forward movement hurled them both toward the edge. Elizabeth's feet lost their feeble purchase and she found herself airborne. Reaching out, she grabbed hold of the hard metal rail beneath her. She felt the weight of Stephanie's body beside her, then her fingers pulling and biting into Elizabeth's skin as she, too, tried to hold on to something, anything.

Inch by inch she felt Stephanie slide lower. "Help me!"

Even if Elizabeth wanted to, she couldn't. She put all her effort into holding on to the one thing that was keeping her from hitting the pavement below.

Then the weight was gone.

There was a scream, but it sounded far away to her ears. And then nothing.

Everything was suddenly still. She felt suspended in time as she hung from the railing, hoping that she could hang on long enough for someone to see her up there and get help.

"Elizabeth!"

Relief washed through her. "Chris!"

His face appeared over the edge of the railing and she couldn't stop herself from crying. She was safe. She would survive. "I've got you," he said grabbing her arms.

"Whoa!" said Paul as he helped Chris pull her back onto the balcony.

As soon as she was safely on solid ground, Chris enveloped her, holding her tightly. "Are you all right?" he asked. "Please, tell me you're all right."

"I'm fine," she said, crying and never wanting to leave his arms.

"Police are here, and an ambulance will be here soon," Paul said. "How are you feeling?"

She didn't answer him right away. Her head was spinning as she came down from her adrenaline rush. "Is she dead?" she asked instead.

The question was directed at Paul, but Chris answered. "Yes. She's dead."

She nodded and leaned back into Chris.

Paul patted his little brother on the shoulder. "I'm going to go downstairs to direct the paramedics."

Chris tilted her head up and kissed her. "Don't ever do that to me again. I thought—"

"I know," she said, trying to soothe him. "I told you I'd never leave you. Did you think I'd go back on my word?"

Chris pulled her close again. "No. Never."

Their little bubble was soon broken, first by the police and then by the return of Paul and the paramedics. Chris stood to the side and allowed them enough room to do their job, but he refused to go more than a few feet. He knew they needed to question and examine Elizabeth, but he also had a hard time not being in direct contact with her. His eyes told him that she was there in front of him and that she was okay, at least physically, but he needed that sense of touch to confirm it. Just to verify that his eyes weren't deceiving him.

The medics cleared her with nothing more than a few bumps and bruises. The two police officers who'd arrived with Paul and Chris questioned Elizabeth. She was amazing, remaining calm through it all. Sentence by sentence, she relived the last two hours of her life in detail.

Stephanie was the other woman, and he couldn't say he was all that surprised. From what he'd learned of Jared, the man was all about appearances, and Elizabeth wasn't fake. He couldn't see her ever truly fitting into the world in which the Carters and Stephanie Manning lived.

"We'll be in touch if we have any more questions, Ms. Marshall." The two detectives stood to leave, and Paul walked them out.

"Are you okay?" she said.

Chris turned to see if she was serious. "You're asking *me* if I'm okay? Shouldn't that be the other way around?"

She blushed, glancing down at the floor. "Well, I know how *I* am."

He chuckled and pulled her down with him onto the couch. "And how are you?"

She sighed and leaned back into him. "Confused. Angry. Relieved."

"Relieved?"

"I never understood her friendship with me. Now it makes sense."

"You're relieved to know that she was only your friend because she wanted to keep tabs on you?" It didn't make sense to him.

"No. Well, yes. Sort of. More, I'm relieved to finally have the mystery solved."

"Yes. And no one is trying to come after you anymore."

"Except for John and Abigail," she said.

"I'm not so sure about that. The judge didn't look all too happy with them when I left. Maybe we'll get lucky and find out they had a hand in this. That would get them out of our hair."

She twisted in his arms. "But I don't think they had anything to do with this. I mean . . . wait. How *did* you find me?"

Chris brushed a stray piece of hair behind her ear before hugging her close again. "Their lawyer, Mr. Haines. He knew about this place and figured that's where Stephanie must have taken you."

"Shawn? Wow," she said. Then out of nowhere, the tears started flowing again. "I didn't think he would ever go out of his way to help like that."

"Hey," he said, increasing his hold on her. "You're safe now. Everything's okay."

"I know. I don't know why I'm crying."

"You've had a stressful day. It's completely understandable. As for Mr. Haines, I wouldn't go thinking him overly noble, if I were you." He chuckled. "After hearing what was going on, the judge told the Carters that if they knew something, they'd better be forthcoming or face being charged as an accomplice. I do believe it was self-preservation on his part."

She laughed. "Yeah, that sounds more like Shawn."

Paul walked back into the room. "They need to get in here and catalog evidence, and I'm sure you'd like to rest, Elizabeth." He guided the three of them to the front of the building and away from all the commotion happening with the cleanup of Stephanie's body.

A cab took them to the hotel, and Chris led Elizabeth to their room. Paul followed, stopping only long enough to take his own bags and disappear to his room next door.

"How does a bath sound?" Chris asked.

She gave him a shy smile. "That sounds lovely. Thank you."

He disappeared into the bathroom and turned on the water to fill up the tub. Wanting to make sure she had everything she needed, he removed a large towel from the rack and placed it beside the bathtub along with soap, shampoo, and conditioner.

He heard movement, and glanced up to find her standing in the doorway. Her clothes were gone, leaving nothing to cover the ugly purple bruises along her wrist, waist, hips, and thighs. Knowing that someone had done this to her angered him, but seeing the evidence of it made him want to weep. She was beautiful. She was precious. She deserved to be taken care of and cherished.

She walked into his arms. He couldn't let go of her. He just couldn't. "Marry me."

"What?" she asked, pulling back to look into his eyes.

Nerves coursed through him. He shouldn't have asked. This wasn't the right time. What was he thinking? She'd nearly died today and . . .

"Did you just ask me to marry you?" she asked in disbelief.

"Yes."

"Wow, I must look better naked than I thought." She laughed, but stopped as she searched his face. "Did you mean it?"

Do or die, he was going to answer her honestly. He didn't regret asking, just the when and where. "Yes."

She smiled. "Well then, yes."

He stood there not moving, trying to process what just happened. "Yes? As in, yes, you'll marry me?"

She nodded. "But I insist on being clothed when I do."

He laughed, pulled her to him, and kissed her. "I love you!" he shouted before kissing her again, slower this time. She responded with the same passion she always did, and it gave him hope.

When the kiss finally ended, she looked at him with such love. He didn't want to leave her side.

"Join me?"

Slowly, she helped him remove his clothing, and they lay in the bath until the water cooled.

As he held her in his arms that night, he thought how lucky he was to have found her. This woman had not only opened his heart to love again, she'd changed his life. He would never let her forget how special she was.

EPILOGUE

THEY SPENT the next few days in Columbus tying up loose ends. When they appeared before the judge again on Friday afternoon, the verdict was swift. The Carters had no real case against Elizabeth, civil or otherwise. They were also given a strict warning not to waste the court's time in the future with frivolous lawsuits.

On Saturday morning they drove home, eager to once again sleep in their own bed. Jan was waiting for them, and she peppered them with questions and fawned over Elizabeth.

Detective Stephens surprised them by showing up on Sunday afternoon. He joined them for dinner and listened as Chris and Elizabeth relayed the events in Columbus, including Carol's visit.

"I was going to talk to you about that," Stephens said. "A store clerk placed her there buying two dozen eggs the morning your car was egged. He also remembered seeing her the morning your tires were slashed. It's circumstantial, but with what she said to you it should get her a slap on the wrist at least, maybe a fine."

"All I want is for her to leave us alone."

"A restraining order might not be a bad idea, just to be safe."

As it turned out, a restraining order wasn't necessary. When Carol was brought in for questioning on the vandalism charges, she decided to turn on the charm. This time, however, she took it too far by actually offering the officer guarding her "a good time" if he let her go. She was promptly charged with soliciting. By the time she was released from jail and paid her fine, she'd lost her job and was thrown out of her apartment. She was too busy trying to salvage her own life to mess with theirs.

Perhaps the most surprising development since their return was that of Detective Stephens himself. When he'd joined them for dinner that first Sunday afternoon, Chris had thought the timing had been random and Jan was just being polite inviting him to join them. He'd been wrong. Since that day, the good detective had been a constant presence at their Sunday dinners. Apparently, *Robert* and Jan were dating.

One afternoon, Chris and Elizabeth were heading back up to their apartment when he said, "I want to take you on a real date."

"That really isn't necessary, you know."

"Humor me. And yes, it is. You've been on a date with my brother, but not me. How is that fair?"

"Fine, fine." She threw her arms unceremoniously around his neck. "So where are you taking me?"

"You'll see," he said.

Two weeks passed and nothing. He didn't mention their date again. Then, on a sunny Friday morning, he surprised her by saying they were taking a road trip. He refused to tell her where they were going, just asking her to trust him.

They stopped along the way a few times for food and to stretch their legs, but he still wouldn't tell her where they were going.

Six hours later, they drove into Nashville. She didn't think anything of it until he pulled off the highway and began winding down side streets. "Nashville?"

"Yes."

"Not that I'm complaining, but why?"

Chris turned into a drive that was blocked by a large gate. He entered a code into a small keypad, and the gate rolled back allowing them entrance.

The paved driveway wound around manicured lawns leading up to a house that looked like something a celebrity would live in. Was this a private hotel?

He parked the car in front of one of the four garage doors before helping her out. "What is this place?" she asked, looking up at the three-story stone mansion.

"This is Gage's house."

"Your brother?" she asked, stunned. "He lives *here?*"

"Yep." He laughed as he grabbed their bags. "Come on. His game's out of town this weekend, and he's letting us borrow his house while he's gone."

She followed him inside, oohing and aahing the entire way. The kitchen was bigger than their whole apartment.

"Feel free to look around," he said. "I'm going to take our bags to our room."

"Okay," she said absently. Her attention was on the mountains she could see through the floor-to-ceiling windows lining the back of the dining room.

She was so caught up in the view she didn't hear him come up behind her. "Beautiful, isn't it?"

"Amazing."

"I arranged for dinner to be delivered in about an hour if you'd like to freshen up. Gage had the lower-level suite made up for us, so it's just down the hall."

As she riffled through her bag, she found that Chris had packed her bathing suit and wondered if that meant there was a pool. *Of course there's a pool. It's a mansion!* She had no idea what else he had planned for the evening, so she took a leisurely shower and changed her clothes. Almost an hour later, she emerged from their room feeling refreshed and ready for whatever he had planned.

As she walked back into the kitchen, a bell rang signaling they had a visitor. "That would be the food. I'll be right back," he said, and gave her a kiss on the cheek. "You look beautiful, by the way."

She'd found a black skirt and fitted shirt in her bag. It looked to be the dressiest thing he'd brought with them, so she'd opted for that.

A few minutes later, Chris appeared carrying several bags of food and a white envelope. He put it all on the large island and set the letter aside.

"What's that?"

"No idea," he said, taking containers out of the bags. "The delivery man said he found it tucked into the gate. It's probably a fan letter or something. Gage is a pretty big deal around here."

She helped him remove the food from the boxes and carry it to the table, or at least she tried to. After the first few tries, he told her he'd get it and to go sit down. This was a date after all.

Along with the food, he also brought a bottle of wine and two glasses.

"You drink wine?" she asked. Beer she'd seen him drink at the barbecue, but she'd never thought of him as a wine person.

"Sometimes." He smiled. "Do you not like wine?"

"No. I do. It's just . . . you strike me as more of a beer and brats man."

Chris laughed. "Well, you have a lot yet to learn about me, Ms. Marshall."

"I guess I do. And I do so love a challenge." She winked. This made him laugh harder and soon she was joining him.

He poured them each a glass of wine. "To us," he said, lifting his glass.

"To us."

They enjoyed their meal, laughing and talking. She didn't think she'd ever seen him this happy. All the worry was gone from his features.

Chris took every opportunity to touch her throughout the evening. His fingers would graze the back of her hand or her wrist, and his foot would rest against her ankle. Just as long as he was touching her somewhere, he seemed to be happy.

When it was time for dessert, he surprised her by standing up and leading her downstairs. "No dessert?"

He smiled at her. "Oh, there's dessert."

The look in his eyes sent the butterflies in her stomach fluttering, her body hoping that the kind of dessert he had in mind involved a bed and absolutely no clothing.

"Come on," he said, pulling her across the room to a large bar. He led her over to a barstool and helped her up.

"What are we doing down here?"

"You'll see." She huffed playfully while he stepped behind the bar.

He disappeared under the counter for a moment before emerging with a pint of double chocolate fudge ice cream and two martini glasses.

Her face lit up. "Ice cream?"

"Yes." He laughed. "I've been told this is your favorite."

"Jan shouldn't be telling my secrets."

He laughed as he scooped ice cream into the tall glasses. "It's not wise to keep secrets from me, Ms. Marshall. I always find out," he teased.

After they'd both eaten their ice cream, Chris cleaned up and led them out to a small patio. The night was clear and warm. With the mountains, it almost looked magical. Chris guided her to a small stone wall near the edge. They watched the last rays of sunlight dipping below the mountains.

She sighed, content. "You've thought of everything, haven't you?"

"Hopefully," he said, suddenly serious.

She looked over at him, concerned. "Chris, is something—"

Her voice cut off as Chris knelt on the ground in front of her. Taking her hands in his, he lifted them to his mouth for a kiss. "I know you've already said yes, but you deserve a proper proposal." Releasing one hand, he reached into his pocket and pulled out a small black box. "Elizabeth Marshall, I love you more than I ever thought possible. I love falling asleep with you every night and waking up to you every morning. I want you with me for the rest of my life. Will you marry me?"

She could feel the tears streaking down her cheeks as he spoke. By the time he finished with his speech, she was so choked up she could barely speak. "Y-yes."

He stood up and pulled her into his arms. "I love you," he whispered, wiping her tears away.

"I love you, too."

She kissed him in a way that wasn't entirely suitable for public viewing. Thank goodness there wasn't anyone around to see. When they finally broke apart, he slid the diamond ring on her finger.

They were lying in bed that night when he asked, "Do you really like the ring?"

"It's perfect."

He breathed a sigh of relief. She couldn't believe he was still worrying about this. Chris had given her so much. He made her feel beautiful and special; things she'd not truly believed about herself for a long time.

She kissed him again, silencing his fears. Chris was one of a kind, and she couldn't wait to spend the rest of her life with him.

***

Are you READY FOR MORE of the Daniels brothers? **Get Red Zone and start reading Gage's story today!** Turn the page to read Chapter 1 of Red Zone.

Sign up HERE or at www.sherrihayesauthor.com to make sure you don't miss any of Sherri Hayes' new releases.

CAN'T WAIT FOR SHERRI'S NEXT BOOK?

Let her know by leaving a review and telling her what you liked about
BEHIND CLOSED DOORS (DANIELS BROTHERS #1)

Chapter 1

It was late by the time Gage Daniels arrived home Tuesday night. He was tired and more than ready for a few days off. Too bad he had to report to practice the next morning.

He tossed his keys in the bowl he had sitting just inside the door as he made his way into the kitchen to get something to drink. He noted that everything seemed to be in its place. His brother and his girlfriend had cleaned up after themselves well after using his home this weekend. That was good. The last thing he wanted was to come home to a trashed house. Not that he could imagine Chris ever partying like that. No. That was Gage's style. At least, it used to be.

Reaching into the fridge, he grabbed a beer and popped the top before taking a large swig. He had spent the last day and a half in Los Angeles with his manager, Mel, at an underwear photo shoot, of all things. Gage didn't dispute he was a good-looking man, but why someone wanted to put him, a quarterback, in a pair of tighty-whities in a magazine was beyond him. He didn't get it.

Mel had set everything up, so at least the previous day's shoot had gone smoothly. That morning had been another story. For whatever reason, his manager scheduled an interview with some magazine he'd never heard of. Apparently they were big in Europe or something. He said it would be good for Gage's image. Although after the interview, he wasn't exactly sure what image they were trying to promote. The woman conducting the interview had pawed at him the entire time.

"What do you like to do when you're not playing football?" She reached out to caress his thigh, her tone filled with innuendo. He knew he had a reputation as sort of a player, but come on! He was supposed to be there on business, not to get in her pants. Business was business. He didn't like mixing the two. Even if he had, there was no way he would have gone for a reporter, no matter how attractive. That was just asking for trouble.

"Swim." He'd kept his answer short, hoping she'd take the hint and move on with another line of questioning. No such luck.

"Hm. Anyone in particular you like to swim with? A girlfriend perhaps?" Her fingers glided suggestively against his arm this time. He leaned back in his chair, away from her. It didn't work. She compensated by leaning in, her top dipping low.

"Surely you don't like to swim . . . alone."

By the time the interview had finished, the woman was practically in his lap. He'd politely excused himself and retreated to the car waiting out front to take him to the airport. The magazine was taking care of the lunch bill anyway, so it wasn't as if he had to stick around to pay.

To make matters worse, someone had recognized him on the plane, and he'd spent the entire flight signing autographs and answering questions. Normally, he didn't mind. Really, he didn't. He loved his fans, and it was part of the job. After his disastrous lunch, however, he'd just wanted to be left alone.

Turning around, Gage spotted an envelope on the counter. How he'd missed it before was a testament to how tired he was, since it was lying there in plain sight. He picked it up and carried it with him upstairs to his bedroom. As much as he was dreading it, he had tapes for this coming Sunday's game to look over.

He booted up his laptop and logged into the team's private account. In the old days—not that he'd been around for the old days, since he'd only been playing professionally for five years—the players would huddle around a single television in one of the conference rooms to watch footage of the other team. He'd done that in high school, and that had been bad enough. This way was much better. Everything he needed to prep for the following day's team meeting was accessible through a website and could be downloaded to his laptop and streamed to his big screen television. Once everything was set, he settled back against his pillows and pressed play.

The team they were playing wasn't doing all that well this year, but their defense was solid. In fact, from what he could see, their defense was scoring as much as their offense. He would need to work with his receivers on protecting the ball. Turnovers could kill a team faster than anything.

An hour into the footage, his gaze drifted back to the envelope he'd brought upstairs. It seemed to be mocking him from where it lay on his nightstand. Picking it up, he saw his name handwritten on the front. It was just like all the others, and he knew what he'd find inside.

The first one had shown up two months ago at the stadium. It had been found by the front office manager and brought down to him. He'd taped it to the front of his locker. At first, he'd thought it was a fan letter, so he hadn't opened it right away. Instead, he'd taken it home. Some of his fan letters, especially ones from women, tended to be slightly more explicit, and he didn't like reading that stuff in front of the guys. In the privacy of his own home was . . . safer.

He knew from the handwriting on the front, however, that what he currently held in his hand wasn't a fan letter. Flipping it over, he took a deep breath, opened the envelope, and pulled out the contents. As with all the others, there were pictures of him and a single sheet of paper that said I'm watching you. These pictures were from last weekend when he'd gone out with some of the guys after the game. A busty blonde was sitting on his lap, making sure he could see all her assets. She hadn't really been his type—he preferred women who could at least hold their own in a conversation—but he was in the mood to party, and she was available. As he'd told the reporter, he didn't have a girlfriend. Although he didn't sleep around nearly as much as he had early on in his career, he wasn't celibate either.

He looked at the pictures again, frustrated. Whoever was stalking him was doing a bang-up job of it. He had been photographed in nearly every public place he'd gone over the last two and a half months, and he'd not been able to spot anything out of place, and it wasn't for lack of trying. Even the night the picture in his hand was taken, he'd thought he'd been diligent. The club was crowded but not any more than usual. People were moving comfortably throughout—socializing and dancing. He'd not seen any indication someone was paying him, or his teammates, any more attention than they normally provoked when they were out in public.

Throwing the letter down on his nightstand, he leaned back against the headboard of his bed and ran a hand through his hair. Tim

Donovan, the team's owner, would want to know about this. He'd nearly flipped a lid when he'd found out about the last one through the grapevine and that it hadn't been the first. Tim had made Gage promise to come to him immediately the next time it happened. He'd even threated to bench Gage if he didn't, and there was no way he would let that happen.

Shutting everything off, Gage lay back on his bed and stared up at the ceiling. Who was doing this and why? It didn't make sense. He was just a football player.

Rolling over, he punched his pillow until he found a semicomfortable position. He'd need to take a detour to Tim's office first thing in the morning. There was no way he was giving Tim an excuse to keep him on the sidelines.

The sun was setting over the smoky mountains on Thursday when Special Agent Rebecca Carson's phone rang, disturbing the peaceful setting. Her job with the FBI often had her traveling across the country. It was rare she was able to sit back, relax on the deck of her condo, and enjoy something as simple as the sun going down behind the mountains. There had been days she'd longed for that moment of peace. Now, it was driving her crazy.

Nearly a month had passed since the agency had put her on administrative leave at the advice of one of their therapists. Sure, it had been a difficult case, and it had ended badly, but her sitting around at home wasn't helping. She wanted—no, she needed—to get back out there. Sitting around doing nothing was going to be the end of her sanity.

She pushed herself up off the lounge chair and walked into her living room to answer the call, hoping it was her boss saying she was cleared to come back to work. Knowing her luck, though, it would be her baby sister needing her help to get out of another jam. Either way, it would be a welcome distraction. "Hello?"

"Carson?"

"Yes," she said, immediately recognizing, Travis Hansen's voice on the other end of the line.

"Good. I'm glad I caught you. Something's come up, and I thought you could use something to do. I know you're probably going stir-crazy sitting at home, and I could use the help."

"Is everything all right? I can meet you tonight if you need me to."

"No, no," he said. "Tomorrow will be fine. You may want to pack a bag, though."

She knew what that meant. Whatever assignment was waiting in the wings, she'd most likely be on a plane before noon the next day. "All right. Where should I meet you?"

"Just be ready at eight. I'll pick you up."

"All right," she said, unsure but trusting her ex-partner and former mentor. Hansen had retired from the FBI, and now ran his own P.I. firm, but they'd stayed in touch. He was one of the few people in this world she would trust with her life.

"See you tomorrow, Carson. Get some rest."

After hanging up, Rebecca walked to her bedroom and began packing. Suits with matching blouses lined her closet. Her sister always gave her a hard time, saying she needed to spice things up a bit with her wardrobe, but she was an FBI agent—she didn't do flashy. Besides, she had been living in sweats and T-shirts for far too long. She pulled out a week's worth of clothing and placed them in her garment bag before zipping it up. The same routine had been gone through so many times, it didn't take her long to pack all but the toiletries she'd need that night and in the morning.

At seven fifty-eight the next morning, she was standing out in front of her building waiting on Hansen. He was punctual and pulled up in his silver sedan as her watch beeped, alerting her of the new hour. He was right on time, as always.

She walked over to the car and slipped inside. He smiled and handed her a cup of coffee before pulling back out onto the road.

"Morning, Carson."

"Hansen." She nodded in greeting. They'd been partners for a little over a year before he'd retired. Although he was perhaps the one person she was closest to in her adult life besides her sister, they still had that professional distance. It was exactly the way she liked it.

"It's good to see you. I apologize for curtailing any plans you may have had scheduled for your time off, but something's come up, and I could really use your help in Nashville."

"No problem. Anything at this point would be better than being stuck at home crawling the walls."

He chuckled. "Good, 'cause we're helping out an old friend of mine."

She looked over at him, questioning.

"His name is Timothy Donovan. He owns the professional football team in Nashville. Something has come up with one of his players, and he needs some help."

She waited for him to elaborate, but he didn't. Although she was curious, it didn't matter. As she'd told him, anything was better than sitting at home doing nothing.

Two hours and a brief argument later, they pulled into the parking lot of a nicer-than-average hotel in Nashville that would act as their base of operations. Halfway to Nashville, she'd finally decided to ask for the exact details of the assignment. Needless to say, she wasn't thrilled with his response. The problem was, either she took this assignment or she went back home again to do . . . nothing.

They checked in, under the guise of a married couple, and quickly set up shop in their assigned room. "I don't like this," she said, staring around the room at the fancy décor. She'd stayed in any number of motels since she'd become an agent four years ago, but none of them had come close to this. This was way above government budget. Of course, the government wasn't footing the bill for this one. It was compliments of Donovan, according to Hansen.

Her nose scrunched up in distaste at the frilly coverlet on the bed. "Not liking the new assignment, Carson?" her old mentor asked, smiling.

He was enjoying her discomfort way too much. "Like you'd be over there grinning if the shoe were on the other foot, Hansen."

"True." He laughed. "Thankfully, I don't look pretty on the arm of a hotshot quarterback."

Rebecca clenched her fists to keep from hurling something at him. Instead, she slipped the hotel key in her pants pocket and walked to the door. "Let's just get this over with."

Hansen kept his mouth shut on the way to the stadium, although she could see he was dying to comment. She liked Hansen. He was a good partner and had always treated her as an equal, even if she had been a rookie at the time they'd worked together. It was probably part of the reason he was getting such a kick out of this.

They followed the instructions they were given and parked in the players' lot. A security guard greeted them, and they were escorted upstairs to a long hallway of offices before he stopped at the last one on their right and motioned they should go inside ahead of him.

An older gentleman, who looked to be in his early sixties, sat behind a large wooden desk. He stood, and rounded the desk to greet them. Giving Hansen a pat on the back, and offering her a firm handshake, he introduced himself as the owner, Timothy Donovan. "I'm glad you were able to come on such short notice," he said directly to her. Then he turned to the man who'd walked them in. "Get Gage Daniels, will you? Tell him I need to see him." The man nodded, closing the door behind him.

Donovan walked back to his chair behind the desk, while she and Hansen took the seats offered to them. Putting her game face on, Rebecca answered in her usual professional tone. "I wasn't told much, Mr. Donovan. Perhaps you can fill me in."

"Of course," he said. Reaching into his desk drawer, he pulled out a large manila folder filled with envelopes. "About two months ago, Daniels, our star quarterback, began receiving these. They're all there with the exception of the first few. He just threw them away. Thought they were a joke."

She flipped through the pictures and letters. They were all of a young man, in his mid-twenties, whom she assumed was Daniels. He was doing various things, from something as simple as shopping to sitting in a bar. What she did notice, however, was that all the pictures included females. "He seems to be quite the ladies' man. Could it be a woman scorned?"

"That's always a possibility, I suppose. Gage is . . . . well, he's young, not bad to look at, and he's an athlete. The ladies like him." He shrugged.

"So, what would you like us to do exactly, Mr. Donovan?" she said, trying to keep the contempt out of her voice.

Donovan stood and walked over to the large bank of windows behind him. He motioned them over and then pointed down to the field. "This is my team. I watch out for them." It wasn't hard to pick out Daniels from the field below. He was in full uniform with his name across his shoulder blades. It helped that the security guard was walking across the field straight toward him, too. "He doesn't know this, and I'd like to keep it that way. I don't want him rattled any more than he already is." Donovan turned to face them, his expression serious. "A security guard noticed something sticking out of Gage's car two days ago. Given the letters he's been receiving, I called a friend in the local PD."

"Explosives?" Hansen asked.

"Yes. Although I'm told it wouldn't have done much damage had it gone off, but that's beside the point. Someone's decided to put a bull's-eye on Gage's back, and I need to stop it." He paused before looking Rebecca in the eye. "Which is where *you* come in."

"Security footage?"

"Checked. There's nothing there except his vehicle. We went back a week."

As much as she didn't like the situation, putting up a fight on this one when Donovan was footing the bill would be difficult. The person behind this had clearly crossed state lines—the pictures were taken in various cities—then delivered them to Daniels, either at his home or to the stadium. A couple even looked as though they'd come through the mail. That was enough to put it on the federal radar. Add in the explosives and even she could admit she was intrigued. They were his last hope before getting the FBI officially involved, and likely the press. Something like this wouldn't stay under wraps for long.

A minute later, there was a knock at the door. "Come in." Donovan yelled.

The door opened, and there stood the man she'd be spending the majority of her time with in the near future—Gage Daniels.

GRAB YOUR COPY OF RED ZONE

ALSO BY SHERRI HAYES

<u>Finding Anna</u>

Slave (Finding Anna, Book 1)

Need (Finding Anna, Book 2)

Truth (Finding Anna, Book 3)

Trust (Finding Anna, Book 4)

Finding Anna Boxed Set (Books 1-4)

Indulge: A Finding Anna Novelette

Change (Finding Anna, Book 5)

<u>The Daniels Brothers</u>

Behind Closed Doors

Red Zone

Crossing the Line

What Might Have Been

Daniels Brothers Box Set (Books 1-4)

<u>Serpent's Kiss</u>

Welcome to Serpent's Kiss

Burning for Her Kiss

One Forbidden Night

Longing for His Kiss

Claiming His Kiss

Tangled In His Embrace

<u>Liberty Crossroads</u>

Seducing Janey

<u>Strictly Professional</u>

Strictly Professional

A Christmas Proposal

ABOUT THE AUTHOR

Sherri picked up her first romance novel when she was twelve and immediately she was hooked. She would stay up reading long after everyone else in her house had gone to bed, needing to see the hero and heroine get their happily ever after. But Sherri never imagined becoming an author.

At the age of thirty, all that changed. After getting frustrated with the direction a television show was taking two of its characters, Sherri decided to try her hand at writing an alternative ending to give the characters the happy ending they deserved.

Since then, writing has become a creative outlet that allows her to explore a wide range of emotions, while having fun taking her characters through all the twists and turns she can create.

patreon.com/SherriHayes
facebook.com/SherriHayesAuthor
bookbub.com/authors/sherri-hayes